Shepherd's call

a SHEPHERD & WOLFE
mystery

COUNIOS & GANE

Shepherd's call

a SHEPHERD & WOLFE
mystery

COUNIOS & GANE

REGINA, SK

Published by Your Nickel's Worth Publishing.
June 2022

Cataloguing data available from Library and Archives Canada.
ISBN: 978-1-988783-77-2

Printed in Canada.
26 25 24 23 22   1 2 3 4 5

Cover © Angie Counios.
Book design by Heather Nickel.
Interior image © Angie Counios.

Production made possible with the support of Creative Saskatchewan.

For Angelica LaClaire
March 9, 1999 – June 9, 2018

**A beautiful child who lived wildly
and loved without condition**

prologue

1

Charlie Wolfe's phone buzzes in his pocket, but he silences the call.

Tonight isn't about him. Tonight is about his girlfriend, Elaina Hollar, and his friend, Tony Shepherd. They're about to graduate high school and become yet more cogs in the industrial wheel of complacent, productive workers. But since it's important to the people he cares about, he's going to give the ceremony's pomp and circumstance his full attention—

Bzzz.

He quietly grumbles before muting it, but the caller tries again almost immediately.

Shit! Who's interfering with his generous spirit? He steps aside to check the caller ID: MELANIE.

Dammit, Mom! Really?

She'd bailed on him at the start of the year and disappeared into the ether. He'd have pretty much been homeless if Tony's family hadn't taken him in. But her vanishing act hadn't stopped him sending out the bat signal in search of her. There wasn't much love left between them—their time together had been rocky at best—but he still worried about her. After all, she was pretty much the only family he'd had, shoddy as it may have been. He has checked all her old haunts—dive bars, old boyfriends—hell, even a bowling alley or two—hoping he'd hear something back, but there's been nothing. And now that he's finally given up on her, sure as shit, she picks *this* moment, Tony and Elaina's special night, to shake up his world again.

"Hey, Shepherd, do you mind helping Elaina inside? I just need to take this."

"Everything all right?" Tony asks.

"Yup, totally fine." Well, not *fine*, but considering his mom's typical behaviour, he's hoping this is nothing more than a check-in. "I've just been trying to track down my mom, and I think this might be her."

Tony doesn't seem to buy it, and truth be told, he wouldn't have believed she'd called either if he hadn't seen her name on the screen.

He motions Tony towards the backstage area of the convention centre's auditorium. "Go on in there before they decide to renege on your diploma."

Tony looks back one last time before joining Elaina at the stairwell that will take them to the rest of the grads.

Charlie steps outside to answer the phone.

"Yeah?" Although he's grateful his mom is calling, he doesn't want to be *too* nice.

"What? No manners, Chuck?" a deep voice growls.

Definitely not his mom.

A chill races down Charlie's back and he does his best to shrug it off.

"Who are you and why do you have my mom's phone?" He tries to play it cool but he's not one for surprises.

"Oh, don't you worry. She's perfectly fine."

Charlie is silent, a still figure among the flurry of graduates. His mind is racing. Who else has crawled out of the woodwork? Hadn't he and Tony caught everyone they'd known about? Could this be someone new? Or worse, someone from his past, from before Tony?

Maybe if he can get the guy talking a little more, he can figure it out.

"What do you want?"

"Again, so *rude*—"

"Look, I'm busy. People are waiting for me."

"Oh, I know, Chuck."

There's familiarity in his tone, like Charlie should know who he is. It puts his back up.

"You can call me Mr. Wolfe."

"You clean up real nice, Chuck. Seems like living on the right side of the tracks suits you."

Charlie glances down at his new clothes, bought for the occasion. The caller is close. Probably watching him . . . maybe for a while.

Charlie's eyes dart across the incoming crowd to the parking lot, looking for someone on their phone, or a car that doesn't quite fit the wholesome school parent suv demographic.

But he's at a high school graduation. Everyone's on their devices, what with selfies and video chats and old-school phone calls from their grandmas. And the road is crammed with limos and classic cars and broken-down beaters.

It's needle-in-a-haystack hopeless.

He needs to flush this guy out into the open.

"You know what? You're wasting my time. I'm going inside." Charlie turns back towards the doors of the building but doesn't immediately enter, scanning reflections in the glass for anyone approaching.

"No, you're not," the voice in his hand snarls. "You'll follow my directions—"

"Or what? You can't do anything to me in this crowd—"

The man chuckles. "Ah, but you're not a lone wolf anymore, are you? You've found yourself a nice little pack."

Charlie swallows hard, his confident veneer slipping.

"Are you quite sure Tony and Elaina made it safely backstage?" the man asks.

Shit.

Charlie whips open the closest door, racing inside.

"You can't save them, Chuck."

He hits the stairs. "The hell I can't!"

There's a smug pause. "Then what about Keya, Ben, and Heather?"

Charlie's stride falters. Tony's parents and sister! Had this goon gotten to them too?

"How do I know you're not bluffing?"

"You really want to test me?"

Charlie grips the handrail at the bottom of the steps, frozen with indecision.

The phone emits another low chuckle. "Poor little Charlie opened himself to the Shepherds, and now it's going to be his downfall."

He's cornered and he knows it.

"What do you want?"

"You're going to go outside. We'll roll up, and you're going to get into the car like everything's cool. Got it?"

Charlie closes his eyes and exhales.

"You goddamn *got* it?!" the man yells.

Charlie's response is barely a whisper. "Yeah. I got it."

Climbing the stairs, Charlie thinks quickly.

The ceremony's almost started; most of the grads and guests are now in the building. The few stragglers are either grabbing a last hit off of whatever they're smoking, or rushing in late.

He considers stopping one of them, but what would he say? "Excuse me, would you mind calling the cops? I'm about to be kidnapped and/or murdered."

And where would that get him anyway? By the time somebody got help, he—or the people he cared about—might already be dead.

He's still running through options when a sleek-looking silver Maserati Quattroporte sedan pulls up to the curb behind a white limo. Two black-suited men—maybe in their thirties—sit in the front seat, sunglasses glinting in the late afternoon sunlight—their goon-ness is such a cliché—but at least they're dressed appropriately for the occasion.

If he can see them through the glass doors, they can probably see him. There's a whole family—teens, parents, aunts and uncles, and old people—between him and the goons, so he's got a chance. Fingers flying, he disables his phone's passcode, then opens his texts and starts typing, but the group of people is called over by an enthusiastic mom and they all step aside, exposing him completely.

He lowers the phone quickly to his hip. He doesn't need the goons to see him on it—not if Tony and Elaina and the Shepherds' lives are at risk.

But dammit! He's only got one word written and he's still got to hit *send*, and he doesn't want to try winging it and accidentally delete the text or close the app.

This is why he loves old technology! An old Nokia would've come in handy right about now. A real keyboard, no fragile screen, and he could drop it out of a two-storey building and it'd break the pavement. Maybe he could've even used it as a weapon to dent in these goons' heads. If he gets out of this predicament, he vows it'll be the next thing he picks up for himself.

He still needs a few more seconds to send his message, but they're watching him, so he steps outside, acknowledging them with a nod before casually walking over.

"A Maserati? Really? You couldn't pick something a little more conspicuous?"

The driver is tough-looking, like being hit with a 2 × 4 in the face is a part of his workout regime. He's definitely called Rocco or Bruiser, or maybe something ironic like Li'l Mike.

"Get in the car," says the goon in the passenger seat. He's smaller than the driver, but sinewy, and probably a brawler too, judging by the scraped skin on his knuckles. Definitely the one who called him.

Charlie's buying time, still looking for his moment, so he lets his mouth run. "Can you even *spell* Maserati—?"

"Stop talking and get in."

"Hey, I was told never to accept rides from strangers. What's your name? Johnny Fingers? Vinny the Knife—?"

"Shut it and get in the back seat—or else." The passenger indicates the Smith & Wesson revolver he's pointing at Charlie.

"Geez, take it easy. Just joshing with you."

As he pulls open the back door, Charlie quickly glances down to check his phone. He's only got one word. Is it enough to make a difference? As he climbs into the car, he hits *send*, hoping it is.

help

3

Charlie whistles as he settles into the back seat.

"Wow. I know this vehicle is all about performance, but look at the interior: Sabbia Poltrona Frau leather seat trim! I don't know if beige is what I'd choose, but whatever. You do you."

He rolls the window down and waves at a couple of girls texting on their phones by the main entrance.

The thug in the passenger seat twists around and yells, "Leave the window alone!"

Charlie is immediately apologetic. "Okay, bossman. Relax. Just checking out the features." He scoots a little ways from the door, careful to leave the glass down in case he has a chance to escape.

Unfortunately, as soon as they speed away, the windows go back up, and the rear door locks click shut.

Bossman turns in his seat. "Give me your shoes."

"What?"

"In case you decide to bolt, it'll make it harder for you to run."

Damn, these guys are thorough.

But as Charlie leans down to untie his sneakers, he works out a new chance to mess with their plans.

"Man, I hate you guys taking my shoes. I really like them."

He leans far enough over to blind their line of sight with his shaggy hair. He slips the phone down by his foot.

"Mrs. Shepherd got me these kicks. She sure didn't like me wearing them to grad, but I can't be expected to tolerate the whole ceremony without a little comfort, right?"

He pops open the camera app.

"But hey, I agreed to let her buy me the suit, so I think we reached a compromise."

He slips the phone by his thigh, and as he pulls his sneakers off and hands them up front, he snaps a pic of Bossman reaching back for them.

"Take shallow breaths. They stink." The goons don't react. "What with the hot day and all."

Bossman grumbles to the driver, who rolls down his window and tosses them out. Charlie watches them skip across the asphalt into the ditch with dismay.

"Hey, man! Didn't you hear me? Mrs. S. is going to be mad! You guys owe her!"

Bossman bends back. "Give me your phone."

"What are you talking about?" Charlie pushes a too-casual tone.

"Don't waste my time. I saw you with it at the convention centre. Hand it over."

Shit.

"Fine. Except—" Charlie tosses the phone past the driver's head and out the open window. "There. Now you guys owe me a pair of kicks *and* a phone. Guess there's no chance of you letting me use the one you stole from Melanie, hey?"

The thug sighs. "Dammit, you're aggravating."

"Depends who you ask."

The driver slows down. "Should we go back for it?"

Bossman considers it for a moment, then shakes his head. "Nah. By the time they find it, it won't matter anymore."

Charlie swallows hard and sinks into his seat. Maybe he's a lot closer to getting killed than he thought.

4

They travel down the thoroughfare that takes them to the freeway. When Charlie leans close to the speaker in the back seat, his furrowed brow confirms his thought.

"You listening to TLC? If you're planning to kill me, don't waste your time. I'll do it myself if you keep playing this crap."

The driver is about to say something and immediately gets a glare from Bossman. He's definitely the one in charge of this little operation—at least for now.

Hopefully, Charlie can get himself out of here before things get worse—as long as he can get them talking.

"You're probably asking 'What's this kid got against T-Boz, Left Eye, and Chilli?—they're one of the best-selling girl groups of all time, with nine top tens on the Billboard Hot 100, and four Grammy Awards? How can he hate them so much?'"

The driver keeps glancing at him in the rear-view, wanting badly to get into it. But he stays tight-lipped, so Charlie pushes further.

"It's the drama. The infighting behind the scenes, the arson, the materialistic excess that lead to their bankruptcy. Of course, I feel bad they signed those shitty contracts—that's the whole issue I have with the music industry—but it's about discipline in the face of adversity—"

"That's it. Pull over!" Bossman yells, and the driver swerves to the curb.

The car screeches to a halt, and Charlie tumbles forward on the slippery leather upholstery and slams into the back of the seat. "Shit. I didn't expect that! I guess that's why they tell you to buckle up."

The passenger sticks the gun deep into his cheek, and Charlie smells the pungent odour of grease and gunpowder.

"Easy, Cass," the driver says. "She wants him in one piece."

Bossman—Cass—glares at the driver, the barrel pushing hard against Charlie's face, knowing that the punk kid now knows his name.

But they are also all aware that this standoff can't go anywhere. Charlie is meant to be kept alive—at least until they get to their destination.

Cass climbs out and opens the back door. "Get your ass out of the car."

Charlie clicks his tongue, shaking his head. "Get in the car. Get out of the car. Make up your mind—"

Cass grabs him by the scruff of his suit jacket, but Charlie's instincts kick in—too many fights over the years—and he shoots his arm up to block. He immediately realizes his mistake and holds his hands up in surrender.

"Sorry." He puts his hands up in a gesture of resignation. "Sorry. Old habits die hard."

Cass whacks his pistol against Charlie's skull, and it hurts like hell.

"For fu—" Charlie rubs his head.

"Kid, I'm about ready to shoot you and tell them it was an accident, if you don't start listening. Get your ass out of this car so we can resolve this amicably."

"Okay. Okay. You win." His head is still stinging as he scoots out of the car.

Cass nods to the driver. "Open the trunk." It pops up and Cass waves the gun at Charlie with mock courtesy. "In you get."

The street is unreasonably quiet, and Charlie wishes a car would come along and see him being held at gunpoint, but luck is against him. He glances inside the trunk. There's a tool box, some rope, and a wad of poly. The outlook isn't great.

"Really?" Charlie asks, playing dumb.

Cass lets out an exasperated sigh. Not eager to experience the repercussions of his stubbornness, Charlie complies.

"Okay, okay. Fine."

Charlie puts a foot in the trunk. "Is this all because of my opinion of TLC? Because I can give them some love. They really brought some serious issues to light—"

But that's all he gets to say before there's a sharp, stinging pain on the back of his head. A numbing pressure spreads across his face, and he tumbles into darkness.

5

Charlie's mind drifts, the gentle back-and-forth sway of the car tugging on an old memory.

He's four years old, lying in the back seat of his parents' car. They're up front, rocking out to CCR on the radio, looking back and singing to him with wild abandon. He wants to sing too. He wants them all to sing. But he can't, because he knows what's coming, right around the corner, ready to tear their world apart.

And then the darkness comes, clouding in on him, sharing the back seat with him, and he's not certain he'll ever be able to escape. He's face to face with the fear that he's locked away for far too long, and before he can escape, it engulfs him.

6

Charlie's eyes jerk open, banishing the wicked nightmare.

He's out of sorts, knocked around, and it takes him a moment to remember that he's in the trunk of a car. His head throbs, and he squints at the pain. A thin scab has formed where they struck him with the gun, his hair matted and sticky with dried blood.

Listening to the steady hum of the tires, he can tell they're out on the highway, but he's got absolutely no clue how long he's been out for, where they are, or which way they're going.

If they had picked him up on any other day, he would have had his trusty backpack, full of all sorts of handy gadgets and tools—perfect for a situation like this. But dammit if he hadn't decided to respect the occasion and leave it at the Shepherds' house.

The tool box. That's got to have something inside that'll help him get out of here. A screwdriver, a box cutter, anything. He feels around in the dark until he locates it by his feet.

He wiggles himself around to get hold of it and pull it close. Damn, padlocked. He's not surprised that it's locked even before giving it a yank to confirm. It's not big, but it's tough enough that he won't be able to break it with only the few hard tugs he'd have room to do.

He searches in the dark for the trunk release. Most cars have them for situations like these. It's often located near the latch with a glow-in-the-dark handle or some other type of mechanism, but there's nothing.

Maybe the tire wrench?

He pushes the rope and poly wrap aside and pulls up the flooring.

Dammit! The whole trunk's been cleaned out. Not even a spare! He feels the sides, hoping to find a panel that gets him into the wiring and cables, but everything is smooth and fastened together tight.

Shit!

His kidnappers are clearly old pros.

Charlie's hot and the space feels tight and cramped and he punches against the sides of the trunk. Not knowing what's going on, not being in any kind of control of the situation, makes him want to kick the shit out of everything. He wants to scream but he knows he needs to control himself. He's been in worse scenarios—far worse.

He's got to gear down.

What does he know? What is the situation?

This settles his thinking. He quits rehashing and worrying about whatever's ahead and focuses on the present.

Right now, he's in a trunk. He doesn't know where he is or where he's going, and he can't change that. He doesn't have any tools to free himself.

The truth is obvious: his moment isn't now. He'll have to wait for it. But when it comes, he'll be ready.

The ride is long and uninterrupted. No turns. No stops. Barely even a yield. Only a straight path into the unknown.

Charlie makes a pillow out of the poly and puts his hands behind his head to pad the bumps. He can't stretch out completely, but he does his best. He won't sleep—that's the last thing he wants right now—but he does his best to compartmentalize and clear his mind.

There's no room for unnecessary distractions now.

A phone rings. The car's speakerphone kicks in.

"Where are you two?"

Charlie strains to hear the muffled sounds of Cass and the driver.

"We're…driving."

"Well, get your ass back to the farm."

"Robert's got us doing something."

Who the hell is Robert? Charlie has heard of a few Roberts around town, but none of them were into kidnapping.

"Don't matter. I want your asses back, now!"

"But, Winston—"

Charlie has also heard of a Winston before, and the name was never associated with good news.

"No! Someone got to Henry, and we need to handle it."

Wait a second.... Someone got to Henry? Who's Henry, and who got to him? What exactly has Charlie gotten dragged into?

"But.... What should we tell Robert?"

"I'll handle him. Get here ASAP, and we'll deal with this quickly!" Winston shouts before hanging up.

Undue hastiness isn't a characteristic Charlie likes—especially when his life is on the line.

He needs to get out of here. He just hopes he's overheard enough to make it happen.

8

Eventually, the car takes a left, and Charlie and the tool box slide into the corner. A roar of rocks strike the wheel wells. Gravel road. Wherever they're going, it's in the boonies, so there's even less of a chance for an easy escape.

Another turn and it feels like the driver is aiming for every pothole he can find. Charlie bangs around, crashing into the trunk lid and back onto the floor repeatedly, until his brain is nearly scrambled.

Thankfully, the car rolls to a stop.

The car doors bang shut, and there's a loud screech and the thud of what sounds like a large wooden door sliding shut. Then, the soft crackle of footsteps on dust and rock as two people move to the trunk. It unlatches and the lid rises.

It's pretty dark, but Charlie can tell they're in an old barn. Hay dust and the heavy scent of manure float in the air. The silhouettes of Cass and the driver tower over him, backlit by the thin strips of sunlight coming through the gaps of a warped wooden roof.

Still reeling from the rough road, Charlie says, "The way you drive, you'd think you just got your licence."

"Get out," Cass says.

"Give me a sec, will ya?"

Cass nods at the driver. "Drag him out, Red."

As the goon leans in, Charlie quickly snaps back and head-butts him in the face.

"Dammit!" Red yells, grabbing his nose, blood gushing over his knuckles.

"I *asked* for a moment," Charlie yells. He knows it was wrong, but his gut wants him to fight.

"All right, kid. You got your one shot. You happy?" Cass pulls his gun. It appears he's done putting up with Charlie's shit. "Now, decide how you want to get out of this car."

Charlie raises his hands in surrender and crawls out.

They're in a large, empty horse barn. Stalls line both sides of the space, and a set of stairs leads to an upper level where old, grey hay hangs over the edge in dirty stacks. There's a door on one side, secured with a rusty lock and chain, so there's only one way out—the wide door they drove in—but a third guy stands in front of it.

Tough as Charlie is, this new guy looks mean enough to toss him through a wall if he tries to make a break for it.

Red turns to Cass, rubbing his head. Charlie hopes it still hurts. "What do you want me to do with him?"

"I got an idea," Charlie grunts. "How 'bout you let me go?"

Red—completely done with him—sucker-punches him hard in the face, and Charlie drops.

"Okay, I deserved that," he says, spitting out blood and making sure his jaw still works. "But if I get hantavirus from this dirt floor, I'm blaming you two."

Red adds a swift kick.

Charlie groans. "Okay. I get it. *Shhh.*"

On the ground, he finally sees a fourth man in the shadows, near the back wall. He's on a cell phone, looking pissed, glaring at Charlie.

He's older, compared to the rest of the thugs, and isn't as much of a brute. He's got a slighter frame and is dressed to the nines. Not business formal, but a $500 pair of jeans with a perfectly fitted sports jacket. This guy must be management, but since he's taken the trouble to be out here, he's probably not shy about getting his hands a little bloody.

Charlie strains to hear what the man is saying into the phone, but catches only bits and pieces.

"I understand that, but these are my guys... No, I don't mean any disrespect to her...I promise—I'll deal with it personally."

Charlie's heard enough to know this is the guy he overheard talking to Cass and Red on the speakerphone.

His mind races, trying to assess the situation and put the pieces of this jigsaw in place before it's too late.

The man ends the call and moves closer, a deep woodsy cologne wafting over Charlie as he strolls over, followed by a base note of stale cigarettes.

"Soooo," he drawls, "you're the infamous Charles Wolfe."

Charlie pulls himself up off the ground and dusts off his clothes before offering his hand. "And you must be Winston."

This catches the man off guard. "How'd you—?" he asks, then adds, "Well, I'd heard you were good, but I'm impressed."

Charlie's quick. "Impressive is my middle name."

Winston clicks his tongue and wags a finger. "Now, now," he smirks. "Don't interrupt."

He leans back against the car, considering Charlie. "You know, over the months, I've had a few of my guys follow you. See who you are, what your deal is, who you talk to. But you always had a knack for losing them—"

"Well," Charlie shrugs, "I'm a pretty private guy—"

Winston lunges and slaps Charlie's face—hard. "I *said* no interrupting."

Charlie's cheek burns. His mouth is full of saliva and the taste of old pennies.

The man isn't done with the lecture. "I know guys like you—digging up people's dirt, playing them off each other, making a few quick bucks. As a businessman myself, I can't fault you for that. However, I'm not particularly fond of your relationship with honest cops like Detective Gekas—"

Who *is* this guy? "Look," Charlie tries, "I don't know anything about you or your business—"

Winston punches him in the gut, and Charlie falls to his knees.

Cass steps forward. "Boss? She wants him alive."

Winston glowers back.

Charlie can barely breathe, barely think. He's running out of time. And options. He needs to save himself—do something, anything, right now.

Winston kneels beside him. "I thought maybe once I met you, saw you face to face, I'd understand you. Get some sense of why you do what you do." He stands, brushes himself off, reaches into his jacket. "Unfortunately, you're an enigma—and I'm not fond of enigmas."

He draws his gun and jams it into Charlie's face.

"Boss!"

"I don't care. He's not worth the effort—"

"I can help," Charlie cries out.

Winston shakes his head slowly. "Look at you. You can't even help yourself, son."

"The person... I can help you figure out—"

"What are you talking about?"

"I can help you figure out who killed Henry."

Winston scowls, leaning close. "And just what do you think you know about that?"

Charlie glances up at the older man, trying not to choke on the overpowering cologne. "Only what I heard in the car."

Winston scrutinizes Cass and Red, his expression making it obvious that they'll catch hell afterwards.

For now, Charlie's own best bet is to make himself useful. "Take me to where they found him."

It's a big ask, but he needs to convince this guy to keep him alive. And if Winston really *has* been having him followed, then he might know that Charlie actually does have a unique set of skills...

"You'd like that, wouldn't you?" Winston scoffs.

"You can throw me in the trunk again. You can gag me. It doesn't matter. Just help me help you."

Winston's finger still rests on the trigger, but the gun is no longer pressed so hard into Charlie's face. "And what makes you think you can?"

"Because it's what I do."

No one says anything. Charlie fears his luck really has run dry. All he can think of is his family.

Winston lowers the gun.

"You got *cojones*, kid, I'll give you that. But, look at me."

Charlie meets his eyes as Winston drops down, getting right in his face, his voice deep and low. "You have until to-morrow—and if you try anything, anything at all, I'm not just going to kill you. My boys are going to lay devastation upon everyone you love."

Charlie swallows hard and nods. He's made a deal with the devil.

Now he just needs to figure out who that is.

part 1

chapter 1

"Tony, what's wrong?" Elaina asks.

I look up from my phone, staring at her, speechless.

We're backstage at the graduation ceremony, surrounded by our class. They are raucously celebrating, diplomas in hand, and I'm ready to throw up.

"Tony?"

I scrutinize Charlie's one word message on my phone:

help

I want to believe it's a prank, but he'd never send a text like this. Not unless he was being dead-ass serious.

Elaina places a hand on my shoulder. "Tony?"

I show her my phone, and her face goes white. I kick into gear. "We've got to find my parents."

"What?" Elaina calls out, but I'm already winding through the crowd towards the exit. I don't know if she's following or not, but I don't care. I'm not waiting.

Chaperones corral students back through the double doors towards their family and friends. Charity Pelton from my homeroom and Randy from my law class have hooked up in the doorway, and I have to squeeze past their excessive kissing and groping to get through.

Outside, it's a madhouse. Families are everywhere, fawning over the graduates. Mothers are crying and hugging, and dads are faking like they don't care.

Elaina's parents call her back into the lobby, and we can't hear them above the bustle and buzz of the busy room. They're obviously not pleased with her taking off.

"Go. Deal with them," I say.

She pauses, hesitant to leave. I want to say something more, something that might make her feel better, but nothing comes out. We both know something bad is going down.

I hug her tight.

She whispers, her voice cracking with anguish. "Tony, please find him."

"I will. I promise."

I twist, searching for my own folks, just as Mom grabs my arm. "Anthony, we'd like to get some photos together—"

"Was he sitting with you?"

"Who?"

"Charlie?" I show her my phone.

She's confused. "I thought he was with you—"

"Mom, we have to get Gekas."

chapter 2

I bust out the doors, Mom and Dad on my heels, sending
Charlie a text:

Dude, where are you?

before calling his number and leaving a voice mail: "Charlie,
call me back."

I dial Detective Gekas next.

"It's Anthony. You need to call me. Charlie's in trouble—"

This'll mean nothing to her. He's always getting into something, whether it's his usual nonsense or breaking the law.

"He's missing—"

Wait. Shit, that won't work either. He went MIA for nearly
two months on me once, and that didn't require calling in
the cavalry. Dammit, Charlie! Why do you have to make this
so hard?

I go with the one thing that scared the shit out of me.

"He's asked for help."

She knows him. With all his skills and resources, if he's asking for help, he's got to be in some serious shit. I hang up.

I can't celebrate now—the photos, the grad banquet, it all goes out the window. Thankfully, my parents seem to get it, only exchanging a look before indulging my urgency to leave.

In the car, I scan through my notifications, hoping Charlie's left some sort of breadcrumb to follow. If he was in trouble, he'd do anything to get me details, up to and including stealing someone else's phone.

There's a couple of messages from friends and lots of notifications on social media about grad, but nothing seems amiss. No new follows or texts from an unknown number. Nothing that sticks out.

If only Charlie was the kind of guy who'd share his location, I could at least track his phone. "Find my friend" is exactly what I want to do. But Charlie isn't much into data-sharing—he's barely on social media.

Speaking of which.... I move over to Instagram. Since he moved in with us and started dating Elaina, Charlie's been trying to be somewhat normal. He got himself an account and posts photos. Never people. Only trees, flowers, landscapes, and buildings. But not one damn selfie.

His last post was from yesterday. A couple of rocks down by the creek. Nothing since then.

I put down the phone and stare out the window. My suit feels too tight, the car too small, and everything too quiet. Dad stares back at me in the rear-view mirror, concerned, but doesn't offer any consolation.

I roll down the window to feel the wind and take in deep breaths. I hope Charlie's safe.

chapter 3

As soon as we pull up to the house, I'm out of the car and rush inside. "Hello?" I call out. I don't really expect Charlie to be here, but I hope for the off chance that I'm wrong.

Only Ollie, our golden retriever, responds with a couple of loud barks from a far corner before racing downstairs to protect his home. He used to be more relaxed, but after being knocked around a few years back during a home invasion, he's not the pup he was. He approaches me with a slight growl, still uncertain.

"Relax, buddy, it's just me," I say, holding out my hand for him to inspect.

He gives it a sniff before welcoming me with a wagging tail.

"Have you seen Charlie?" I ask, but all Ollie offers is love. I give him a quick scratch behind the ear, then dart past him to Charlie's room.

The blinds are open. The late afternoon sun warms the space. Everything is in order. Charlie's bed is made, his dresser neat, his poster of Pink Floyd dust- and fingerprint-free.

Charlie's always been a private guy; he keeps personal stashes everywhere, storing them in every nook and cranny. If he knew what was coming, maybe he's left a hint that'll give me a direction.

"Time to make a mess," I say to the empty room. "I'll apologize to you later, Charlie."

His dresser is first. I yank out drawers, dumping clothes on the floor. He doesn't have a lot—his wardrobe is sparse—but I still go through every single piece of clothing, shaking out T-shirts, socks, and underwear. I don't hesitate.

I run my hand along the inside of every drawer before pulling them out and checking the bottom of each one. Under the last one—yes!—a manilla envelope.

I peel it off and look inside. It's empty.

"Shit!" I shout.

Mom calls up from downstairs, "Language!" Even in these stressful moments, she polices my manners.

The find is encouraging, though. If there's one, there's got to be more, and they can't all be empty.

I dump out the stacks of paperbacks in the nightstand, flipping through each, before searching the drawer and behind it. I find another envelope, but again nothing's in it.

What could've been in there? And why doesn't he trust us enough to keep the contents around?

In the closet is his backpack. He carries everything in it, and—like a magical bag of tricks—sometimes it seems endless what he pulls out. I dig through it, searching each pocket and seam and finding heavy-duty sealed plastic bags filled with water tablets, a Snickers bar, a candle, a lighter, wool hiking socks, underwear, a small first aid kit, a length of nylon cord, two glow sticks, ten $20 bills, his lock-pick kit, duct tape, charging cables, two large garbage bags, and a container of Tannerite he bought at the lake last summer.

But no clues as to where he might be.

Beside the backpack is a box that's half full. Inside are old video games, CDS, a scarf, and two picture frames, face down. I remember them. Last year, Charlie slapped my hand away for trying to look. I flip them over.

The first frame is empty, but the second holds a picture of a man and a kid with short hair, sitting on a couch, holding a football, in the middle of a high five. It's a stock photo, which seems like Charlie's kind of joke.

I turn it over and pull off the back and cardboard spacer. A small photo falls into my lap. It's ripped in half, but it shows a man, maybe in his late twenties, with dusty-blond shaggy hair. He stands along a shoreline, mountains in the background, holding up a big fish on a line. He's smiling, the edges of his mouth creasing in deep wrinkles, a cigarette hanging loosely from his lips.

Is this Charlie's dad?

On the back, handwritten in smeared, discoloured marker are the words: *Sasquatch Lake, 1999.*

I turn it over again and study the jagged tear. A red pail floats in the air beside it, the kind you'd buy a kid from the local resort store. Someone's got to be holding it. Charlie?

None of this tells me anything about where he is now, but it feels like something. Maybe I've opened a little window into his past, and if—no—*when* I find him, I'll have to ask him about it.

I slip the photo in my pocket and continue the search.

I finish up in his closet, then move back to the centre of the room. I open his desk, search behind the poster, check the light fixture, pull apart the mattress and box spring, crawl under the bed, but find nothing else. Search complete, I'm standing in the middle of a mess, and all I've got is a torn photo of some dude from years ago.

Dammit, Charlie! Why do you have to be so private?

Mom appears at the door. She's obviously pissed at the mess. "What are you doing?"

"Nothing." This couldn't be further from the truth.

"Since you're doing nothing—" she eyes the mess, "come down for tea."

This is Mom's signal that she and Dad want to have a heart-to-heart. Usually, it happens when I'm in trouble, but as far as I know, I haven't done anything … yet.

The thought of talking it out over tea gives me a headache. "No thank you."

This catches Mom off guard. Usually, I'm a little more compliant. "Anthony—?"

"No, Mom. Not right now."

She's not pleased with my answer. She and Dad always tell my sisters and me that the foundation of a strong family is clear communication.

"Please. I just—I don't have it in me at the moment."

She sighs deeply. She's not happy, but she heeds my wishes.

"Fine," she says curtly. "But if you care about your friend at all, you'll tidy up this mess now before he gets home."

chapter 4

After cleaning up Charlie's room, I drag my ass into my own, feeling absolutely wiped. The highs and lows of the day are taking their toll, and I'm crashing hard.

My suit feels crumpled and constrictive; my tie is wrapped around my throat like a noose. I need to get undressed and into something more relaxed, but partway through changing, my phone blasts The Who's "Who Are You?" and scares me.

"Jeezus!" I shout.

"Language," Mom calls again.

I check the caller ID to see Gekas's name. Charlie must have changed the ring tone for her number at some point. I shake my head as I answer the call.

"What happened?" Gekas asks.

I appreciate the directness.

"Honestly, I have no idea. We were at the grad ceremony. I was backstage, and thought Charlie was with Mom and Dad, but when we were done, I looked at my phone, and there was a text from him that just said 'Help.'"

There's a pause before she says, "Anthony…"

I already know where she's going.

"This *isn't* some sort of practical joke." I pace the room. "Charlie can be a goof and a troublemaker—and yes, sometimes he's an asshole. But he'd never mess with me like this."

She's quiet on the other end before responding. "I know you're concerned, but Charlie's not a child. Maybe, if he were younger, we'd send out an Amber Alert, but the truth is he's likely gone off somewhere on his own."

I can't believe what I'm hearing. "Detective—!"

"For now, we need to wait. He's a very capable person. He's gone through a lot. He's strong, tough, and resourceful. One quick text from Charlie can't be a call to action."

"Detective—it's just that—"

"Anthony, I want you to stay put for twenty-four hours. Charlie's not a vulnerable person, and it isn't out of character for him to slip away from time to time." Her tone is firm. "We need to be patient."

"But—"

"Anthony."

I exhale and give a half-hearted "fine" before hanging up.

chapter 5

I fall back on the bed and stare at the ceiling.

I understand that Detective Gekas doesn't want to jump to conclusions, but my gut tells me she's wrong. Charlie hasn't just taken off.

What am I missing? What loose ends have I not thought of?

There was that phone call right before we went in to the ceremony. He said it was his mother, but she's been AWOL for most of the school year, and it's weird as hell that she'd be calling, let alone at that moment. But he hadn't seemed to question it too much, so I'd simply accepted it. What if it *hadn't* been his mom? And if it wasn't, then who on earth could it have been?

Then I remember the thick envelope Gekas gave Charlie a couple months ago. He never showed me what was in it, but I imagine it was full of secrets from his past. Was there something of value in there? Had Gekas even considered it when I talked to her?

I pick up the phone and try to call her back, but it goes straight to voice mail. Dammit, why wouldn't she answer? I just talked to her!

I hang up, squeezing the phone so tight that I actually have to stop myself before I accidentally break it.

Twenty-four hours.

It's a long time to wait while my friend is missing. I've lost too many people in my life already. I don't want to lose another.

I pull out the photo of the man and look at the back again: *Sasquatch Lake.* I punch it into Google, and it comes back as a provincial park in British Columbia near the town of Chilliwack.

Charlie once said he'd gone out to B.C. to visit his dad. Maybe he lives nearby. I try *Wolfe Sasquatch Lake* in the search bar but only get hits about howling wolves.

Dammit.

I lay back in my bed, staring at the ceiling, not ready for sleep. Too many questions and not enough answers.

Charlie, where the hell are you?

Tomorrow, I'm going to start finding out.

chapter 6

After the horse barn, Charlie's kidnappers drove him south-east, judging by where the sun was in the sky. At some point, they'd turned off the highway and down another gravel road that probably only a handful of locals knew about.

No sign of where they are, though.

As the sun settles below the horizon, they pull into an old farmyard that boasts only a few rusty grain silos and a boarded-up house. But when they go inside, it's stocked full of food and beer, and beds to sleep on.

Well, at least for the kidnappers. Not for Charlie.

They drag his ass down to the basement and lock him into a windowless room with nothing but a dirty mattress that smells like vomit.

He definitely isn't sleeping on that, so he props himself in a corner, using his suit jacket as a pillow, and stares at the bare ceiling light until they shut it off from a switch upstairs.

What he wouldn't do for his lock-picks. Or even his shoes. Absently, he rubs a bit of warmth back into his cold feet. Alone in the dark with his thoughts and memories, he avoids the nightmares by focusing on those he cares about. He hopes the Shepherds don't think he'd just ditch them.

What he wouldn't do for the room they had given him, its soft bed and warm blankets. Or the delicious aromas that waft out from Mr. Shepherd's kitchen. Charlie's mouth nearly waters at the memory of the jerk chicken Ben had made for his wife's birthday a while ago. He'd even imported pimento wood from Jamaica, wanting to make it just like the meal Keya had grown up with.

And Charlie's pretty sure Tony's mom—the whole family, really—hadn't expected a white-ass boy from Canada to pull it off. But Tony's dad had outdone himself—and Keya had had to admit that it was as good as her mama's. Well done, Ben.

But Charlie's pretty sure that it was Keya who had let him have a roof over his head. She runs the Shepherd household with a firm hand, but it was her kindness and empathy that had let Tony bring him in like a stray to share their home.

And Tony...Tony's *got* to know something's majorly wrong by now; he and Charlie have been in enough shit together. And somehow things always turn out better when Tony's around.

But not here.

Charlie has to get out of here before Tony comes looking for him. He needs to focus on the next step.

Where the hell was he? And more importantly, who the hell wanted him in the first place? He'd better figure out how to survive long enough to find out.

chapter 7

Charlie must've fallen asleep at some point because he wakes to the driver kicking him. "Time to go."

When they step outside, the sun hasn't risen yet.

"Don't suppose we could get a coffee?"

They shove him in the back seat, Cass piles in beside him, Red drives, and Winston takes shotgun. The gravel road quickly devolves to a cow trail, and tall grass scrapes the sides as the Maserati's undercarriage takes a beating. Eventually, a shortcut through a field returns them to the highway.

Something, however, is different. The road signs are all in miles per hour, and the deejay on the radio gives the temperature in Fahrenheit. Did they sneak him past the border?

"I've got to warn you, fellas. I didn't bring my passport."

"Shut it."

"Just don't want you to get into trouble—"

"Quiet."

In the front passenger seat, Winston's been prickly all morning. He treats Charlie like some bullshit task he doesn't want to deal with. Cass, slumped beside him in the back, is also in a mood. Charlie can't be sure, but he's guessing Cass is none too happy with Winston forcing this detour down south. And Red? Well, Red just seems pleased to be behind the wheel, listening to tunes. Charlie figures Red hasn't been out of the office—or whatever these goons call it—for quite some time; he's clearly enjoying the outing.

"Seriously, a coffee would be nice," Charlie says again.

"No," Winston grumbles.

"Even some crap from a gas station will do. Or an energy drink—?"

"I said *no!*"

"Then how can I do my best work?"

"Your best work?" Winston scoffs.

"Well, you must've brought me along for a reason, right?"

"And I'm regretting it already."

Charlie's nothing if not persistent. "But if you buy me a coffee and tell me what's going on, then I can start figuring out what happened to Henry."

Winston twists in his seat to glare at him. "You really think you're that good?"

Charlie shrugs. "Of course."

"Wow, you're an arrogant son of a bitch."

"Probably."

Winston grunts and turns back around, saying nothing.

This is a problem. Charlie can only earn their trust and maybe get out of this if he solves Henry's murder; trouble is, they aren't telling him anything because they *don't* trust him.

He needs a different approach. The question is: what the hell would that be?

chapter 8

Red turns down a driveway, travelling towards three Quonset sheds in the middle of an oilfield. Charlie scans the area, but there's no sign of a house. They pull up and park in front of the largest shed.

Nobody moves.

"Is this the place?" Charlie asks. "Can I go in and look?"

Again, nothing.

Cass leans forward. "Boss, you want us to take him inside?"

Winston gives a curt nod.

Charlie climbs out of the car, taking a big stretch. "Gah, that feels good after a long drive."

Cass shoves him forward as Red unlocks the shed.

Inside, it's dark and smells of grease and gas. Red wanders into the black, though Cass and Charlie stay by the door.

"You really need to stop running your mouth," Cass mutters. "If you don't shut up, I'll shoot you myself."

"Well," Charlie retorts, "if you don't give me something to work with, this is a waste of everyone's time."

Cass glances back at the car. "Fine. But only to get us back on schedule. What do you want to know?"

"Who's Robert? Your boss?"

Cass blinks. "How did you . . . ?"

"Paying attention is my superpower."

"What's it got to do with Henry?"

"Nothing, I just want to know what he wants to do with me."

"You know what? That's none of my business. Or yours."

There's a deep *thunk* somewhere at the back of the building, and bright fluorescents burst to life above them. The space is open and wide with two big semi tractors parked in the middle. One wall is lined with a long workbench, filled with drawers and cupboards and every tool imaginable.

"Henry was a trucker?"

"Yup."

"But he worked for you guys? What'd he haul? Stolen goods? Drugs?"

"Among other things."

Cass and Charlie meet Red as they walk to the back of the metal shed, Charlie watching for stray nails and screws on the cold cement floor. These goons aren't likely to take him for a tetanus shot if he happens to step on something in his sock feet. A V8 engine hangs from the ceiling on chains, its cylinder head pulled off and pistons exposed.

"Shame he won't have a chance to finish rebuilding that," Charlie comments.

There's a large plywood structure against the opposite wall. It's been segmented into separate rooms, each door padlocked.

"Storage units? What did he keep in them?"

"Never mind," Cass grunts, pushing Charlie along.

Along the rear is a broken-down motorhome.

"Are you telling me he lived in that?"

"Why not? It's got everything you need," Red says.

Charlie can't argue with the logic. He never understood why anyone would buy a massive house for a family of four. If he'd learned anything from life on the run with his dad, it was that you didn't need much.

But living in a rusted-out RV in the back of a dark Quonset? That's getting pretty weird.

The interior isn't much better. Stained green shag carpet, matching plaid upholstery and oily fingerprints everywhere.

Charlie doesn't say anything right away, taking time to study the place. A dark-brown splotch of blood has bloomed across the back of one of the dining seat cushions. On the table a litter of dirty dishes and beer cans surrounds an ashtray overflowing with stubbed-out cigarettes.

"What happened to the body?"

"We've got guys who deal with that sort of thing," Cass says.

Charlie sighs. "Really messes up my crime scene."

"Yeah, well, we like to keep our business away from the cops."

Charlie shakes his head. Alas, poor Henry. Dude had probably been dumped somewhere in a hole on the back forty.

He wanders down the short hallway to look in the bedroom. A row of dog-eared romance novels fills the shelf under a television. A pillow has been pushed up against the closet divider. Between the sheets is another ashtray.

Something is off.

"Was the TV on when they found him?"

Cass and Red shrug.

"You don't know?"

"We can find out if you want—"

"It was." Winston appears, mounting the steps. He's holding his gun. "Time's up, kid."

"But you barely gave me a chance," Charlie argues.

"I don't give a shit," Winston snaps. "Sitting out there, I realized how nice it was not listening to you spout off."

"Wait!" Charlie stammers.

"No. We're done."

"Boss, she said she wants him alive—"

"Don't matter." He nods to Red and Cass. "Drag his ass out, so we can wrap this up."

Charlie tries to pull away, but Cass and Red have him.

"Henry's not the only victim, is he?" he shouts.

Red and Cass pause.

Winston glares. "What'd you say?"

"More of your guys are dead, right?"

"What're you getting at? What do you know?"

"Nothing!" Charlie throws up his hands, then points to the bloodstain. "But whoever killed Henry moved him over to the table before shooting him."

"So? What's that got to do with anything?"

"This was definitely a crime of revenge."

"Yeah? How so?"

"Look, Henry was watching TV in the back and smoking cigarettes." Charlie points to the ashtray on the table. "In this one, he stubbed them all out. But in the bedroom, there's a cigarette burnt right down to the end. He wouldn't have let that happen unless he was interrupted."

"Feels like a stretch, kid." Winston begins to lift the gun.

"Think about it!" Charlie adds. "The killer came in while Henry was watching TV. Whoever it was had the drop on him—they could've easily shot him in the head right then. But they didn't. They moved him to face his executioner."

"So it was retribution—we figured. It's a hazard in our line of work. What's that got to do with the rest of our defunct colleagues?"

"Revenge and crimes of passion usually involve a lot more bullets. *This* was cold. Calculated. An execution. Your killer is someone who's had a lot of practice."

Winston stares at him, and Charlie hopes he's said enough.

"Congratulations, kid. You earned yourself another day."

chapter 9

I wake to the smell of coffee and breakfast.

I don't know what time I finally fell asleep last night, but it was late. I'm pretty sure the rest of the house had gone to bed long before my eyes even closed.

Today is the first non-holiday weekday since I was five years old that I don't have to think about going to school. I can sleep in as long as I want. I'm not, though.

I check my phone for new texts. There's a shitload of notifications from my socials about the after-grad party, but nothing from Charlie.

I do find a few from Elaina asking if I've heard anything. They were sent about half an hour ago. She probably had about as good a sleep as I did. I respond:

> **Sorry. Haven't heard
> anything. You?**

> **No.**

**Let me know if anything
changes, please.**

Absolutely.

I've been there. I know what she's going through. I wouldn't leave her hanging without information.

I jump out of bed, get dressed, and head into the kitchen.

Dad's at the stove, cooking eggs. "Look at you, getting up early. I guess old habits die hard."

I catch his look, and he and I both know that's not the reason.

"Hungry?" he asks as he pours me a cup of coffee.

"Sure. I'll have something."

Dad pulls eggs and toast from the warming tray and sets it in front of me. It's a huge stack, way too much for just him and Mom and me to eat.

He looks it over and forces a smile. "Seems like I've gotten used to Charlie's appetite. Any word from him yet?"

"No."

Dad furrows his brow. "Definitely unusual."

I nod as I take a piece of toast and dump an egg on top. I don't have much of an appetite, but I want to support Dad in his effort. I fold my pile of food in half before taking a bite, the yolk smooshing out the end.

Dad builds a similar one, topping it with bacon.

"The other day, he convinced me to make egg nachos. Cheese, chips, bacon, peppers, tomatoes, and fried eggs, all baked in a dish, with a side of salsa and guacamole."

"And?"

"It looked disgusting but tasted delicious."

"He does like to experiment."

Dad turns back to the stove to focus on the eggs but keeps talking. "I agree. Sometimes the only way you're going to figure something out is to try it on your own."

I glance over at him. Is he telling me to go look for Charlie? I decide to test the waters. "I'm thinking about going over to Gekas's office after I'm done eating."

"Sounds good." He nods towards the car keys at the back door. "You can take my car as long as you promise to fill up the tank before you come home."

"Of course."

"Don't be late. We don't need your mom worrying."

He and I both know that he'll catch hell as much as me if I'm late.

"Got it, Dad. And thank you." I give him a hug before heading upstairs.

chapter 10

I drive to the police station and park out front, digging deep into Dad's cupholder for change to fill the parking meter.

The officer on duty asks if she can direct me to where I'm going, but I point to the stairs and move past her.

The second floor has Criminal Record Checks, where I assume she thinks I'm headed, but I skip past it and climb to the third floor, where Gekas's office is. In the hall outside the stairwell is another desk, this one with a waist-high wooden gate barring my way.

I turn to the admin assistant behind it. "I'm here to speak to Detective Gekas."

"Does she know you're coming?"

"Yes."

It's a lie. We never actually discussed it, but I'm pretty sure she knew I'd show up at her office at some point today.

He directs me to a row of chairs, and I take a seat.

People come and go, arms full of folders and paperwork. There's a background hum of machines and phones ringing.

It's a pretty busy place, and I try to distract myself with the buzz of it all, but my mind keeps slipping back to Charlie.

If the phone call wasn't from his mom, who could it have been? Who has a vendetta against him? The question should probably be, who *doesn't* have one? Even though he's helped a lot of people and done good in this world, he's also pissed off as many others with his willingness to break laws and bend society's rules to meet his own needs. I'd hope that someone we've come across wouldn't want to hurt him, but in my short time of being around Charlie, I've learned never to assume anything about anyone's intention—ever.

I check the time. It's been twenty minutes. What the hell?

I go back to the desk. "Is she going to be much longer?"

The admin assistant looks up. "I'm not sure."

"Can you let her know I'm here?"

"I have."

"Can you let her know again? Please," I add.

He raises an eyebrow. "Take a seat. She'll call you when she's ready."

I ignore the advice, lean on the wall, and pull out my phone.

> **It's Anthony Shepherd. I'm here.**
> **Could I see you please?**

I watch as DELIVERED flips over to READ with the current time-stamp. I wait for the typing indicator to bubble up.

Nothing.

I wait a few more seconds before sending another.

> **I know you're busy. It won't take long.**

I have trouble staying still and move to the other side of the room so I can look down the hallway towards her office. The door is open, but it's just around a corner, so I can't see much inside. I scan for any signs of movement—shadows, reflections off the glass door. Nothing.

I send one more.

Please. I have questions.

The door opens, and two police officers emerge from her office and scowl my way. I glance away, embarrassed by the attention, but when I see her come out, I advance towards her, only to be stopped by the magnetically-sealed wooden gate.

"Detective Gekas?" I call out.

People poke their heads out of offices to look, embarrassing me more.

"Anthony."

Finally. "Did you get my texts?"

"Yes. I was in a meeting."

"I want to talk to you about Charlie."

"Anthony—"

"It's been almost twenty-four hours—"

"It's been fourteen hours."

"Don't you care? He risked his life to save yours!"

She glares at me, and the admin assistant looks back and forth between the two of us. Gekas nods to release the catch that seals the gate and waves me back.

"Five minutes. That's all you get."

chapter 11

Gekas directs me to her office, and once inside, points me to a chair. "Sit."

I don't have time. *Charlie* doesn't have time. My mind is teeming with questions. "Detective—"

"Sit!"

She's done with my bullshit, and I know I'm not going to get anywhere if I don't start listening. I flop into the chair, trying to act less like a scolded child and more like the seventeen-year-old that I am.

She circles around to her side of the desk and eases into her office chair. Her desk is covered with files, and although it's been nearly two years since I was last here, the piles haven't changed. Even the stained coffee cup looks like it has the same number of dried rings around the inner edge.

She leans forward, clasping her hands in front of her. "Anthony, I know you want to hear something different, but it really is a matter of waiting twenty-four hours."

"Did you check the cameras at the graduation ceremony?"

She sighs. "When it's someone like Charlie who's over the age of sixteen and no longer a minor, we have to consider that maybe he left on his own."

"But did you?"

"Yes."

"How about getting officers on the street to look for him? Or maybe you could send out an APB or BOLO or something official like that?"

"Anthony, there's nothing to communicate—"

"Yet."

"He's not a missing person."

"He will be if you don't do something," I mutter.

This pisses her off, so I reset, going through the list of ideas I'd assembled in my head last night. "Can you track his cell phone?"

"You know this isn't an active investigation, right?"

"Yes," I agree, but persist anyway. "Have you found it?" Charlie should be more than a missing teenager to her. She and I both know this.

She pauses before nodding. "An officer recovered it."

Charlie's lost his phone? *That* can't be good. And it's clear she's at least somewhat concerned to have sent someone to check out the area. "Where was it?"

Again, she doesn't answer immediately. She knows that whatever she tells me, I'll use it to follow up on my own.

"Outside the convention centre—"

"In the parking lot? Or along the street? Was it near the intersection? On the north or south side—?"

"It was in the middle of a boulevard." She sighs again. "But before you get any ideas, its location gave no indication as to which way he was going."

My brain is buzzing. "Did you open it up and look at it? Is there anything on it that might tell us where he went?"

Begrudgingly she admits, "It was pretty beat up but still functional, and there *was* a photo taken around the time he texted you—"

"Of who? Did someone take him?"

"Anthony, stop! The image is blurry and backlit. We can barely tell if it's a man, a woman, or a dog—"

"But it's *proof*—"

"It doesn't mean anything except that Charlie took a bad photo then lost his phone. People lose their phones every day. People leave town every day. Other than the text he sent you, there's no indication of suspicious activity."

She makes it sound so reasonable.

"But he got a call, right before we went inside. He told me it was from his mom—"

"Yes, and against my better judgment, I checked the call logs this morning—"

"And?"

"There was one call."

"From?"

"His mother."

I scowl. "That can't be right."

"Anthony." Yet another sigh. "There's nothing here. No sign that anything insidious happened."

I argue. I can't help it. "But if it *was* his mom, he wouldn't just disappear and not let us know where he went!"

Gekas rubs the bridge of her nose between her thumb and forefinger. "What if I told you that over the years we've spent a lot of resources dealing with Charlie Wolfe. A lot. And over and over again, we've brought him home kicking and screaming."

I ignore this. "A couple months ago, you gave him a big envelope—"

"No."

"And once you showed me a file here, in this office—"

"No."

"I could *help*—"

"This conversation ends now."

"Can't you just tell me what you know about—"

She slams a hand down on the top of the table. "Anthony. Stop. We're done."

The frustration of the moment hangs between us, and I glare at her, not backing down.

She leans forward, clearly working to relax the tension in her face, to appear sympathetic. "Anthony, I'm not giving up on him. I will let you know if I find anything, but for now, we've done everything we can."

She rises, moves to the door, waits for me to follow.

I'm pissed off and push my way past her.

"Anthony?" she calls after me. "If you hear from him, you'll let me know, right?"

I turn back and nod once, sharp and sullen. But she's just gone from being an ally to being another obstacle in the way of finding my friend.

chapter 12

I step outside the police station to find a parking ticket on the windshield.

"Shit," I grumble, jamming it in my pocket. I add it to my growing list of a lousy day. I drive away, and my frustration slowly boils into anger.

Gekas is so tight-lipped, I can't stand it. Sure, she's always professional, and she cares—but this time there's something else. Not indifference, not exactly. But it's almost like she's making excuses or denying the reality of the situation.

I'm tired of waiting around. It will lead to nothing but suffering and misery. If she's not willing to look for Charlie, then I'm going to find my own answers.

But where do I start?

The guy definitely knows how to keep a secret. It's like he has a genetic predisposition to be reserved.

I go through my list of leads, people who know Charlie. The choices are limited. I've only seen his mom once, down a hallway and late at night. I never even spoke to her. I know his dad is somewhere out in B.C., but I don't know his name, and the photo I found yesterday is the first hint I've ever had about what his dad might look like.

Charlie doesn't have a lot of close friends, either—I'm probably his closest—but when I first met him, he was mostly alone, and all the times I'd tried to track him down, it was like chasing a ghost.

He used to hang out with Robbie at his old school, but they're definitely not buddies anymore. There's Elaina, and maybe a couple more people from my school, but no one that knows him any better than me.

There are, however, a lot of people around the city that he helps or trades intel with. I barely know any of his connections, but I *do* know two who might just be able to offer some insight as to his whereabouts.

I think it's about time to pay them a visit.

chapter 13

I travel north to Fran and Donny's.

Technically, it's her house—she owns it—but Donny stays there, along with about a dozen or so street kids that rotate through the place every week. Some have jobs, but most rely on other forms of income. Doesn't matter, though. She lets them hang around for free because she likes the company.

The place looks the same—rundown and uncared for. The cream-coloured three-storey house looks ready to collapse in on itself. The grass has been trimmed, but whoever cut it also took out a section of the small picket fence that runs around the edge of the property. Plywood has been hammered over one section of the living room window, and the front door hangs wide open. Two kids, maybe fourteen, sit on the steps, passing a vape back and forth and laughing at something on a phone. I go past; they don't even look at me.

On my first visit, I'd felt uneasy entering the place, but this time I've got a job to do. The smell of smoke, dust, and B.O. punches me in the nose as soon as I step into the front entry. I skip the ritual of removing my shoes and stroll into the living room, knowing the sticky floors are layered with dirt. Two large garbage bags of clothes—labels still attached—are in the corner, the thin plastic of one gutted and spilling its overstuffed innards. There's a couple of new recliners as well—most likely picked up from a back alley or lifted straight from a house they B&E'd. A girl is crashed on the couch, and another kid plays on a computer—also new—but he's got his back to me, headphones on, so I breeze past.

In the kitchen, a short, blonde-haired girl with a septum piercing cooks scrambled eggs for two boys who must be around five years old. Way too young for this place.

"Is Fran around?" I say.

"Who's asking?" the girl responds.

The two kids watch our conversation, heads ping-ponging back and forth.

"A friend of Charlie's."

"I don't know a Charlie."

"Just tell me, is she around?"

"No." She turns her back on me and dishes food onto the boys' plates.

I'm not interested in waiting around and go on up the back stairs to find Donny. The second floor is a mishmash of people lounging in the hallway and crowding doorways. I'm just another random teenager, so I move past without resistance.

The door to Donny's attic loft is closed, the air pungent with incense and weed. I'm about to knock but shake my head. I don't need to be polite with this guy.

"Donny?" Silence.

"Donny, I'm coming in."

chapter 14

I push open the door, and a cat shoots down the stairs, scaring the shit out of me.

The room is dark and dingy, but a haze of patchouli and nag champa swirls in the sunlight that breaks through the curtains at the far end of the room.

I find a light switch, but it only turns on the twisted heap of Christmas lights on the floor by my feet. At one end of the room there's a mattress on the floor, and just like last time, a human-shaped lump lies under the sheets.

On this side of the room is Donny, splayed back in his chair, eyes closed. A pair of Beats headphones hugs his head. I assume they're stolen.

I walk over and kick his foot.

He opens his eyes. "Oh, hey there, shiny boy." He makes it sound like he's been expecting me, but his eyes betray him. I can tell he's annoyed that I've dared enter his inner sanctum. "Did you finally come to dust up those clean kicks of yours?"

"Is Charlie here?" I ask, ignoring the question.

He snickers. "Aww, is the bromance finally over?"

"Knock it off. Have you seen him?"

He catches the crack in my voice, and sits up, chair creaking as his feet hit the floor. "Oh shit. This is something else." He scrutinizes me, and I have to force myself not to look away. "What is it? He steal your lunch money? Because we all knew that'd happen sooner or later."

I'm just about ready to punch this pasty trash bag in the head. Trouble is, it's clear Donny suspects he's getting a rise out of me. Worse, he'll try to use that against me.

"You're angry—understandable—but whatever's bugging you is more than just Charlie's old habits." He studies me a moment longer. "Ah. You're worried; something's happened to him." A smug smile spreads across his face; the gap between his front teeth shows. "I'm thinking his past finally caught up to him."

What does he mean by that? What does he know? I want to ask, but when Donny smells weakness, he's like a shark in chum-filled waters. But given that it took him a little longer to read me than last time, I deduce that he actually doesn't know much. My only two questions are *What does he know?* and *Can I get him to tell me?*

"Do you know where Charlie might be?" I ask.

Donny's cockiness grows; he thinks I'm at his mercy. He stretches back in his chair again, crooking his arms behind his head. "What's your name again, rich kid?"

I don't want to give it to him—I don't want to give him *anything*—but I'm sure he'll figure it out sooner or later. "Shepherd."

He grins, the gap showing again. "All right, Shepherd," he says icily. "I don't know if your buddy told you or not, but he and I go way back. We were bruthas *long* before you ever entered the picture."

Really? He's going for the jealousy angle? Doesn't matter. It's not going to work. Charlie told me that before I met him he used to live at Fran's and do illegal things for Donny, but also that it didn't last. Charlie was smart and worked his way out of the situation.

But do any of his past connections have a bearing on his current disappearance?

"Look, do you know anything about him or not?" I ask.

The greasy smile reappears. "Well now, *that* information is gonna cost you."

When Charlie had come to Donny in the past, he'd offered a trade, and Donny's favourite currency was information—the kind of power that could get you into places not even money can buy.

"I've got nothing for you," I say.

"Oh, shiny boy, we all have something to bargain with."

"I'm not bargaining."

"Come on. Look above, look below, and I'll tell you where you need to go."

He's trying to be cryptic and deep, but all it makes him sound like is a douche.

"Listen, nutsack—"

"No, you listen. You come into my den, telling me you want info, and then say you've got nothing to offer? We all have something special to share."

"What are you talking about?"

"Aww, we all know a guy like you, Mr. Popular. You must get invited to *all* the parties..."

Ah, I see how it is. To him, I'm just some rich kid who hangs out in the homes of other rich kids, which makes me a treasure trove of valuable information for a guy like Donny. I could give at least a couple of passcodes, places where keys are hidden, the layouts of rooms, and where the valuables might be stored. Damn, I might even know the schedules of some of these people, when they'll be out of the house for activities, or on vacation.

I'm not going to betray those who've trusted me, but a guy like Donny doesn't understand that. He's such an asshole that he'd steal his own grandma's medicine, then sell it back to her at a higher price.

I might be able to use that to my advantage. "I don't know..."

Donny's grin grows. "That's fine. I'm sure Charlie will be okay."

I give a dramatic sigh. "All right, fine. But if I give you this information, how can I trust that you even know where Charlie is?"

He shrugs. "You give, and I'll tell."

I need to proceed carefully. "Okay, but before I start sharing, I want to set some rules on this transaction."

Confident in his position, he eases even further back into his chair. "All right. What's your terms?"

"One-for-one trade. One piece of my info for one of yours."

"Of course."

"And I'm not trading for anything I already know."

He laughs. "And how am I supposed to know what you already know?"

Donny's grinning, but there's something forced. I'm betting he's playing a fake, but I have to be sure. "I'm not trading for anything you've got about Chan, Lock, Padders, or Foy."

He nods, but half of these names are from Charlie's past, and the others I've made up.

"And don't tell me about the hangouts I've been to, like the Sugar Dough Shop, the Box, or Ollie's." Throwing in my dog's name seems like a nice touch.

He tries a poker face, but squints momentarily, and it's all I need. "Fine. That it?" he asks, too vain to admit he doesn't know shit.

"Yup. Nothing else."

"So, are we going to do this trade?" He's hungry for the deal.

"Nope." I grin, holding it long enough that he feels the burn.

"Why not?"

"Because you're bluffing."

He forces another smile. "The hell you talking about? Of course I'm not."

"You didn't recognize anything I just said, not even Charlie's workplace."

"Don't you give a damn where your friend is?" he splutters.

"I do," I say. "But you've got nothing to offer."

"But me and Charlie used to roll together—"

"Yeah, but apparently that means shit, or else you'd know something."

He flies out of his chair, coming at me, getting in my face, but I stand my ground, ready for him to strike. He doesn't. He and I both know I'd kick his skinny bag-of-bones ass.

"He'll never be your brutha," he shouts at me, but it's all bluster.

"Donny," a female voice ventures from under the blanket. "Quit being a dick."

"Shut up, bitch," he yells.

"*You* shut up—bitch," the lump snaps back sarcastically, then adds with a giggle, "Shepherd there called your bluff."

I walk over to the voice, leaving Donny trying to act tough.

"Do you know anything about where Charlie could be?"

She rolls over and pushes a little deeper into the corner. "If anyone knows anything, it'd be Fran."

"Any idea where she is?"

"No, but when she's back, I'll give her your number."

A frizzy thatch of bed-tousled red hair pops out from underneath the blanket, and she hands me a bedazzled phone.

I punch my number in and hand it back.

"Thank you," I say, and mean it.

"Ah, it's about time somebody did something for Charlie. He's a good dude."

chapter 15

I jump back in the car, happy no one from the house had decided to ransack it while I was inside.

There's still plenty of time in the day, and Donny isn't the only asshole Charlie knows. The second is Joseph Lock, the slimy businessman Charlie had used to leverage his way out of his situation with Donny. Charlie did similar jobs for Lock, too, trading information, but it wasn't long before he had realized that Lock, and people like him, were always willing to pay a lot to screw each other over, so Charlie took advantage of them all.

Lock works downtown, so when I hit the city core, I pull onto a narrow street overshadowed by shiny metal and glass high-rises. Parking is limited, and I struggle to find a spot.

Last time we were down here, Charlie made me park down a back alley in a secret garage filled with high-end cars. He said spaces were offered 24/7/365, with security and a concierge service that delivered almost anything you could want, and the only way you could get a spot was through a high-stakes auction. Charlie might've been ballsy enough to park there, but I'm not, so I patiently wait for someone's grandma to pull out of a metered spot along the street.

Parking is only half the battle. Getting access to Lock's office, a real estate firm called AE and Associates, might be tricky without Charlie. I'm hoping I can summon some of my friend's brashness.

I dig into Dad's glove compartment and grab the plastic pouch that holds the owner's manual, hoping to pass myself off as a courier delivering documents. The ruse isn't perfect, but hopefully it'll get me past the gatekeepers.

I push my way through the revolving door into a large open lobby with chandeliers and white, polished-stone floors. It's beautiful, but having seen it through Charlie's eyes, I know the ugly underbelly of the place, so it doesn't impress me much.

A turnstile with a swipe card-reader blocks my path to the elevators. Thankfully, Charlie introduced me to the security guard stationed next to it a while back.

"Hi, John."

John's tall, stone desk is a mini-fortress, solid and imposing. He drops the newspaper he's reading just low enough to peer down at me. His face is its own granite barrier.

"Do I know you?"

"My name is Tony Shepherd. I'm a friend of Charlie Wolfe's."

Immediately, his face softens, and he offers a smile. "Oh, right. I remember—you came by with him earlier this year. What can I do for you?"

"I'd like to go up and see Mr. Lock."

And just like that, the frown returns. "Is he expecting you?"

"No, but—"

"Look, you seem like a nice young fella—"

"I only need a few minutes," I plead.

"Why do you need to see that man?"

Maybe John will understand the urgency. "Charlie's missing," I blurt. "I want to ask Mr. Lock if he's heard from him."

John's torn. I can tell he wants to help, but he's also got a job to do.

"I'm only asking for a couple of minutes," I say again.

John shakes his head. "He's not going to help you. Guys like Lock only know how to take."

"Yeah, but my friend is missing—I have to try."

John nods, on board, but barely. "All right. I'll let you up, but only because Charlie's a good kid."

He hits the button underneath the desk and the turnstile flashes green.

"But don't stay up there too long. The stench of guys like Lock can be hard to wash off."

chapter 16

I ride the elevator up to the twentieth floor and step out. The long hallway opens onto the offices of AE and Associates straight ahead.

I walk the long hallway to Lock's office, but hold off before the final approach. If I go straight in, I'll only butt heads with the receptionist and draw attention to myself. I'd like to keep this on the down-low as much as possible.

I slip behind a column and wait for my opportunity.

The last time I was here, the secretary was more robot than human, barely showing any emotion, and it's no different now. Through the glass door I watch her answer the phone with a dead-eyed stare, and when someone comes to her desk, she barely acknowledges their existence.

The elevator *pings* behind me, and I pretend to answer a call. "Yeah, just arrived, then off to Wolfe and Co.," I say to an imaginary boss, as a man and woman pass me and walk into AE and Associates. The secretary glances up briefly, but is interrupted by a man from the back office.

"Kelli, can you give me a hand with the coffee?"

From the look on her face, this isn't the first time she's dealt with this moron. She pushes away from her desk and leads him down the hall.

Perfect. As soon as they disappear around the corner, I slip inside and make a beeline for Lock's office.

The door is open, so I walk inside. Lock's there, bent over the keyboard at his mahogany desk. I startle him.

"Who the hell are you?!"

"A friend of Charlie Wolfe's."

This does not ease him, and he reaches for his phone. I step forward and press the button that disconnects the call. "Just give me a minute." I'm ridiculously calm.

"Why? You another junkie kid looking for quick cash?"

I've been called a lot of things, but "junkie" has never been one of them. Donny must've found his way here and tried to make his own deals.

"Not even close. Charlie's gone missing."

"Look, I don't know anything."

"Have you seen him?"

"Not lately." Recognition flutters across his face. "We've met, haven't we?"

"Yes, a few months ago."

"Right, right, right..." He tries to come up with my name.

"Anthony Shepherd."

"Right, right, right..."

"Do you have any idea where Charlie might be?"

Lock leans back in his chair in a contemplative pose, hands behind his head. He even swings shoeless feet up onto the desk. It's a study in relaxation. It's utter bullshit.

"Like them?" He indicates his socks. "Vicuña wool. Had them shipped in from South America."

Did he intentionally stick his feet on the desk just so he could brag? Unbelievable. This guy is truly the weirdest douchebag I've ever met.

"What about Charlie?" I ask again, exasperated.

"Listen, if I knew where he was, I'd help. A missing Mr. Wolfe does me no good. Without him, I'm s.o.l."

Though I'd like nothing better than to smack him across the face with the hefty bulk of the owner's manual, I'm desperate for info. "Any idea what might've happened to him?"

He plucks up a brass golf ball sitting in a display tray on his desk and rolls it between his palms, bringing it to his forehead now and then like he's praying to the gods of sport.

"To be frank, I'm not surprised that Charlie's disappeared. He's always walking the line." He points at me. "Have you checked with any of his miscreant friends across the tracks? They're always taking advantage of his charity."

Funny that Lock doesn't see himself in the same category as Donny's crew—they both abuse Charlie's skills.

I shake my head. "They didn't have anything for me. Do you know anyone else who might—" here I choose my words carefully, although this guy's so dense, he probably wouldn't recognize an insult if it bit him, "'employ' Charlie's services?"

He laughs. "I could throw this ball and probably hit a dozen people who've used him…" He pauses, realizing I may actually go and *talk* to one of those people, so he backpedals. "However, not everyone's going to be as forthcoming with their assistance as me…"

I realize he's already forgotten my name—again. For a highly paid corporate dude, he sure is dense. "Anthony," I repeat.

"Right, right, right…Anthony." He turns to the window to ponder. Again, I'm pretty sure this is all staged. He studies me. "Look, Anthony, I'm sure Charlie's fine. He'll show up when he feels like it. Of course, anyone that Charlie trusts as much as you, well, they must also have a similar set of talents." He leans forward, clasping his hands together. "You seem like someone who's good at keeping secrets…or perhaps learning them?"

He pauses, and it occurs to me that in the silence, his statement has twisted into a question.

"Are you—are you asking me to do Charlie's work?"

"Well, since he's not around at the moment…"

"Because he's missing!"

"And if I hear something, I'll let you know. But for now, give a little, get a little—am I right?"

I've heard enough. Personally, I'd like to reach over Lock's desk and wipe the toothy grin off his face, but he's not worth the trouble. "I'm not exploiting my friend's disappearance for a little profit."

"Aww, don't be sore, sport. It's just good business. I'd pay you well."

It doesn't matter what he's offering. I'm out of here, slamming the door in his face. The sooner I leave this corporate slime factory, the better.

chapter 17

I fume quietly as the elevator takes me down to the lobby. Not only did I waste my time getting absolutely no help from Lock, but I was also reminded what a sleazeball he is.

Why can't Charlie work with normal, decent people?

Except I know the answer: normal, decent people don't get involved in Charlie's kind of business.

As the door opens and I head across the lobby, John waves me over. "That was quick," he says, folding up his newspaper.

"Yeah. He didn't know anything."

"Doesn't surprise me. Lock's just a peon."

"What do you mean?"

"Well, although he's got some money and a little power, he's not really anyone. But while you were up there, I got a call. Seems like someone wants to speak to you."

This is a surprise. "Who?"

"Lamay."

"Is that Lock's boss?"

John considers. "Not really. But Lamay's someone with a lot more knowledge about what's going on in this town."

The thought of encountering yet another frustrating dead end exhausts me, but if I don't follow every lead and something happens to Charlie, I will never forgive myself.

"Where do I go?"

chapter 18

John sends me to a narrow set of stairs near the elevator. I follow the winding steps downward until I reach a blank, grey door that looks like it leads to the bowels of the building. But when I open it, it's nothing like the dark, steam-filled Freddy Krueger basement I imagined.

On the other side is a clean, brightly lit area. High-end industrial machines hum quietly along lengthy and spacious corridors. Everything is immaculate. Either they recently put a fresh coat of paint on everything, or it's part of the daily sweep and mop and maintenance.

There are a number of people down here, too. Not just building maintenance and janitorial staff, but office workers pushing rolling carts filled with boxes of mail and files. This place is a whole other world, an underground corporate system unseen by the city above.

I've barely had a chance to take it all in when a dude in a suit with a "don't mess with me" face approaches. I wouldn't be surprised if he works nights as a bouncer.

"Good day, sir. May I see your ID?" The words come out scripted—polite but cold.

I yank the lanyard that John gave me out of my pocket. It's a pink laminated card with the word GUEST written in bold.

"You're just visiting for the day?" the suited security guard asks.

"Hopefully not even an hour."

He nods, holding up the lanyard. "Keep this visible at all times while you're down here." He waits until I slip it on before continuing. "You know where you're going?"

"I think so. I'm looking for—"

"Listen, I don't want the details. Just get moving, and get out of here as soon as possible. Understood?"

I nod.

He moves back to his spot beside a cement post.

I take out the directions John scribbled on a page from the financial section of his newspaper. They look like something between chicken scratchings and hieroglyphics.

The first arrow says go right, so I go that direction down the passageway between the machinery. There's a number of intersections and detours that split off from the path in multiple directions, but John has drawn shapes beneath the instructions to show me what to look for.

The first one is easy: EXIT.

I turn left when I see the red glowing sign.

But the next one looks like an upside-down U or a gravestone. Ah. There's an archway up ahead, and I walk through it to a new section. The hallway shudders as a truck thunders overhead. I must be under the street.

I continue on.

Several more security people linger in corners, but office workers are now scarce. The ones I do pass have different coloured lanyards; none of them are pink like mine. I feel like I've stepped into some weird spy movie.

I go down a corridor that runs the length of a city block, before turning right, then left, and a final right to arrive at a locked metal fire door. There's an intercom on the wall, and a small camera in the corner above stares down at me.

I can't find a call button, so I knock. The solid door absorbs the sound. Nothing.

I pound again. Harder, louder.

The intercom crackles. A man grumbles. "Password?"

I flip over the newspaper to read the word John has written down. "Polyglottal."

Seriously?!

The door opens a crack, and a tall, slim man in an Adidas track suit blocks my way. He looks nothing like the security dude in the suit. He's definitely got a scumbag-from-a-British-gangster-film vibe. Oh, this is definitely the sort of thing Charlie would lead me into.

"What do you want?"

"I'm here to speak to Lamay."

"Get lost."

"Wait. I was told to come."

"Yeah? By who?"

"John."

"Don't know any John. Beat it."

"No, wait—"

He goes to slam the door, but I shove my foot in before it closes.

He glares at me. "You better remove that before I do it for you."

I trust he will, but I'm not budging. I need to see Lamay.

If Charlie were here, he'd probably do something drastic like throw a smoke bomb and dart past in the confusion. Fortunately—or unfortunately, I can never decide—I'm not like him. But diplomacy isn't going to work either.

I need to combine Charlie's strengths with my own. I dig deep and find something between cockiness and "too tired to give a shit."

"Why don't you open the door before this becomes a real problem."

Tracksuit sneers. "Yeah? From who? You?"

"I'm sure Lamay would love to know that you're wasting my time."

"Please. Lamay's not even my boss."

Then who is? Never mind. I have to ignore this and keep pushing. "Yeah, and everyone's going to want to hear what I have to say."

"And what exactly is that?"

"That's between me and Lamay," I sneer.

"Get out of here, you little shit."

Damn. This isn't working. Desperate times call for desperate measures.

"Fine. Then *you* explain to everyone why no one told them about Charlie Wolfe."

This catches his attention. "But didn't they—?"

"Pick him up? Yeah, way to go, genius! We know. This is about the impact."

He's getting pissed. "And what's that?"

"Why would I tell you? I don't know who you are! But instead of letting me deliver this time-sensitive information to Lamay, you're wasting my time at this door."

I feel him ease back, and I push my way in.

There's another long hallway on the other side. A tall stool and a bar table sit behind the door, with a bottle of water, a book by Ken Follett, and a small bag of beef jerky on top. I have no idea how many hours Tracksuit's been stuck here, but it seems like an awfully boring way to earn a paycheque.

"Hey—!" He whips a snub-nosed revolver out from the waistband of his pants.

My stomach drops. I'm sweating—a lot—but I'm too far in to react to my fear.

"Great! Just great," I yell. "I give you the password, Lamay's name, Charlie's name, and John's—who you don't even seem to know—and you're *still* waving a gun around? How about instead of screwing everyone's day, you move aside and let me do what I need to do."

I turn on my heel, abandoning him. Every step down the hallway feels like a mile. I think I can feel the gun trained on my back, and hope against hope that he's doubting himself enough not to shoot.

Seconds feel like minutes until I arrive at a service elevator. The inside is wide, white, and sterile. Almost like something from a hospital, except there are only two buttons on the inner panel. I slam on both, hoping either one closes the doors. Tracksuit is still staring at me down the hall, gun in hand, as I back all the way inside.

After an endless wait, the doors finally roll shut in front of me, and I breathe a huge sigh of relief.

chapter 19

I can't believe how stupid I am. I really should've let my parents or Gekas—or someone!—know what I was up to. If Tracksuit hadn't folded, I would have been screwed—or worse, ended up on a milk carton.

The elevator rises, and the doors open without even a *ping*, and I face a room filled with glass and light. The floor glows with frosted panels, and the wall to my left has a mirror that stretches the length of the short corridor. But on the right loom tall, tinted floor-to-ceiling windows that reveal the city for miles: the lake, the government buildings, and the urban sprawl stretching to the countryside and far beyond.

Charlie would love this.

Unfortunately, my fear of heights says otherwise, so I keep close to the inner wall until I push through the door at the end of the hall.

chapter 20

I step into a dark room.

My eyes take a moment to adjust, and once they do, I'm surprised how tight the space is around me. I'm sure if I stretched my arms out, I could probably brush the navy blue walls on both sides with my fingers.

Directly in front of me is a deep, rich walnut counter with space for only two wood-and-leather barstools. On the wall behind it are shelves filled with premium alcohol.

I suddenly realize what I've walked into.

Earlier this year when Charlie took me to the garage with the high-end cars, he pointed out a door that he said led to a series of passages all over downtown, including an exclusive club high above the city.

This is it—except Charlie had said it was the size of a small apartment. This isn't much bigger than a utility closet.

The only other person in the room is a tall, muscular balding man in his thirties with a hard-set jaw and a keen stare, standing behind the counter. He's dressed formally in a vest and a white button-up shirt, his sleeves rolled midway up his forearms.

Before I can say anything, he smiles. "Welcome, Anthony."

"You know me?" I ask, trying to keep my voice steady.

The man chuckles. "Of course."

"Are you Lamay?"

He shakes his head with a soft chuckle, and I'm startled by how disarming it is.

"I'm Kosmos, barkeep of this establishment." He offers his hand. "Regrettably, Ms. Lamay is unavailable."

Another dead end. This annoys me. "What's that mean?"

"She's travelling and won't return from Europe until next month."

Next month? What a waste of time. The whole day has been an exercise in frustration, with me getting all the exercise. It's like I'm running back and forth on the court but not moving the ball anywhere.

I head for the door.

Kosmos calls out, "Perhaps I might offer you a drink before you leave?"

"Why? I came to speak to Lamay—"

"*Ms.* Lamay—"

"Honestly, I don't give a—"

His friendly tone takes on a firm edge. "Anthony Shepherd, I appreciate your frustration, but if you want to find out who has taken your missing friend, I insist you show her some respect, and take a seat."

The mention of Charlie stops me in my tracks. "What do you know—?"

"Manners, Anthony."

"Please, just tell me." I can't take much more of this.

He raises a hand. "In due time. Now sit, and let me fix you a drink." He searches behind the bar. "I think I've got something that'll satisfy both our needs."

Swallowing my impatience, I reluctantly hop onto a bar stool, setting the owner's manual on the seat beside me.

As he gathers items, I study the space—who knows if I'll get another chance?

The whole counter gleams, and the upholstered leather is soft to the touch. The lights are low, and the corners of the room drop into shadows and muted silence. Every bottle label is aligned perfectly straight so I can read them; there's nothing out of place. Not a smudge or a speck of dust.

Kosmos fills two glasses with ice. He grabs a small bottle and shakes out a couple of drops in each.

I raise my eyebrow, and he grins. "Just bitters to add some flavour."

He tops each drink with ginger ale and pushes one of the glasses towards me.

I'm willing to give it a try. The spice definitely has some zing, but it mixes nicely with the sweetness of the soda.

"What *is* this place?"

He gestures to the room.

"It once belonged to Ms. Lamay's grandfather, who was a lawyer. Back then, it was a quiet escape from the hassles of the day for him and his colleagues. They built it into the backroom of their office." He reaches out, touching the wall beside us. "Behind here is what is now one of the most powerful law firms in the country."

For the first time, I notice the faint outline of a door cut into the wall.

"When her father didn't pick up the legal baton, her grandfather passed the keys on to Ms. Lamay when she made partner." He chuckles. "I don't think her parents, God rest their souls, even knew the place existed."

He takes a sip, savouring the flavours.

"When she took over, she transformed the bar into something far more impressive than her grandfather ever conceived. Ms. Lamay is industrious; she saw a big opportunity for her unique and affluent clientele. She expanded downstairs, and set up the garage and concierge service, always focused on her grandfather's singular vision: to create a place of respite for all who enter."

He leans over his drink, looking down at the ice floating at the top of the glass, but when he looks back up at me, he's close, and I can feel his gaze cut through me.

"In the beginning, it was easy, but as her business grew, so did the needs of her clients. She did her best, but often their demands were far too onerous. To accommodate their requirements, she had to make sacrifices—moral ones—and work with the wrong types of people."

"What sort of people?" I ask softly.

He leans back, his face grave. "That's where you and your friend come into the story."

chapter 21

Kosmos tops up his drink, not with ginger ale or bitters this time, but with a bottle of booze he brings up from a shelf below the counter. He twirls his glass, listening to the ice cubes tinkle before choosing his next words.

"A few months ago, we had a reservation. A woman from out of town, with deep connections to the folks who had . . . appropriated this bar."

"How deep?"

He sighs. "Organized crime."

"You mean the Mob?"

He nods. "They once held sway across Canada, but after their boss was killed a few years ago, the whole organization suffered. There are still pockets that exert force—one being here, in the city—but they aren't what they used to be."

I'm not sure I want to know, but I have to ask. "What does this have to do with Charlie?"

Other than Donny's guys, we'd never had any encounters with any sort of gang, especially one as truly serious as the Mob.

"The woman from out of town was looking for your friend."

"Did she say why?"

He shakes his head. "She only asked his whereabouts."

"And what did you tell her?"

"Nothing. At the time, she knew more about you two than we ever had."

"Like what?"

"She knew where you lived, who your family was—"

"What about Charlie?"

"Well, she knew he'd been in trouble with the law quite a bit and at one point was tracking his movements through Western Canada—"

"What do you mean? When was this?"

"Before he moved here."

This hits me like a bombshell. I knew he'd visited his father in b.c., but I had just assumed Charlie was from around here originally. I file all this information away, focusing on my present query.

"So, if she knew where I lived, why did we never see her?"

"Oh, she watched from a distance, but since her time was limited, she had some of the local crew keep an eye on you."

I lean back in my seat, head spinning. As far as I knew, neither of us had ever been aware of their presence.

"So then Mr. Tracksuit downstairs—?"

"One of theirs. He's undoubtedly reported your visit to his bosses already, but since they have your friend, they're likely not worried about you too much."

"I may have blundered that. He wasn't too keen on letting me in."

"Even with the password?"

I shrug.

"Well, we'll make sure you leave by the emergency exit."

I return the discussion to Charlie. "Why didn't either you or Lamay contact me and tell me about this sooner?"

"As I said before, you had stayed out of our business so we stayed out of yours. In fact, until you spoke to John half an hour ago, Ms. Lamay hadn't even been aware of Charlie's... departure."

"Do you know where they took him?"

He shakes his head. "From what Ms. Lamay has gathered, he's been taken out of town. She doesn't know much beyond that."

I'm amazed by how quickly the elusive Ms. Lamay has been able to gather even what little she knows—especially from across an ocean.

I finish the last of my drink, the bitters now catching in my throat on the way down.

I pull out my wallet. "How much do I owe you?"

Kosmos waves me off. "Courtesy of Ms. Lamay." He pushes a latch in the wall, and the secret door swings open, revealing another dark room—this one full of regular filing cabinets. "Safe travels, Anthony."

I duck down to get through the passage, then pause. "This woman who was looking for Charlie—"

"Yes?"

"She had booked a reservation?"

He nods.

"What was her name?"

"It was probably an alias."

Even so, it might be useful. "What was it?"

"Anthony, I caution you against this. She's dangerous—"

"Just tell me."

"I don't think she'll stop until she's done."

"*Please.*"

Kosmos sighs. He knows I won't go until he gives it to me. "She called herself Cousin Rachel."

I don't recognize it. Never heard it before in my life. But still, a shiver runs up my spine.

Charlie, what have you got us into?

part 2

chapter 22

The road trip back from Henry's was remarkably different than the trip there.

They had spent the day at a safe house on the border, waiting for nightfall to make their cross-country run over the line and back to the farmhouse. But Winston was no longer treating Charlie like a piece of trash—more like a pop can he might get a nickel back from for recycling.

They still stuck him in the basement, but Cass surprised Charlie by showing up at his door with a sleeping bag, one of those cheap ones you find at a gas station. Winston must've sent him to get it.

"So, where to now?" Charlie asks, as he unrolls the bedding out on the floor.

"All depends on Winston."

"And what about Robert? I thought you were supposed to deliver me to him."

"We'll get there soon enough" is the reply.

"And where's *there*?"

"None of your business."

"Hatley," Winston announces, cutting Cass short. All it takes is a look, and Cass retreats back up the stairs.

Charlie can smell the mix of fresh air and cigarette smoke on Winston. He must've been outside, pacing, considering what to do next.

The choice to share information is a new tactic.

"And what's in Hatley?" Charlie knows the place—had lived there briefly once—but it is an old tourist town with not much going for it.

"Don't know and don't care." Winston leans against the door frame, squinting. "Do you know why Robert wants you?"

"Nope. Do you?"

The question pisses Winston off. He's easy to piss off. Winston sucks his teeth and shoots Charlie a look before turning on his heel and locking the door behind him. The light goes out shortly afterward.

So much for conversation.

Charlie settles into the sleeping bag.

He isn't in control of this runaway rocket ship yet, but he is slowly making his way into the cockpit. He's made some headway with Winston—he's certain of that—but will it be soon enough? Planet Robert looms in the distance, and he really needs to avoid a crash landing. And what about home base? The Shepherds are no doubt worried. But it could totally mess him up if Tony attempts a rescue mission.

No point stressing about it, though. He'll have to see what tomorrow brings. They haven't killed him—yet.

So, seriously, how bad can it be?

chapter 23

Holy shit! The Mob has Charlie.

The thought keeps running through my mind as I stumble my way through the law office. People stare, probably wondering who this kid is that's just wandered out of their file room. I travel down the hallway, the owner's manual from Dad's car still in my hand, but I don't even try to pretend that I'm a courier. I only want an exit, so I can get out of here.

I shuffle into an elevator, and thankfully no one follows. As I descend, I collapse against the handrail, doing my best to process everything Kosmos has just told me.

How the hell did Charlie get mixed up with the *Mob*?

The worst we've ever encountered is Donny's s'kids—and the biggest trouble *they* got into was vandalism and basic B&E's. The Mob is all about organized crime: drugs, money-laundering, human trafficking, extortion. It's too big.

The whole idea seems equally ridiculous and equally plausible all at once. Yeah, we've never had a run-in with them, but since Charlie showed up, I've seen a whole side to this city that I never knew existed—hell, I've seen a whole side to *life* I never knew existed.

And who is this Cousin Rachel?

Has Charlie ever mentioned her? Does he even *know* about her? Is she the reason he's missing? Is she the one who took him? And what can she possibly want from him?

The elevator doors open, and I remember I'm no longer in John's lobby, but several blocks from my car. I keep my head down, slip past the security desk, and step outside.

My phone buzzes. I've missed a call. All the cement and metal of the building obstructed the signal. Or maybe Ms. Lamay and Kosmos have set up signal-jammers to block cell phone reception. Nothing would surprise me anymore.

I don't recognize the number, but there's a voice message. "Tony? It's Fran. Call me."

I call her back immediately. Maybe she's got something.

"They told me about Charlie," she says breathlessly.

By "they," I'm guessing she means the redhead under Donny's blanket. I'm pretty sure he would never step up on his own.

"Is there anything you can tell me about Charlie's past that might help me find him?"

"Oh, Tony, I'd like to help, but I really don't know much. He was a good boy when he was here and never a bother, but he never really said much. Even when he helped out cooking and cleaning, he stayed pretty much to himself."

"What about his parents? Did he ever mention them?"

"Oh Lord, I never even thought about Melanie. She must be frantic with worry."

I roll my eyes. Melanie has barely made an appearance in Charlie's life since I've known him. The only time I'd ever seen her was back when Charlie was in the hospital. As soon as she'd seen me, though, she'd bolted.

She probably doesn't even know he's gone.

"What about his dad? Did Charlie ever mention him?"

"No, he never spoke much about him."

"How about a name? Or where he used to live in B.C.?"

"Hmm. He did once tell me his dad's name was William, but never mentioned anything about B.C."

"How about his life before the trailer park? Did he ever talk about where his family lived before they moved here?"

"No. Not really..."

Hope rushes out of me.

"He did mention one place a lot...Snowberry, I think?"

"Snowberry? What's that? A town?"

"I assume so."

"What did he say about it?"

"Not much. Only that he liked wandering along the creek after school. I wish I had more, but you know Charlie. He's not one to share much about himself."

Oh, I'm aware. Trying to make sense of Charlie's past is like singing a song with only half the lyrics.

I just hope it's enough.

chapter 24

After I hang up, I open my browser and search *Snowberry*.

There's a bunch of information about the plant, but nothing specific about a place. I try to narrow it down with different phrasing: *Snowberry Saskatchewan, Snowberry Alberta,* and *Snowberry B.C.* Still nothing. I even try each place with *snowberry town, snowberry street,* and *snowberry lane* but only a few locations pop up, like nurseries or B&Bs in the mountains. But no place that looks like it has a creek nearby.

Next, I try *William Wolfe B.C.*, and about a dozen names pop up around the province.

Okay, this feels more promising.

I save the results to my notes app and retry each name, adding the town in with each search. I trim down the list a bit using social media accounts, local news articles, and pictures that prove the men are obviously either too young or too old. A few results match with other searches, so I leave them with a question mark. But a few bring up absolutely nothing, and I star these black holes as definite possibilities.

I open up 411 and work through the list of maybes and definites to find contact information. I find phone numbers for four of them, leaving only two without any contact information except the town. One of them has a middle initial C. I put a second star beside both of them.

I'm ready to call the first number, but something in my gut nags at me. What if there's a reason Charlie hasn't told me anything about his dad?

And why did he never mention that he wasn't originally from around here? Could this Cousin Rachel be the reason?

Also, what if I actually do find his dad, and he freaks out and—I don't know—goes on the run, like Charlie is prone to do? Then I'd be in worse shape than before.

My eyes float back to the two William Wolfes with double stars. No way to call them at all. Only way I can talk to them is to show up at their door. I type the town where the first one lives into a map: Juneau. It's high up, just past the northern part of the province, in Alaska. Difficult to get to but not impossible.

I type in the second one, the one with the C: Sardis.

Much easier. Just off the Trans-Canada Highway.

But what really catches my attention is the lake in the top corner of my screen. I zoom in.

Sasquatch Provincial Park.

Just like the one in Charlie's photo. And less than an hour away from this double-starred William Wolfe.

Suddenly, a really dumb idea starts to form.

chapter 25

But first things first.

Dad said he wanted a full tank in the car before I got home. I'm going to need it because I've got a very big ask of my parents. I drive to the nearest station, and while the tank fills, I pull out my phone for the second part of my plan.

I open my contacts and bring up Aunt Ayana.

She has a condo out in B.C., but she's rarely there. She works in the art department on movies and hops all over the world on big shows.

I hit *call*.

The phone rings several times. I worry she's sleeping. She usually has a fourteen-hour workday and sometimes isn't even in the same time zone.

She answers. A party blares in the background.

"Tony! My boy!" She's in a good mood. Maybe even a little drunk.

"Hey, Auntie. Did I wake you?"

"Don't be a smart ass," she yells over the noise. "I'm allowed to celebrate after a long week."

"Where are you?"

"New Orleans."

"Working with anyone famous?"

She laughs. "You know I don't kiss and tell. What can I do for you?"

"I'm calling for a favour."

She's distracted suddenly, muffling the phone so she can order a drink. Then she's back, not skipping a beat. "Careful what you ask for. I'll never say no to you."

That's what I'm hoping for.

"I was thinking it's time I visited Vancouver," I say. "Just like Heather and Jodi." Both of my sisters had gone out to the Coast after graduating high school.

"For how long?"

"A week. Maybe two?"

"And when should I expect this visit?"

"I was hoping in the next couple of days?"

"Ha, ha, very funny. You know I'm not there."

Yes, I do. "Uh. I was hoping to be there for my birthday."

She's quiet on the other end, and I can't tell if she's distracted or annoyed.

I push a little harder. "After the couple of years I've had, I figured I should do something nice for myself."

She still doesn't answer, but this time I keep quiet. No need to seem desperate or over-manipulative.

"Have you talked to your parents?"

"Not yet. I thought I'd float the idea past you first."

"Anthony, you know you are always welcome to visit. But I would've preferred showing you around—"

Dammit, she's going to say no.

"But I think you're right—you deserve a change of scenery. Let this be my birthday gift to you."

I nearly choke. I can't believe she said yes!

"Thank you, Auntie."

"All right, I've got to go. Text me the details after you've talked to my sister."

I hang up, elated, but know my biggest challenge still lies ahead.

chapter 26

I wait until after supper before asking my folks.

As soon as Mom starts clearing the supper dishes, I take the leap. "Do you mind if we have some tea?"

Mom's eyebrows go up—she's immediately suspicious, but she puts the kettle on. While we wait, I dig into her collection and choose one of her special rooibos blends. It's a big ask, so I might as well do it right.

"Anthony, is everything—?" Dad ventures, but I cut him off quick.

"It's all good. I just have a favour to ask."

Dad looks at Mom, and Mom looks at me. "Fine, while the water heats up, you can do *me* a favour and help with the dishes."

I oblige, filling the dishwasher and starting to hand-wash the stuff that can't go in.

The kettle whistles, and Dad pours the water to steep.

"It's Charlie, isn't it?" Dad says. It's not really a question.

"It is," I say from the sink.

"You know he's a survivor," Mom says.

"I know."

"But…"

"Let me get settled before we start." I finish the last dish, drain the water, and head over to the island where my parents have already perched. "I know what you're going to say: you like him, but he gets into a lot of trouble."

Mom glances at Dad. "It just seems that every bad situation you've been involved in lately—"

"He's right there, a part of it," Dad finishes.

"Yeah, keeping me safe." My voice raises in volume, and I force myself to calm down. Getting into an argument isn't going to help anything.

Dad begins again. "Don't misunderstand us. We think of Charlie as a part of this household. But he's got a wild side—"

"And we've always expected the day would come when he'd leave," Mom adds.

I can't really deny what they're saying. Charlie has always been one to keep his distance, constantly yo-yoing in and out of my life. Even after he moved in, I wondered how long he'd stay. But I need to move the discussion away from Charlie and on to me.

I grab the pot of tea and pour out three cups. "It's been a crappy year. Actually it's been *two* crappy years. And now Charlie's gone missing."

Mom wants to take issue with my phrasing, perhaps put more blame on Charlie, but I don't give her the chance. "But you're right. There's nothing we can do until he contacts us."

I test my tea, seeing if it's cool enough before continuing.

"I'm wondering about taking a break. Get away and refocus before university."

Mom's back goes rigid, but Dad leans forward. "Okay? Where are you thinking? Toronto? Somewhere down in the States?"

Here goes nothing. "I was hoping for Aunt Ayana's."

"Is she even home?" Mom asks.

Instead of lying, I avoid the question. "I called, and she said I could stay for a bit." Before she can question this, I add, "I was hoping to drive out—take my time. I haven't been through the mountains since I was a kid. I'd maybe do it in a couple of days, celebrate my eighteenth, then come home."

This distracts her. "You want to be away on your birthday?"

"Yeah, I was thinking so. Maybe check out the city. Aunt Ayana's always talking about taking me to a club."

Again, not a lie. She *has* talked about it.

Dad and Mom glance at each other again. Mom's pained face says it all. "Anthony—"

Then something surprising happens. Dad reaches out and clasps her hand. "I think it's time we let him go."

Mom and I are both a little shocked. He almost never contradicts her.

Dad continues, "Over the past few years, you've seen and done and experienced a lot more than anyone your age should have to, even more than someone *my* age. I can only imagine, son. If we can't trust you to travel out and visit with Ayana for a few days and make it back safely...well then, I don't know what it'll take."

Mom shakes her head. "I'm not ready to let him go, and I hate this idea—"

"Hey, I'm right here," I put in, attempting to keep it light.

She glares at me, and I shut my mouth. "However, I do understand what you're saying—and maybe it's time we..." She shifts in her seat. "Maybe it's time that you get out on your own."

"Really?" Before she can change her mind, I jump up and give them a big, all-encompassing bear hug. "Thank you!"

I only hope it'll all be worth it.

chapter 27

I'm up early the next morning and loading the car. Mom appears at the doorway in her pyjamas and bathrobe. Ollie stands beside her.

I grab my backpack and Charlie's from a pile and toss them into the trunk, hoping she doesn't recognize his.

She shifts on her feet. "When you said you were going, I thought it'd be in a couple of days."

I've already thought of a response. "Didn't want to rush, especially if I'm checking out the sights along the way."

Dad comes out of the house with a small cooler and hands it to me. "I've packed some water, lunch wraps, apples, and bananas—as well as my delicious muffins."

"Are these your classic hemp-seed, multi-grain, fruit-filled, all-organic ones Mom forces me to eat, or are they the double chocolate chip ones you hide for yourself in the freezer?"

Dad scowls. We both know it's nothing but healthy for me. I shove the cooler down on the floor in front of the passenger seat.

"Behave yourself at Aunt Ayana's," Mom says.

This kicks me in the gut. I grab them both, pulling them into a hug to cover my guilt. Even Ollie squishes between us for one final pet.

"I expect a phone call at least once a day," Mom says.

"Yes, ma'am."

Might be difficult, given my intentions for this trip, but I'll need to if I don't want my folks to put an end to everything.

"And don't get sloppy with your eating. Your dad packed well for you, so no stopping for chocolate bars and soda."

"Okay."

"The Okanagan is full of fantastic fruit—"

"Easy, Mom! I got this."

She sighs and gives me a final squeeze before pushing me away. "Okay, get on the road before the traffic gets busy."

Dad gives me a solid pat on the back. "See you in a couple of weeks."

I climb into the car and back out of the driveway. Seeing them standing there watching me leave, knowing I'm lying to them, bugs the hell out of me. I give a quick, final wave before focusing on the street ahead.

There are a dozen ways this might go wrong and a dozen other ways I could've done it differently. But in this moment, this feels like the only right way.

I drop the car into drive and head for the thoroughfare out of the city.

All right, Charlie, let's go find you and your dad.

chapter 28

"Stop here."

Charlie wakes from a nap to see that Red's pulling the Maserati into a gas station.

They're on their way up north to the location of another murder. It happened months ago, but Winston apparently still wants Charlie to look around. Feels like a fishing expedition, and Charlie's the one on the hook.

Winston twists around. "You, stay put." Then, a crack in the armour. A small one. "Coffee?"

Geez, maybe Ol' Winston *has* read the Geneva Conventions. "Uh, sure…"

"Cream? Sugar?"

"Black?"

"Black. Right. Naturally."

Winston climbs out, along with Red, who goes to the pump to fill the tank, leaving Charlie and Cass in the back seat.

"I don't suppose you could let me use the washroom since we're here?" Charlie asks.

"Yeah, right," Cass says. The sarcasm is thick.

"Seriously. It's an outdoor one. See?" Charlie points. "You can walk me over, wait by the door, make sure I behave."

Cass pins him with a look before opening the car door. "Keep an eye on him," he says to Red, who's still filling the tank. He heads inside the station to grab the bathroom key.

Charlie scans the vicinity—hoping for his chance.

Shit.

Winston's at the coffee stand at the back of the store, but he's watching.

Cass returns to let Charlie out of the car. "Remember: do anything stupid, and you die slow and painful. Got it?"

"Never expected anything less."

He leads Charlie across the parking lot. He unlocks the door to the toilet and gives it a quick once-over before stepping aside. Cass's smirk says it all.

Inside is the blandest bathroom Charlie's ever seen. The walls are bare, the floor concrete, and everything is lit by a dim LED embedded in the ceiling. The toilet and sink are formed out of pressed metal, and the mirror is a polished plate of steel. A prison bathroom has more warmth.

Charlie shuts the door and leans against it. He doesn't actually need to go, but the momentary space, being away from those guys for even five minutes, here of his own volition, is enough to give him a breath of relief regardless of any odour.

Outside, Cass's phone rings. Charlie hears him answer, but can't hear anything he's saying, even when he presses his ear against the door. Suddenly, there's the crunch and scuff of gravel. Cass has done something surprising—he's walked away. Charlie's sure of it.

Bless people's need to pace while on the phone.

Charlie waits until he's positive that Cass isn't right outside, then unlocks the door and peeks out. Sure enough, Cass has taken his call over to the air pumps. He's facing Charlie, but not making eye contact.

Now or never.

Charlie slips out and alongside the station to scope out the others. Winston is nowhere to be seen, and Red is scrubbing bug guts off the Maserati's windshield.

No one's watching him.

A three-quarter-ton truck pulls up next to the building, blocking Cass's line of sight. The driver jumps out and goes into the gas station, taking the keys with him.

But the door is unlocked.

"How far do you think you'd get?" Winston says beside him.

"Just trying to figure that out," Charlie answers, trying not to sound disappointed. "I *could* maybe hot-wire the truck..."

Winston hands Charlie his coffee. "But it's never easy without the proper tools."

"Right," Charlie agrees. "So maybe I hide in the back of the cab."

His captor considers this. "As long as no one sees you."

"Right."

"But then," Winston takes a slow sip of his own beverage, "what about the Shepherds? Or Gekas? The second you disappear, we make a call."

Charlie nods.

"You got me there," he sighs, like the whole thing's a hypothetical. "Though maybe I could somehow warn them before you saw I was gone?"

"But who could they trust?" Winston responds, turning cold, flat eyes on Charlie. "Doesn't take much to leverage a cop these days."

"True...," Charlie says, taking as nonchalant a sip of what's supposed to pass for java as he can. Still, he has to suppress a shudder, despite the warmth of the coffee, despite the heat of the summer sun.

And that was the heart of Charlie's problem. These guys had backups for their backups, and all roads led back to the threat against people he cared about.

No, the only way out was through.

He'd have to cooperate—at least long enough to identify the mystery woman who's pulling the strings. But once he's found her, he'll stop at nothing to keep those he loves safe.

chapter 29

I pull onto the freeway and turn on the stereo. The radio blasts some Top 40 garbage, and I scramble to switch over to Bluetooth. Smooth beats fill the car as I ease into the long journey ahead.

Bing!

I check my notifications.

It's Elaina.

Any news?

Shit, in my rush to chase after this, I forgot to tell her what was up.

I dial her number, and the car speakers broadcast her voice when she answers. "Tony? Where are you?"

I shout above the rumble of the tires on the highway.

"Travelling."

"Wait! Did you find out something about Charlie?"

I pause, considering how much to tell her, not wanting to get her hopes up. "Just following a couple of leads." I hate sounding like some sort of detective.

"Do you know where he might be?"

"Not really."

"But you know *something*?"

"I might know where his dad is."

"Really? Where?"

"B.C."

"Wow. I always figured Charlie was dumped out by aliens during a fly-by."

It's good to hear she's still got a sense of humour, even under the circumstances.

"What town does he live in?"

"Um, I've got a few options—"

"Wait? You don't *know*?"

"Not exactly…"

"Okaaay…"

"I don't suppose he ever mentioned Snowberry?" I ask.

"What is that? A town?"

"Not sure."

"But it's connected to Charlie?"

"I think so."

"Well, I'm sure it's something," she says, trying to sound hopeful, but I can tell she's losing faith in my chances.

After an awkward silence, I change the subject. "No one really knows what I'm up to out here, so I'd appreciate it if you didn't mention it."

"Okay. But you'll keep me in the loop? Tell me if you find out anything?"

"Of course."

She thanks me and hangs up. The music fades back in.

Maybe Elaina is right to be skeptical. Maybe I'm only chasing Charlie's ghosts and won't find anything.

But I have to do something.

chapter 30

By the time I get to Medicine Hat, I'm exhausted and cross-eyed. A person can stare at only so many rolling fields.

A giant tepee appears on the horizon, and I realize it's a point of interest. Perfect.

I pull off and park. The place isn't too busy; there are only a few cars. In the distance, people wander the valley like bobbing black specks.

I climb out and stretch. Being folded into a pretzel for four hours is the last thing a tall guy like me needs.

It's a beautiful day, so I grab one of Dad's veggie-and-meat-stuffed wraps from the cooler and wander to a spot to eat. As I munch away, I read a sign that says the giant structure is called the Saamis Tepee, originally built for the 1988 Winter Olympics in Calgary.

A cute young woman, maybe in her early twenties, walks out of the valley with her dog. She's got a relaxed, easy presence. Cut-off jeans and blonde hair tucked under a New York Yankees baseball cap.

She smiles at me, and I smile back.

My girlfriend, Sheri, has been gone nearly two years now, and I told myself this spring that it was finally time to let go and get back to living my life.

It's a conscious choice. But not an easy one.

As the woman walks past, I take a quick second glance. She catches me and gives a wink as she climbs into her car.

She drives away, and I take a selfie in front of the big metal structure and send it to Mom and Dad, adding a thumbs-up emoji below. Might as well appease them as long as I can, because the moment they figure out what I'm up to, there'll be hell to pay.

chapter 31

It's late afternoon when I make it to Calgary. Although I'm tired and could use a break, I continue driving, hoping to arrive in Golden right after sunset. It's just over the halfway point to Vancouver, which means tomorrow I can make the final push through B.C. and start the search for Charlie's dad.

The beauty of the Rocky Mountains amazes me, and I can't help but gawk at the steel-grey peaks growing on the horizon. I'm so transfixed, I barely notice the sign that zips past me.

Wait? What was that?

I pull over to the side of the highway, then shoulder-check and drop the car into reverse.

The driveway reappears.

A cattle fenceline stretches all the way to a grove of trees in the distance. A windmill rises above it, spinning angrily. And a ranch sign stretches beside the road: BLUEBELL FARMS.

I quickly pull out my phone and type *Snowberry Farms Saskatchewan.*

Nothing.

I delete *Saskatchewan* and enter *Alberta.*

The top result is a Snowberry Ranch west of High River. No phone number. Only an RM listing.

What if…?

I open the map. How much will it take me off schedule?

Almost an hour and a half to get there, plus looking around, then driving back. That'll put me three or four hours behind.

There's no guarantee it means anything. But if I don't try, I'll only regret it.

I take a moment to switch off my phone's location services—no sense having my parents on my case first thing—then pull back onto the highway, turning at the next crossroad to drive to High River. In the rear-view mirrors, the mountains recede in the distance.

Fingers crossed this detour is worth it.

chapter 32

Following the map's GPS, I turn onto a back road before entering High River.

Gravel kicks off the tires into the wheel wells. I wince at every stone striking the underbody of Dad's car. Here's hoping I don't encounter any fast-moving vehicles that kick up a rock and crack the windshield or dent the hood.

Cows are everywhere, grazing on the tops of hills and down along creeks. Foothills roll towards the mountains, and old wood barns are tucked among bluffs of trees. You'd think an old western town might be over the next rise.

I take a couple more lefts and rights, zigzagging down increasingly less maintained roads. I even have to backtrack when my path disappears into a pasture.

I go another half-mile before seeing a small farmhouse nestled on the side of a wooded hill. If it didn't look so run-down, it could be a postcard, with the way the Rocky Mountains rise up behind it in the hazy distance.

I drive a little further until I find a weed-riddled driveway. Hanging above it is a sign of warped and twisted lumber: SNOWBERRY RANCH.

This must be the place.

I turn towards the house and travel alongside vast pastures. There's not a single cow in sight here, though.

I pull into the yard and am underwhelmed by how shitty and small the place looks.

A little green-and-white farmhouse squats in the centre of the yard, along with a small red barn and a tiny, tilting shop. A few horses are corralled behind the barn, and a line of granaries runs down one side of the windbreak. But there's not much else except a collection of rusted vehicles buried in the trees. An old camper looks like it fell from the sky and impaled itself on a thicket of poplar trees sometime in the last half-century.

As I pull up to the house, two border collies rush around a corner to greet me. They seem friendly enough, despite their barking, so I open my door to let them investigate my scent. One remains cautious, but the other comes in for some pets.

"Sadie, get over here."

A woman in her sixties stands on the steps of the small porch, a shotgun cradled in her arm.

Shit. Although she's not pointing it at me, coming here unannounced *might've* been a bad idea.

"What do you want?"

Definitely not a pleasant tone.

"My name is Anthony Shepherd, and I'm wondering if you might help me out? I'm looking for information about a friend of mine? Charlie Wolfe?"

"Never heard of him," she responds, a little too quickly.

It's like she's practised for a moment like this. Challenging her might not help, especially while she holds that shotgun, but I didn't come all this way for nothing.

"Are you sure? I heard he might've lived here a few years ago."

"Like I said, I don't know anything."

"It's just that he's disappeared, and I'm worried."

She squints when I say this, like it means something to her.

"I'm not asking for much. Just a little information. Maybe you knew his father—?"

She comes off the steps, the gun still not pointed at me, but turned a little more my way. "Listen! What did I tell you? I never heard of him."

"Please, if you know anything, it'd really help—"

"Why's he matter to you so much?"

"Because," I struggle to put it into words, "he's like family—"

"And yet he took off? Doesn't sound much like family to me. In fact, sounds like the kind who'd only bring a lot of trouble your way."

Geez, she sounds a little like Mom.

"Might be all to the good that your buddy ditched you. Now, I'm asking you politely to get the hell off my property."

Her dogs are beside her. Sadie doesn't really seem to care, but the other one has his hackles up and gives a low growl.

I'm done here, whether I like it or not.

chapter 33

Back on the main road, I take stock of the situation.

My gut tells me the woman at Snowberry Ranch knows Charlie, but for whatever reason, she isn't sharing.

I don't want to leave it alone. I'm sure he was here, now more than ever.

If he lived here before he moved to Regina, there's a good chance he went to school somewhere close. A quick search shows a school in a village not far from here.

Hopefully Charlie went there, and they still have his school records—names, previous addresses, anything that might flesh out his background a bit more.

I drive towards it, knowing full well what I intend to do when I get there.

chapter 34

The village is small—a couple of streets and maybe a hundred people—and it doesn't take me long to find the school.

Since it's summer holidays, the place is deserted. The parking lot is empty, and no cars are on the street in front.

I drive past and pull behind a car parked down the block. I grab Charlie's backpack and climb out of the car. If Charlie knew what I was about to do, he'd be razzing me.

In a place this small, any stranger is going to be noticed, so I need to keep evidence of my presence to a minimum. I rush across the street, searching for cover. The front of the building has a few bushes, but it's way too exposed. I duck around the corner.

Unfortunately, this side is no better. The schoolyard faces another street, and I worry that someone could be watching from their front window. I slip into the long shadows of the setting sun, hoping to disappear out of sight.

A single double-door entrance is tucked into an L-shaped corner at the back of the school. I unzip Charlie's backpack and dig out his lock-picks from the bottom. I've used his ring of bump keys before, but never on my own.

I check the brand name of the lock and find a couple of options. I'm absurdly pleased to find the one that fits, and slip it in, adjusting it until it clicks. Then I tap the end with a small rock, just hard enough to jostle the pins inside the lock and jam them into place as I turn the key.

After the third try, I unlock it and dart inside, quietly pulling the door closed behind me.

chapter 35

I stand in a centre hallway that runs the length of the school. I listen cautiously for any movement, but there's nothing.

I need to find the office. Based on my drive-by, the front door should be on the right side, so I head in that direction.

From the look of things, the maintenance staff have already begun the summer-break cleaning. Ladders and scaffolding are everywhere, and the desks and chairs have been shoved into the corridors, barricading the path.

I hop up, moving from one desk to the next. They're all different sizes, some for Kindergarteners and some for high school students. Must be what happens when you go to a small-town school.

I step nimbly off the makeshift obstacle course and work my way down the hall. At the junction of the hallway and front door, there's a trophy case along the wall and an entrance to the auditorium/gym. Across from both is the office.

I peek through the window, making sure no one's inside, before testing the door.

Locked.

I pull out Charlie's bump keys again and find one that matches, but realize I've left the rock behind. It doesn't stop me. I pull off my shoe and give the key a soft hit. It doesn't work, so I give it another try.

"Hello?" a voice calls out from somewhere inside the gym.

Shit.

I scuttle past the office and dive around the next corner.

Footsteps approach. I have to get out of here!

I wiggle the knob of the door closest to me. It's unlocked, so I slip inside.

chapter 36

The whole room is dark.

I bump my way to the back, moving by touch, trying not to make a sound. Copy machine…shelves of paper…whoa, big panel of buttons! Glad I didn't hit any of those—might be the PA system or recess bell.

There's a short hallway around the back corner of the prep room, and I find another unlocked door.

On the other side is the staff room. Past it is the office. The late afternoon sun slices through the closed vertical blinds to light my way. I want to celebrate, but fear it'd jinx my luck. I move across the carpeted floor of the empty staff room and peek into the office.

Yikes! A mustached guy with short hair and a Mötley Crüe T-shirt is chewing a sandwich in the main hall outside the office window next to the door I'd just tried to jimmy.

I duck out of sight, hoping he hasn't noticed me. When I look again, he's gone.

I play it safe anyway and crawl into the office, concealing myself behind the front desk.

I survey the room. Principal's office, vice principal's... and a long row of filing cabinets along the side wall. I cross to them on all fours and open a drawer.

Bingo.

Hundreds of students files, all organized alphabetically. I locate the Ws and flick through them.

WOLBERG, WOLD, WOLENSKY, WOLEFARD, WOLHART...

Nothing.

I check again, making sure I didn't miss anything. Nope. No Wolfe here.

Maybe I'm wrong and Charlie was never at this school. Or maybe these files only include current students. I pull out WOLENSKY and flip through it.

Sure enough, Clara Wolensky was in Grade 7 last year, and according to the gold stars stuck at the top of her file, she was on the honour roll.

I shove her file back where I found it, but notice it's been recycled. Some kid named Lawson has had his name crossed out on the opposite side of the tab.

I thumb through others and find a few more like it, but they're in no particular order. I thoroughly check the drawer before moving on to the one above it. Again, a few recycled ones, but none with Charlie's name.

I've pulled open another drawer, when suddenly—

"What are you doing?"

My hands shoot up, and I turn to face Mötley Crüe guy standing in the doorway.

Thankfully, he seems more confused than threatening. "Do I look like I'm going to shoot you? Put your hands down."

I lower them.

"You want to explain to me what you think you're doing in here?"

I opt for the truth. "I'm looking for a friend."

"And you figure an empty school is the place to find them?"

"I think he—my friend—lived here once. I was hoping to find his school records."

"Doesn't sound like much of a friend if you got to bust in here to do that."

He's got a point.

I shrug. "I'd trust him over anyone."

Mötley Crüe rubs his nose with the back of a hand. His fingers are filthy and blue from whatever chemicals he's been working with. "What's your name?"

"Tony Shepherd."

"But you're not from around here?"

I fess up. "No, I'm from Saskatchewan."

He nods then motions me over. "You wanna come out of there?"

I'm nervous about what he might do next, but slide the drawer shut and move slowly towards him. He opens the door and leads me out into the hallway, but instead of disciplining me, he merely retrieves his half-eaten sandwich from a folding ladder.

"I'm not in trouble?"

"Nah. Most kids don't break into a school looking for paperwork."

He bites into his sandwich, and I cringe at whatever is all over his hands. "So, Tony Shepherd from Saskatchewan, who's this friend of yours?"

"Charlie Wolfe."

He drops the sandwich, mouth gaping like he's just found out aliens are real. "Charles? You've seen him? He's okay?"

"Do you know him?" Holy crap—jackpot!

"That kid—that kid..." he stammers, and I can only imagine all the shit Charlie must have pulled on this guy.

But I'm wrong.

"He was one of the sweetest kids I've ever known."

chapter 37

"Excuse me? Are we talking about the same Charlie Wolfe?"

"Short kid, big shaggy mop—"

Definitely sounds like him.

"Kind and considerate to everyone he met."

Or maybe not.

"I'd arrive at school every morning, and he'd already be here. He'd greet me at the door with a 'Hello, Mr. Whitaker,' and then he'd want to help me mop floors or empty the garbage."

Whitaker wipes his hands on his shirt before sticking them on his hips in contemplation. "You're definitely not gonna find his file in the cabinets. He left, oh . . ." He trails off, trying to do the math.

"Maybe four or five years ago?" It's just a guess.

He nods. "Yeah, that's about right. So those files'll be down at the board office. But . . ." He seems to disappear again in thought, then crosses to the trophy case. "Yeah, yeah, yeah." He moves slowly along the long shelves, searching up and down until finally he stops to push a dirty finger against the glass. "There."

I stand beside him and study the picture he's pointed to. It's hard to see in the dark hallway, but the photo is of a small group of kids holding certificates. Attached to the frame is a short list of names recording their achievements.

Whitaker pulls out his key ring and unlocks the case to pull out the picture and hand it to me.

Holding it, I walk over to the light spilling through the front windows and scan the faces.

Whitaker follows and points to one kid in particular. "There."

As soon as I see the dirty blond hair, I know it's Charlie. But it's not the Charlie I know. Sure, he's younger and shorter, but he's gentler, too, with a gigantic, goofy grin on his face. I've never seen him look so innocent.

"Like I said, one of the nicest kids I ever met."

The date on the small plaque says 2007. I scan the list of names typed on the label below.

CHARLES WOLFE (CONSCIENTIOUSNESS).

Seriously?

I turn to Whitaker. "What else can you tell me about him?"

"Let me see. Oh, I guess Charles and his dad lived around here for about a year and a half."

"Not his mom?"

Whitaker shakes his head. "Nope. As far as I knew, it was just the two of them."

And where was Melanie during that time?

"Pretty sure they moved here from Penticton. William never said much at the best of times, but from what Charles told me, sounded like his dad had worked the fruit farms there. Then he came here to work as a farmhand out at Snowberry Ranch for the McLachlans."

"Yeah, I stopped by there. She wasn't the friendliest."

Whitaker lets out a soft huff. "Doesn't surprise me. Never were the easiest to get along with. At the start of this year, they had some folks bust into their house while they were away. Now they're suspicious of everyone."

I wonder if Cousin Rachel had anything to do with it.

"They never paid him well, but William didn't ask for much. Just room and board."

"That's it?"

Whitaker nods. "They gave him a camper and a little something for food. It wasn't much, but it didn't seem to bother either of them. Charles talked it up like it was a palace."

This doesn't surprise me. Charlie isn't much of one for excess or extravagance.

"Do you have any idea why they left?"

He shrugs. "No one really knew, but it wasn't all on the up-and-up."

"What do you mean?"

"We were expecting a big winter storm, and Charles promised to help me shovel the next morning. When it hit, it was a doozy. Drifts more'n six feet deep around the doors. Took me hours to dig out."

"Charlie didn't help?"

"Never showed. Didn't think anything of it: he lived on a farm and until they'd dug themselves out, I figured we'd not be seeing anyone. Then the next day came and went, and still no Charles, so I ask the office, and they say they haven't heard from anyone. By the third day, the roads were clear, and all the farm kids were back in school."

"But not Charlie," I say.

Whitaker nods. "Apparently his dad came to pick up supplies in town before the blizzard hit, then up and told the McLachlans he quit and was moving on. He packed Charles up and cleared out that night."

"Did something happen? A falling out, maybe?"

"No one knows." He stares at the image, the youthful shadow of my friend. "I was so damn pissed at William for leaving during that blizzard—especially with Charles. You know, I never wanted anything bad to happen to them...but if someone had at least found their vehicle...at least I'd've known."

I know how he feels. Right now, all I want are answers.

And to know my friend is safe.

chapter 38

After thanking Whitaker—and using the front door to leave—I get back on the road. I'm way behind schedule.

To make matters worse, Mom and Dad are calling, but I don't answer. I'm not in Golden yet, like I said I would be, and this could be a real short trip.

Back in the mountains, I pull into the first hotel I find and check in. It's not the cheapest—I've only gotten as far as Banff—but it'll have to do. I skip the elevator, take the stairs two at a time, and rush to my room.

I phone the house, hoping Dad isn't the one who answers.

Unfortunately, he does. "Do you know what time it is?"

"Sorry—"

"Sorry's not going to cut it. I stepped up for you. Let you take the car—"

"Is that Anthony?" Mom calls out.

"I'm putting you on speaker."

"Wait—"

Mom's on the phone now. "Where are you?"

"At the hotel."

"Only now?"

"Well, I did do some sightseeing—"

"Don't be a smart ass," Dad barks.

"You should've called," Mom adds.

"Sorry," I say again.

"We're trusting you to be responsible—" Dad says.

"I *am*!" I bristle.

"Then you need to start showing it," he finishes.

"We aren't asking for much. We simply want to know you're safe," Mom says.

"Fine," I mutter.

Mom is suddenly alone on the line, no longer on speakerphone. "Tony, we know you're old enough to be doing this. It's hard sometimes, letting you grow up."

I hear what she's saying, but I'm still pissed—and since I'm talking to just her right now, Dad must feel the same way.

I exhale slowly. "I need you guys to trust me."

"We do. It's just… You just have to give us a bit of time."

They need to let me make my own choices—but if I don't acknowledge their need to know I'm all right, especially after everything that's gone on lately, there's a good chance they'll shut this rescue mission down.

"Okay," I say finally. "I'll check in more often."

Mom sighs a breath of relief. "Thank you. Now, go get some rest. You have another long drive tomorrow."

chapter 39

I toss and turn throughout the night, stewing over the call with my parents. I wake up early. Between Charlie and my parents, I can't sleep. Might as well drive. I decide to get on the road.

The tourists aren't out yet, only a couple of man-bun dudes packing for a hike up the mountain. I wish I was in the right frame of mind for a run; it's a gorgeous setting, and might help burn off my frustration.

Instead, I grab a small coffee from the shop next to the hotel and get back into the car, waiting for the jolt of caffeine to take effect as I open my phone and search for Charlie and William's names in Penticton.

Nothing comes up; no big surprise. Still, in addition to visiting the William Wolfes on my list, I decide to take a detour and check whatever records might be in the town library in Penticton.

Besides, Mom *had* suggested going to the Okanagan.

I text Gekas next; it's been a couple days since I checked in.

Any news on Charlie?

The text remains unread, so I search all my social media, checking again if there's any message or anything odd that might be from Charlie. Still nothing.

Hoping to head off any parental commentary, I send them a short message:

Leaving soon.
Sightseeing on the way.
Might be out of cell range.

Mom texts back immediately:

Let us know where you are
throughout the day.

Geez. She's up early.

I clench my jaw and send her a thumbs-up.

The constant monitoring annoys me, but the last thing I want is to be dragged home—and it *is* their car—so I've got to at least try to keep them happy. And the spotty cell coverage in the mountains is a good excuse to keep my location app turned off. My biggest fear is that they'll get suspicious and call Aunt Ayana. They can't really ground me anymore, but they'd sure make my life a whole hell of a lot tougher if they found out what I'm actually doing.

I've got to find some answers before that happens.

chapter 40

I drive into Golden two hours later and go straight to the first address on the list of William Wolfes. The idea of meeting Charlie's dad is exciting, but it's promptly extinguished.

The place is a retirement home.

I walk inside anyway and check the registry at the door. Sure enough, there's a Bill Wolfe living here, but it seems unlikely that he's the right one. The photo I found in Charlie's room suggests he should be a lot younger.

Still, I make my way towards the dining room, where the residents have gathered for breakfast. I tell an attendant I'm a friend of the family, and he points me across the room to a gaunt old gentleman in a wheelchair, who looks like he's about a hundred years old.

It's definitely not Charlie's dad.

I awkwardly excuse myself and get back on the road, feeling a little discouraged.

The next stop is Sicamous, but it too is a dead end. This William Wolfe is a young twenty-something, probably not much older than me, on his way out the door to shoot hoops with his friends. I apologize for interrupting and head back to the car.

Damn. Two failed attempts.

I try not to dwell on it as I cross them off the list, and resume my travels towards Penticton.

When I arrive in town in the early afternoon, I go straight to the library and find the archives room. Like many of these places, it's silent. Only the occasional cough or quiet tap of a keyboard. Even my footsteps are consumed by the crushed carpets.

I locate a computer and type in *Charlie Wolfe*.

No results.

I try *William Wolfe*.

Again, nothing.

Dammit.

According to Whitaker, William never said he was from here. He'd only gotten that impression from the stories of a young boy. Maybe wires had gotten crossed, and the school janitor had misunderstood. But I'm not coming back this way, so I might as well try everything.

Bill Wolfe

Nothing.

Charles Wolfe

Again, nothing.

William+Charles+Wolfe

One result pops up.

William Charles & son [photo], August 8, 2007, pg. 10.

What the hell? William Charles?

Having done this once before with Charlie, I go to the reference desk and they send me to the drawers where all their microfilm is stored. I locate the roll and load it up in a viewer, zipping through the daily newspapers, searching for the date and page number.

Eventually, I locate it and roll to a stop on a full two-page photo spread celebrating the annual Peach Festival. Image after image of people celebrating the weekend.

And there in grainy black-and-white, two of its attendees: Charlie and his dad.

Except the name isn't William Wolfe.

Just like the search record stated, the caption before my astonished eyes reads: William Charles... and his son, Mercury.

Seriously—what in the double hell is going *on*?!

chapter 41

I slump back in the chair, trying to comprehend what I've just seen.

Mercury Charles?

Either it's an alias or the greatest practical joke Charlie has ever played. Or Charlie Wolfe isn't his real name at all. And if that's true, then why isn't it?

Charlie has always kept quiet about his past, and I've always assumed that he was just the kind of person who liked his privacy. Oh, I more or less knew that *something* had happened, something personal. But first there was Cousin Rachel and the Mob, then Charlie and his dad skipping town on the McLachlans, and now Mercury Charles!

Looks to me like they were on the run.

I stare back into the viewer and scour the rest of the page, but there is no other information except the photo. No address, no info about what William did in Penticton.

I take the microfilm back to the receptionist and return to the computer to search *William Charles*.

The screen fills with a ton of hits. There's a couple of companies as well as records about an old political cartoonist, a politician, a Canadian fur trader, an English wrestler, and a judge. There's also a lot about Prince Charles, Prince William, and Prince Harry. After scanning a few more pages of search results, I see it's more of the same, and give up. There's nothing more about Charlie's dad.

Next, I try—and I really can't believe it—*Mercury Charles*.

Nothing. At least not in Canada or during Charlie's time on this earth.

Shit!

Like everything else in Charlie's past, it's another dead end.

chapter 42

Frustrated, I leave the archives and drive to the beach at the north end of town. Even though it's a weekday, the place is busy, and I choose a spot away from people so I can be alone with my thoughts.

It's hot and there's not a cloud in the sky. The waves roll in, swishing against the shore, and I regret not bringing a swimsuit. Nothing would clear my mind better than a dip in the water.

I text Mom and Dad, and tell them I'm taking a break from the drive. I lay back and close my eyes to relax, but it doesn't take long for the questions to start to swirl.

Mercury Charles?

What the actual hell?

Searching for Charlie has only led to more questions, as well as the not-insignificant realization of how little I truly do know about my friend. I would have hoped that after all we've been through, he'd at least have trusted me enough to tell me that Charlie Wolfe isn't his real name.

There has to be a reason for all of it: not telling me, being on the run, the reason for his name change to begin with. The questions tumble like rocks in a washing machine—heavy and difficult.

How many other towns had Charlie and his dad lived in? Was it just Snowberry and Penticton, or were there other places in between? Also, why can I not find any record of Charlie and his dad in search results, even under their new—old?—names? Unless William Charles and Mercury aren't their real names either?

And I still don't know why they were on the run.

Charlie's mom wasn't with them in Snowberry, and after seeing that photo in the newspaper, I doubt she was here either. Was she the reason all this had happened? Maybe they were trying to escape from *her*. But then why go back to her in Regina? Or was that the reason Charlie's dad no longer lived with them? Also, is that why Charlie doesn't seem to think much of his mom—?

A flash of brown-and-white fur zips past, dousing me in sand.

"I'm sorry!" A woman hurries over to me. She's around my age, darker skin—maybe East Indian. She has a nose ring and wears her hair in two long braids that hang down on either side of her shoulders.

She's stunning. Literally—I'm momentarily speechless.

"Spirit!" she calls out. A young German shorthaired pointer bounces at full speed through the shallow waves.

"As soon as I open the car door, he forgets his manners and beelines for the water," she says to me. "Doesn't matter whether someone's in his way or not."

I stand up, dusting myself off. "That's okay. My pup is pretty much the same way."

"Spirit!" she calls again, holding up a tennis ball. This catches his full attention, and he's poised, ready for her throw. She tosses it hard over his head, and he hurtles into the lake to retrieve it.

"That'll give us about ten seconds before he's back," she says, her full lips flashing a beautiful smile. She puts out her hand. "Lakshmi."

"Tony."

"Nice to meet you."

Spirit returns, dropping the ball at my feet before shaking off, catching us both in the spray.

"Oh my god! I'm so sorry—again!"

"It's all right," I laugh. "I feel honoured."

Her mouth quirks into a smile. "You should."

I pick up Spirit's ball and give it a really good toss, hoping that'll buy us more than a few seconds this time.

"Are you from around here?" I ask.

"Yup. You?"

"Passing through."

"Are you heading out for tree-planting?"

"No..." I'm not sure how much I should say, but my mouth keeps talking anyway. "I'm looking for a friend."

"Oh? Someone special?"

"No—it's... well, it's just... complicated."

"Does one of you want something more?"

I realize what she's asking. "Oh! Yeah. No. Not like that. He's just... guarded."

Spirit returns, and Lakshmi tosses the ball this time. She sits down beside me, and I'm surprised by her forwardness. I don't know anything about her at all except for her name and that she owns a dog with boundless energy…but her self-assurance and inquisitiveness is really attractive.

"So, why is it complicated?"

I think about how to phrase it. "I thought we were close, but lately I'm starting to learn how little I really know him."

"Does that make you think less of him?"

I shake my head. "To be honest, it only makes me worry about him more."

"So then what does it matter?"

I pick up Spirit's ball, holding onto it a little too long. The dog gets impatient and carefully tries to take it from my hand. I give it a weak-assed toss before continuing. "I guess it doesn't. But if I can't make sense of it all soon, I worry that I might fail him."

"Has he never failed you?"

Answering truthfully is tough. It means telling her all the reasons why Charlie has had to save my life, while avoiding all the emotionally difficult parts. Thankfully, Spirit brings back the ball just then, and I pitch it hard down the beach.

"I have a question," I say, sidestepping hers.

"Sure. Ask away."

"How bad would things have to get for you to disappear?"

"Me? Disappear how?"

"Pack your bags, change your name, never be heard from again."

She smiles. "Sounds interesting, but I've got plans this weekend. Sorry."

I laugh. "Sorry. Just a hypothetical."

"This is about your friend?"

I nod.

"Is that why you're looking for him?"

"Not this time. But it's a definite factor in his past."

Lakshmi leans back and looks up at the clear blue sky. I let her think. It's not every day that a complete stranger asks you such a suspicious-sounding question.

Spirit trots back once more, but drops the ball this time and collapses at our feet.

"You know, if it were me," she says slowly, "I wouldn't try to disappear. That's impossible. Once your info's out there, it never goes away. What I'd try for is diversion. Misdirection. Decide you're going left, then make everyone think you're going right."

I admire her ingenuity. Kind of reminds me of Charlie.

"But to get in a situation like that? It has to be bad. Somewhere along the way there's been some suffering."

It's a sobering thought. "What do you mean?"

"Either your friend created it or he's the recipient."

Knowing Charlie's methods, I'd expect him to have caused it. But something tells me that's not the case. "Do you think there's anything I can do to help him?"

Again, she ponders the question before answering.

"I don't think so. Suffering is a storm, and your friend is caught up in it right now. All you can do is be there when he needs you."

I stare out over the water. Lakshmi's right; Charlie *has* been caught in a storm. But I need to find him before I can help him weather it.

chapter 43

Before I leave Penticton, Lakshmi insists that she and Spirit take me on a tour. We walk along the beachfront, stopping at the Peach Ice Cream Shop before continuing to the pier.

I tell her about my parents, my sisters, and the less thrilling parts of my life. I skip over Sheri, Mike, and the more inexplicable adventures Charlie and I have been on.

She tells me about her family's emigration from Mumbai and her travels throughout the world.

I'm amazed by her intrepid spirit. She plans to work hard for half the year to save up money so that she can take long trips around the globe during the other half. Her infectious energy makes me wish I could jump on the next plane and join her.

Unfortunately, our time together runs out.

"Tony, it's been a pleasure, but I have to take Spirit home and get to my serving job."

I'm not ready for this moment to end, and there's a pang in my heart that I haven't felt in a very long time.

Lakshmi pulls out her phone. "Give me your number in case I ever get the urge to see how you're doing."

I enter it, and she takes the phone back. She holds up the phone for a photo. "Okay, give me your best angle, Tony. But no duck face."

The words aren't lost on me, and I smile at the serendipity.

"Now," she says, "give me your phone.... You know, in case you're ever around here again in the next six months, and you want to look me up."

She snaps a photo of herself, and my heart skips a beat.

I give Spirit a final scratch across his shoulder blades before they go.

She turns to leave, walking backwards, drawing out the goodbye. "You know, you're pretty awesome, Tony Shepherd. And no matter what you find out about your friend, I don't think you'll fail him. It's not who you are."

I walk back to my car, memorizing her smile. There's a bounce in my step, and I can't stop grinning.

chapter 44

Until I see the time.
   Shit.
   I've fallen behind schedule. Again.
   I grab my phone and text Mom and Dad.

Sorry. Running late.
Fell asleep on the beach.

Dad replies:

What beach?

I forgot to tell them about my detour. Crap.

Penticton. Thought
I'd take the scenic route.

Dad doesn't answer immediately; the typing indicator bubbles for a few seconds.

So you'll be in Vancouver around 8:30 tonight?

I do a quick calculation. It's tight, giving me only forty-five minutes to spare.

Yup. I'll text you when I arrive.

chapter 45

Except this is a lie.

After leaving, I pull out my list of William Wolfes and look at the last one with two stars beside it.

It's very close. And I've come this far already.

I travel to Chilliwack then turn south towards Sardis. The map on my phone sends me through the town and onto a winding road along the tree-lined Chilliwack River. Cows graze along a fenceline, and houses are barely visible in the hills. The forest disappears, and modest homes sit in the middle of large, lush yards, their shadows lengthening in the golden light of early evening.

The whole area feels both wild and carefully manicured all at once. Little lanes divert down side streets that disappear around wooded bends. Many of the yards have gates and fences, but they're built from fallen logs, rocks, or shrubs. Eventually the road I'm on becomes a switchback, and I drive up a gentle rise, lined with well-established mobile homes tucked into the hillside.

My phone announces that I've arrived at my destination, and I pull into the small driveway of an ordinary, single-storey blue house. At first glance, the place has an untended, natural feel, like it's been forgotten for years. The grass has been mowed, but the yard doesn't show the care that some of the neighbouring homes do. Moss grows on the roof, and a blue tarp covers the peak. Some of the siding has been pulled off but not replaced.

Yet, amidst it all is a small, crooked sign, probably purchased at a church craft sale, that says HOME in white letters on a blue background.

"All right, William C. Wolfe with the two stars, let's see who you are."

chapter 46

I go up the walk, ring the bell, and wait patiently, hoping it's not too late in the day for a visit.

If this is Charlie's dad, I have so many questions that need answering. Not just where Charlie might be, but what happened to them in the past, and why they were on the run for so long.

I listen for activity inside.

Nothing.

Maybe no one's home. Maybe they've moved.

I ring the bell once more. From the depths, a muffled woman's voice calls out, "Coming!"

There's a couple of latch *clicks* and *thunks* of locks being opened, then the door swings open to reveal a middle-aged woman with a soft expression.

"Yes?" She's smiling even though she holds a pair of yellow rubber gloves and it looks like she's in the middle of cleaning toilets.

"I'm sorry to bother you. I'm wondering if William Wolfe lives here?" I go out on a limb. "William Charles Wolfe?"

"I'm sorry, but I'm afraid he can't help you." She steps back to close the door.

"Wait...!" I don't shout, but I know I sound desperate. "Is he home?"

The smile fades a bit. "Who are you?"

"My name is Tony Shepherd. Mr. Wolfe doesn't know me, but I'm friends with his son."

Her lips tighten.

"Please, I won't be long."

There's a moment of long decision before her shoulders drop. She exhales. Then she swings the door open and allows me inside.

chapter 47

Inside, the house smells clean. Flowers and plants adorn the front hall, and sunlight pours through the windows. The living room is open and bright.

The woman pulls off her gloves. "I'm Julie."

She leads me into the living room, which is small but cozy, showing none of the wear and tear of the home's exterior. Two chairs face a television, and a couch rests against the far wall. It feels homey, but there are very few pictures.

I notice the front door has a heavy padlock.

"Will?" Julie calls out. "You've got a visitor." She turns to me, "He's out back, but I try not to surprise him."

We pass through the bright white kitchen; its open glass cupboards show neatly organized dishes. The sink is empty, and the counters are spotless. There are no magnets or pictures on the fridge.

Something is going on.

"When we first found out, I really deliberated whether or not to contact Charlie, but I was really impressed with how well he handled everything," she says off-handedly. She must think I know what she's talking about, but I'm definitely in the dark.

She unlocks the sliding door to a closed-in porch that overlooks the backyard. "Will, did you hear me? You have a visitor."

I come into the porch, and there's William Wolfe, sitting in a comfortable patio chair, wearing a Blue Jays ball cap, covered in a blanket, watching a squirrel at the feeder outside his window.

At first glance, he's rugged and handsome. I can see Charlie in his profile. But when he turns my way, the youthful, piercing look from Charlie's photo is gone, replaced by an empty stare. He looks lost, a shadow of the man I expected to meet.

"Will?" Julie repeats. "This is Tony."

I take a step forward. "Hello, Mr. Wolfe."

He doesn't reach up to shake my hand.

Julie steps forward. "He's a friend of Charlie's."

"Char . . . arlie?"

"Yes, Charlie. Your son."

He studies me and guffaws. "Oh, I don't know about that."

Realizing he thinks we've said that *I'm* Charlie, I stammer, "N-no, I'm a friend of his. Charlie's. I met him a while ago."

"Uh—yeah. Well, I don't think he . . . be that much more."

I glance at Julie, lost.

She interprets. "No, you're right, Will. I don't think he's that much older than Charlie either."

"Uh, yeah, I'm actually just a little older. My birthday's in a few days."

"I would've a year…we'd-would be having, uh…" He struggles to get his thoughts out amidst a jumble of words. He tries again, "This time of year…year she'd he'd would have…"

"Yes, Charlie came to visit last year," Julie says, helping him. She turns to me. "It was the first time I got to meet him. We were both really happy to see him."

"Is he still on?" he asks her.

"Not anymore."

"He's off?"

"Yes. Charlie isn't here."

His brow furrows as he registers this.

Julie looks at me. "Where *is* Charlie?"

"That's actually why I'm here. He's missing. I was hoping Mr. Wolfe could help me find him."

William grabs at his blanket, twisting it in his hand. "Wish she-he be…be?" He tugs the bundle of cloth towards him. "I can't get him. Yeah, I take in my car…ah no, I'm not on-in car-ar."

"No, William. You can't drive anywhere," Julie cautions.

Under his sleeve, I notice a tattoo on his arm: a compass, just like Charlie's.

I lean in. "Mr. Wolfe? Do you know where I might find Charlie?"

He tries to recognize me. "What's that? That be…not be-be." A frustrated look crosses his face and his eyes shift to Julie. "Lost all them…I can't get the…the damn thing go."

I'm in the right place, but Charlie's dad can't help me. His mind and words are fighting him, and he's losing the war.

This whole trip suddenly seems completely useless.

chapter 48

"Why don't we take Tony back inside to get him something to drink?" Julie says, more to me than to William.

He doesn't say anything, but allows Julie to guide him through the door and direct him into a chair in the living room.

She motions for me to join her in the kitchen. "I make a great homemade iced tea out of Earl Grey and bergamot," she says, pulling a pitcher of it out of the fridge and pouring me a glass.

I take a sip. "It's delicious." I look towards Will. "How long have you two been together? Charlie hasn't told me much about his dad."

"That doesn't surprise me. Almost five years."

"And how long has he been…?"

"This way? Only a couple of years. It's all fairly new."

"What happened?"

She sighs. "Lung cancer first, which led to vascular dementia, and what doctors now think is latent Alzheimer's.

Things are steadier now—" She laughs to herself. "When it rained, it poured for us, it seems. We both know we're living on borrowed time."

My phone vibrates in my pocket, but I tap the button to ignore it.

She takes a small glass of iced tea to William and helps him drink, carefully wiping his spills with a towel. She returns to the kitchen.

"Not really what I was hoping for when I first met him, but he was a good man—no, he still *is* a good man—and I won't abandon him. We've made so many good memories in the short time we've been together. But I'm not fooling myself. The William I met is gone now."

William enters the kitchen.

"Do you want more iced tea?" Julie asks him.

"Oh, I wouldn't mind."

Julie turns to get his glass, but he's already in the fridge.

"Is he okay?" I ask quietly.

"Oh, he might make a mess, but it's nothing we can't deal with," she says, just as quietly. "Things tend to be more difficult for him later in the day."

She goes to pour him a small amount and helps him get it to his lips without spilling. I feel bad for her and her situation, but admire the love she shows. She has an easy, relaxed approach to what must be a very stressful life.

She turns back to me when William wanders back to the living room. "He used to be full of adventure. Loved to hike and camp. Always dreamed of owning a cabin. This place was the closest we got."

"Did he ever talk about Charlie?"

"Always. He always regretted leaving."

I hesitate to ask, but I'm here now. "Do you happen to know why he did?"

"We kept very few secrets between us, but he never really talked about his life before B.C."

"What about his wife, Melanie? Did he ever say anything about what happened with her?" I can tell this might be a difficult topic, but Julie is kind enough to answer.

"I think he cared about her. Once, anyway. But something must have made him leave his child."

"Did he ever mention anything about where they might've lived?"

"Like I said, he didn't talk much about the past." She pauses before adding, "Sometimes at night, now, when he's really struggling, he says some things..."

My phone buzzes again, and I silence it.

"What kind of things?"

"Oh, peaches and horses and fishing.... After his diagnosis, I discovered he'd been a locksmith. He'd spend hours in bed, believing he had to file keys and reset safe combinations."

Like father, like son, I guess.

William is back, this time beside me. "I gotta get home down there now but can't get her." He shoves his Blue Jays ball cap into my hands.

"You should feel honoured," Julie says. "That old thing's been his favourite these past few months."

I offer the warmest smile I can muster, but it all just makes me sad. "No, thank you, Mr. Wolfe. This is yours." I hand it back to him.

"Yeah, yeah. No. I can't get him, no, them in…'cept you don't—can't get that."

I glance over at Julie, but she's struggling to make sense of it too.

He pushes the cap back into my hands, and I feel bad rejecting it a second time, so I take it. "All right," I say, "but I'm going to give it to Charlie when I see him."

He struggles with his broken English and broken thoughts. "No…he—she…take…Charlie."

I stare at him, confused, but my phone buzzes a third time, and I know that whoever is trying to get a hold of me isn't going to stop, so I excuse myself to find out who's calling.

It's Mom and Dad.

Then I see all their text messages, and my stomach drops.

Tony, call us.

Call us back now, please.

Call us now.

CALL NOW

I step outside to answer. The texts are from both of them, so I'm not sure who's safest to talk to.

It's Mom. "Aunt Ayana called. Wondered if you got to her condo safely. Do you know why that would be?"

Might as well bite the bullet. "Because she's out of town."

"Wow, your powers of deduction are amazing, Anthony."

Oof… When she's angry, her sarcasm really lets loose.

"Where are you?" she asks.

"B.C." I consider mentioning that I'm actually headed in the right direction, but I'm pretty sure it won't help.

"And what exactly are you doing?"

"Taking in the sights?" I probably should've said that as a statement.

"Don't get cute, son. Do any of these sights have anything to do with Charlie?"

"Yeah." There's no point in lying. I'm clearly neck deep in sewage already.

There is a long pause. Never a good sign.

In these quiet moments, I always imagine that she's like a wizard in a movie, summoning the surrounding energy before turning the enemy to dust in a blast of smoke and flame.

"This is not acceptable." Her tone is flat. "It's deceptive and manipulative, and this little escapade is over."

"Mom—!"

"*What*?" she yells, and I shut up immediately. I've never heard her so angry.

But I have to try. I have to.

"I just can't—" I fight back the wave of feelings buffeting me. "I just can't handle another call from Gekas…telling me I've lost someone else—" I choke on the words.

"Enough. Turn around now and we'll settle this when you get home." She hangs up without even saying goodbye.

It doesn't matter.

There's nothing I could've said to make things better. I lied to my aunt and my parents when I should've been honest with all of them.

Worse, I still don't know where my friend is—and my chance to find him has just run out.

Dammit, what the hell happened to you, Charlie?

part 3

Charlie cranes his head towards the warm sun; the wind gently blows through his shaggy hair. He's feeling pretty good. Yesterday, they'd gone to a lawn bowling green on the outskirts of Saskatoon, where another one of their men had ended up dead a couple of months ago.

Normally, that length of time would've put a damper on any investigation, but Winston walked him through the crime scene, trying to recall every detail.

Charlie wasn't sure, but it felt like Winston had something on his mind. Like he was searching for a very specific answer. Charlie just couldn't figure out what it was.

The victim, Maurice, had been on the bowling green all afternoon. He'd finished his game and had been relaxing alone on a bench while his buddies finished their end. Next thing anyone knew, he was slumped over with a hunting knife buried in his chest.

Access through the front gate was by key card, and all the staff members had been accounted for. After walking the perimeter, Charlie found a blind spot by a work shed that someone could've used to climb the fence, blend in with others before stabbing him, and then leave the same way before anyone noticed.

"It's a different weapon," Winston said.

"But a similar M.O.," Charlie said. "Whoever did it wanted to get up close and personal, so he would see their face."

That night, they holed up in a house in the city on a quiet street. It looked like somebody's grandma's house and felt like the Ritz after the last place. Charlie had been upgraded to a room with flowery wallpaper, doilies everywhere, and an old wrought-iron frame bed that squeaked when he lay on it.

This morning, Winston had tossed Charlie a pair of knock-off Crocs. Charlie had choked back his immediate response—having earned the shoes, he was reluctant to lose them. Winston had further surprised him by stopping for coffee before they left the city. And not shitty gas station coffee, either, but a legitimate hole-in-the-wall that ground its own beans. They had fresh baking, too, and Winston had even sprung for sourdough doughnuts topped with saskatoon berries.

So yeah, all things considered, Charlie's feeling okay.

The trip to Calgary was long, but as they hit Deerfoot Trail, the dread that's hung over him the past few days fades a little. He's not yet free and clear, but he's got some control now, and with it comes a sliver of hope that he'll find his way out.

It's close to supper, and his stomach is rumbling, so when they pull in to a restaurant, he doesn't think anything of it.

Then he sees the name. *Sullivan's.*

His stomach drops, and he's ready to vomit. Suddenly, he no longer feels like everything is going to work out.

chapter 51

Are they messing with him? Is this their idea of a joke?

"Let's go."

Rarely does Charlie's brain shut down, but all he can hear is a ringing in his ears as panic sets in. "Give me a sec. I'm taking it all in." He tries to calm himself, taking slow, deep breaths.

Why hadn't he realized? Of *course* these guys would be connected to this place.

Winston's prickliness has returned. "Get out of the car." He nods to Red, who exits and opens Charlie's door. On the patio, people are eating food and drinking beer like nothing's ever happened here.

"No."

Red grabs him by the scruff. "Yo, get your ass out the car."

"I don't want to."

It can't be a coincidence. They must know.

"We're not asking, you little shit. Get out of this car and get in that goddamn building." Cass clips every word.

"No."

Charlie readies himself for Red's attack, but instead Winston hisses, "Give us a moment."

Cass backs off and glances between them before climbing out of the car himself.

Winston leans close to Charlie, the smell of cigarettes and musk making for an uneasy blend. "I don't know what's going on with you, but you need to get inside."

"Do your worst. I'm not going."

Winston's ready to go ballistic, but he makes a visible effort at patience. "I need your help in there."

"Why? What aren't you telling me?" Charlie wants to know.

For the first time, Winston hesitates. "I need you to tell me what you see."

"What are you talking about? All of these murders are open and shut. You and I both know it." Charlie glances at the restaurant then back to Winston. "Unless you think this one is different."

"That's what I'm hoping you'll tell me."

chapter 52

It feels like the worst case of déjà vu.

Charlie has known about this place for nearly three years but never had the balls to come. He was scared what answers he'd find. Then, a couple months ago, Gekas handed him a police report from a murder that had happened here seven years ago.

The victim was Tommy "The Falcon" Sullivan. The man responsible for most of the heartache in Charlie's life.

Charlie had known about his death, but always held out hope that there would be more to the story. Gekas's file had pretty much ended that. Probably exactly what she was hoping for: to help him move on from his past. Sure, he pored over it for weeks, studying every detail and photo, but in the end, any answers seemed to have died that night with Sullivan.

But now, if Winston's brought him here, suspecting more to his death, then maybe things *aren't* finished. And maybe Charlie's past isn't quite finished with him yet either.

chapter 53

The restaurant is in full swing. Families and couples fill the tables, and heaping trays of burgers, steaks, pizzas, and spaghetti flow out of the kitchen. This place is all about the meat, grease, and carbs.

The decor is a tchotchke mishmash of red-checkered tablecloths, wine bottles, olive tins, and autographed movie and music memorabilia. One of the walls is covered in pictures of celebrities standing beside a huge hulk of a man. Charlie recognizes Sullivan—he knew the man's face long before Gekas had given him the folder—but seeing it now only makes him angry.

But he's got to play it safe. None of them seems to know Charlie's connection to this place, so it's best to keep it that way. So he only says, "Who's the guy?"

"Tommy Sullivan. He owned the place."

Yeah, the piece of shit did a little more than that. But Charlie needs to play it cool.

"Owned?" he asks naively.

"He's the reason we're here."

Didn't Charlie know it.

A woman greets them at the door. "Table for four—?"

"Chelsea, I've got this." A tall, thin, perspiring man rushes over. "How you doing, Winston? Haven't seen you here for a while."

"Been working, A.J. I was wondering if we can look around for a bit?"

A worried look crosses the sweaty man's face. "Are there concerns?"

"No, no. Just want to show the kid around."

A.J. glances at Charlie, trying to sort out who he is. He's leery but clearly has to comply. "Sure, sure..."

Winston turns to Red and Cass. "You two grab seats at the bar."

Red is halfway there, but Cass looks reluctant. "You sure, boss?"

"It's been a long haul. Go. Relax." Without waiting for Cass's reply, Winston pushes Charlie to follow A.J. to the back.

The kitchen is bustling. Cooks shout. Food sizzles. Flashes of fire and smoke dance off the grill.

As they wind through the ordered chaos, several of the workers look up and call out to Winston. He nods back. When they arrive at a door at the rear of the building, he turns to A.J. "If you don't mind, I'll take it from here."

"You sure there's nothing I can do for you?"

"Don't worry. Everything's okay."

A.J. nods, and hands over his keys before leaving.

"You're pretty popular," Charlie says.

"I grew up here. Started as a busboy, then moved on to doing side jobs for Tommy before he brought me on full-time."

"He mentored you?"

"Suppose so."

Winston unlocks the door and opens it to an office. It's small and cluttered, without any windows or ventilation except for a small standing fan in the corner. Shelves are filled with old menus, flyers, and office equipment, and the desk is covered with paperwork and receipts.

For Charlie, it's like being in the belly of the beast. He expected revulsion, but all he feels is a deep sense of emptiness. He pushes it down. The sooner he gets out of here, the better.

Winston begins. "Seven years ago, Tommy was working late. It'd been a busy night, and the staff had left. Just him and Joey, his bodyguard. Joey went out for a smoke and returned to find this."

Winston hands over his phone, showing Charlie a grisly photo of the crime scene. This wasn't a police photo. This was from someone who'd stood here, long before the cops showed up. The body is slumped forward in the chair, face against the desk, eyes wide.

The asshole never even saw it coming.

Charlie zooms in and counts five bullet wounds, all in his back.

He studies the room now, and finds the imperfection of a bad putty-and-paint job on the back wall. Another hole. The killer emptied the entire gun. This was a crime of revenge.

Charlie steps back into the kitchen and finds the back door. Two big metal bars prohibit anyone from pushing the door open without removing them.

"Are these new?" Charlie asks.

Winston shakes his head. "Tommy never let his guard down. That door was secure the night he was killed, and Joey, A.J., and the head cook had all checked it at least once throughout the night."

"So the killer left this way—but how did they get in? And where was the bodyguard? In the front?"

"Yes."

"So no entry that way. What about the cameras?" Charlie points to two in the corners of the kitchen. He had also noted a few up front as they'd come in. "They should have caught the murder and the escape that night, right?"

"They should have—but the cameras went on the fritz just before it happened."

Interesting. Despite his disgust with the man, Charlie's intrigued. It's like one of those old one-minute mysteries he read as a kid. "Does all the footage go to a security company?"

"Nope. All in-house on a system downstairs."

"Show me."

Winston leads him past the office, down a set of stairs to the basement.

The area is well organized and well lit, but there are still enough shadows to add a sense of eeriness. Coolers and fridges line one wall. There's a large walk-in cooler at the back, and shelves and pallets of dry goods fill the rest of the space. Beside the stairs is a small closet containing a high-tech server rack. Redundant drives record multiple feeds off a TV that displays several camera angles throughout the restaurant.

Charlie checks the lock on the closet. "It'd be easy enough to pick this and mess with the wires," he says. "But they'd still have to get down here without being noticed."

He wanders the aisles, studying every corner of the basement. No windows down here, and the only access is through the kitchen and past the office. "Could they have snuck in during a shift, then hid somewhere—maybe down here?"

"We checked the cameras and questioned the staff. Nobody saw nothing."

"So then they came when no one was around and had access to the alarms. Who has keys?"

"Tommy, A.J., and the two assistant managers. And we know they're all clean."

Charlie considers this.

"What about someone outside the restaurant? Like a painter or plumber or someone—"

Winston shakes his head, grinning. "Like I said, kid. You're impressive. Took me weeks to figure it out."

"Hold on—you already know who did this?"

Winston nods. "The company with the cleaning contract had a woman working there for nearly a year; she quit just before the murder. I think she copied the keys and slipped in one morning, hid somewhere, and waited for Tommy."

Charlie swallows hard, the darkness closing in. "But you don't have her on camera. Do you have any idea what she looks like?"

Winston shakes his head. "Fake ID, fake name. Hell, probably dyed her hair or wore a wig. She's a ghost."

"You think she's the same person who's been taking out all your guys?"

Winston nods. "That's my theory."

Charlie considers his next words carefully. "Then why me? Why drag my ass all over the place if you know who the killer is?"

"I needed an outside opinion."

It's not the answer Charlie expected. "Why?"

"At first we thought it was a vendetta—another family moving in—so we prepared for war. But nothing happened. Then two years later, she comes back and starts wiping out all our old guard. Many of them went underground, into hiding—but she found them too."

"Doesn't seem like she's a professional," Charlie mutters, thinking aloud.

"No," Winston agrees. "What she did to Tommy was a mess."

"But she *does* seem to have improved with time."

"Exactly. And now she's getting at us with info no one on the outside should know."

"Someone on the inside is using her to move up the ranks, maybe."

Winston nods. "And I think I know who it is."

"Who?"

"Robert."

"Ah. Any relation?"

"Tommy's brother," Winston says. "Tommy's murder put him in charge."

Charlie realizes what Winston's saying. "And that's why you're hanging on to me? To help prove you right?"

Winston nods again. "But if we're wrong, kid, it's both our necks in the noose."

chapter 54

As they walk back upstairs, Charlie's mind is buzzing.

He's suddenly found himself in the middle of a Shakespearean tragedy, in which brother kills brother, and each of them—Winston, Red, Cass, and Charlie—has a part to play. He's pretty sure his old English teacher, Mrs. Melcher, would've loved the irony.

And if Robert is leading this coup, where does that leave Cass and Red? Their orders were to deliver Charlie to him—are they in on it? Or are they just doing what they're told?

And what *does* Robert actually want with him? Up to this point, Charlie has barely heard of Robert's existence. Do he and Robert have some sort of unfinished business he's not even aware of? As far as Charlie can recall, Robert Sullivan doesn't make an appearance in any of the police files or news articles he's researched, so where does this—there's no other word for it—*gangster* fit into Charlie's past?

He needs to get closer to the situation, and he has the solution. He hates using it—it's like hitting launch on a nuke—but it'll lead him right to the centre of this shitstorm.

Cass rises as they return to the bar. "What did the kid say? Same as the others?"

Winston nods. "Different technique, but yeah, same M.O."

"Jeezus," Red mumbles.

"What now, boss?"

Before Winston can answer, Charlie interrupts. "So, guys, it's been fun, but I think we're done."

"What're you on about?"

"Like you said, whoever's out for blood has been careful—they've left nothing behind. There's not much more I can do."

Winston glares at him. "You know what this means, right?"

Charlie shoots him a sardonic look. "Yup, but I figure it's time I meet Robert and see what he wants."

Winston shakes his head. "Kid, I can never tell if you're actually smart or just too damn stupid to know better."

"Well, I guess we're about to find out."

chapter 55

I'm beyond exhausted.

It's nearly 11:00 p.m. two days later, and my house glows like a beacon in the darkness. Great. The folks are still up, waiting to yell at me.

They'd insisted I turn my phone's location services back on so they knew where I was every moment of the day. The whole thing pissed me off so much that I didn't call home once. If they wanted to know where I was so bad, they could look.

Now, though, I just want it over with.

I grab my bag and walk up the steps, pushing open the door, ready for the ambush.

But nothing happens.

No Mom, no Dad standing at the door ready to tear my head off. Not even Ollie has come to greet me.

Did I just spend the last 1,600 kilometres worrying about this moment, and none of them even has the decency to show up?!

Fine. They can come to me. I'm not giving them the time of day. No "Hello!" No "Hi, Mom and Dad, I'm home!" and definitely no head scratches for the pup.

I'm trudging up the stairs to my room when I hear voices in the kitchen.

Three voices.

My defences fly back up, and I drop my bag in the middle of the hall.

Okay, then. Here we go!

I take a deep breath, priming myself for a fight, and step around the corner.

Mom and Dad are at the island with a woman that I don't recognize. Everyone has a cup of tea. A fourth waits in the empty spot.

My empty spot.

Damn, they've been waiting for me. All *three* of them.

But who the hell is she?

There's no hint of a therapist or social worker in the way she looks. She's in her late forties, thin and fair, with leathery skin over-baked by the sun. She's wearing an open cardigan sweater over a halter-top and jeans. A hint of hairspray and cigarettes wafts from her.

"Anthony," Mom acknowledges me. Her tone says *I'm relieved you're home*, but she's also not getting up to give me a hug, which speaks volumes.

I figured as much.

Dad's a little less welcoming and doesn't smile when he sees me. "Take a seat."

"I'm fine where I am."

"Anthony, please," Mom says, pouring my tea.

It's only a few steps from here to there, but it feels as long as my entire trip home. I take a seat, clasping my hands on the table, and try to calm the storm brewing inside me.

The woman extends her hand. "Tony, it's nice to finally meet you."

"Who are you?" I have no patience for any of this. I'm exhausted, defensive, and frustrated.

"Manners, son," Dad snaps, drawing breath to say more.

Mom reaches over to take his hand and he closes his mouth on whatever else he might've said. "This is Charlie's.... This is Melanie."

chapter 56

Charlie's *mom*? What the hell?

"I've heard a lot about you," she offers.

My anger bubbles over. "Oh, really? That's great. Because I've heard absolutely nothing about you!"

"Anthony, you watch yourself—" Dad's about had it.

Mom squeezes his hand. "Please, you two." She looks at me. "Melanie's here because she's worried. She wondered if you know anything about Charlie?"

"If I *know* anything? Are you kidding? Yeah, I 'know' about him—"

"Anthony!"

I ignore Dad. "I know he likes dark roast coffee, and he keeps his room cleaner than my mother. I know he's tough and smart and a serious son of a bitch with a golf club. And no matter how shitty his life gets, he rarely complains. I know that he'd go to the ends of the earth for anyone he cares about, and I know he didn't deserve to be left in some trailer park shithole by someone like you!"

No one in the room speaks right away. Not even Dad.

At some point, I have stood up, my hands balled into fists, my chair skidded away.

"Anthony?" Mom gently touches my hand. "Will you sit, please?"

I take a breath and pull my seat back towards the table.

My words struck hard, and Melanie wipes away a tear. "I'm happy Charlie's got the family he deserves," she whispers.

I stare at her. "What the hell does that mean? *You're* his family!"

Mom reaches out, squeezing my hand. "Melanie's been telling us about her time with Charlie—"

"Her *time* with him? What are you talking about?"

"I'm not Charlie's birth mom. I'm his stepmom."

chapter 57

As soon as she says it, giant pieces of the puzzle fall into place.

"You don't seem surprised," she says.

"After everything I've learned about Charlie in the past two days, it's almost the least shocking."

She smiles. "Let me guess? Mercury?"

"What's that?" Dad asks.

"Not what, who," she says. "Just a little nickname Charlie had."

A quick glance from her tells me she knows the truth.

"Do you know who Charlie's birth mom is?" I ask.

She shakes her head. "William and Charlie never really spoke about her."

"Not a friendly split?"

"No... I think she died of an overdose."

"Wait, who is William?" Mom asks.

"Charlie's father," I answer.

Melanie raises an eyebrow. "You know him?"

I pause, glancing at my parents. "We met a couple days ago."

Melanie's eyebrows draw together. "How is he? Is Julie taking good care of him?"

There's no malice in her voice. Only kindness. Perhaps my understanding of her—much like Charlie—hasn't been as accurate as I'd thought. "You know about him...them?"

"Bits and pieces. I had heard he wasn't well and that he had someone caring for him."

"He's taken care of. She's loving and very patient."

She flashes a smile. "She'd have to be. He was a handful when we were together. I couldn't imagine him now."

"When did you two meet?"

"Not long after they arrived at the trailer park. William quickly became known as the resident handyman. He'd shovel snow, help you move, or take stuff to the junkyard. He was always helping others. Well, sure enough, as soon as I met him, I immediately fell for him. He was such a good-looking man."

"And when did you meet Charlie?"

"Not long after we started dating. At first, Will was cautious about introducing us, but once he did..." She smiles as she remembers. "He was such a sweet boy."

I can't help but laugh. Even Mom and Dad are smiling.

"I know. Not the terror that he is now." Her smile fades as she realizes what she's just said. "I shouldn't have..."

Mom offers her hand. Even though I know Mom has never been Melanie's biggest fan, I admire her kindness towards this woman.

Melanie continues, "Charlie was only eight when we met. He was quiet and withdrawn. But William took us out for ice cream, and we were walking back, and Charlie took my hand in his sticky little fingers." There's a flicker of another smile as she thinks about the memory.

"I cared for him … I care for him still—and we had a good relationship at the start."

"What changed?"

"William got a job hauling. He'd be gone days and weeks at a time. By then, we were living together, and I'd look after Charlie while he travelled. We spent Christmases and birthdays and Easters together."

No wonder Charlie called her "mom." She was practically the only family he had.

"Then William was gone longer and longer, and I could feel him getting restless. The two of us just grew apart, I guess." She stares into her cup, studying the last bit of tea at the bottom. "Then one day, he said he had a long haul out east and that he'd be gone for a while. He never came home. I called and texted, but he never responded. Then one day, the number was disconnected."

I'd always thought of Melanie as a negligent parent, but I can't imagine the pain and confusion of suddenly being dumped and left with someone else's kid.

"At first, me and Charlie handled it okay, but it wasn't long before anger at being abandoned wrecked everything."

"For Charlie?"

"For both of us. I was in over my head. And as Charlie got older, his attitude grew. I wasn't his mom, and he felt rejected. But it got harder, and I started to struggle too." She shakes her head, admonishing herself. "I began self-medicating and drinking too much, and hooking up with assholes…" She glances up and whispers "sorry" to my parents.

Mom squeezes her hand again, and Dad pours her a fresh cup of tea.

She sniffs back the tears. "It's a time I'd like to forget." She dips her used tea bag in and out of her cup, trying to squeeze out the last bit of flavour. "I didn't realize it at the time, but Charlie was trying to protect me from myself as much as from the men I brought home. But I was too blind, too sick to see and understand."

She takes a sip, wincing at the bitter flavour. Dad offers sugar but she declines.

"We fought a lot, and finally just stopped talking. Unfortunately, my moment of clarity came too late. I came home to find the trailer seized, and Charlie gone. But despite everything, he'd still leave me messages and tell me where he was."

A flash of anger returns, and I can't help but blurt, "You *knew* he was here, but you didn't call?"

She nods. "Well, I lost my phone…" She catches my expression at this excuse, and looks away, unable to meet my eyes. "But mostly I was embarrassed. Ashamed. He was better off without me. I was no use to anyone at that point."

Ah. There's the real reason.

She trails off and fights back tears, until suddenly her face hardens. "But to be honest, it was also a relief. I wasn't responsible for him anymore. Maybe I wasn't there for him, but I also couldn't screw him up anymore."

She doesn't wipe away the tears this time, just lets herself feel the pain.

"When I lost him, I knew I needed to face my demons. I did whatever I could, whatever therapy was out there: counsellors, hypnotherapy, acupuncture, reiki. Eventually I got myself into a twelve-step program, and I've been clean for three months now."

There is a heaviness in the room.

Melanie leans towards me. Her tears have washed away her makeup, and her eyes are puffy and tired.

"I know what you and Charlie did. I know what you can do." She reaches towards me, then stops herself, clasping her hands tightly together. "Can you find out where he is?"

I don't have the heart to tell her that he might not have left on his own. "I'm sorry—"

"Please?" she adds, as if that's what I'm holding out for. "If he's not at his father's, maybe he went to Hatley?"

"Hatley?"

She nods. "Alberta. It's where they lived before moving here."

Another piece. But Mom and Dad are right here.

"I can't—"

"Not even for your friend?"

The words cut deep. "I'm sorry."

My refusal crushes her, and I can't help but feel her pain. But in this moment, it's the only thing I can say.

chapter 58

I wake in the middle of the night and can't get back to sleep.
I can't settle my thoughts about Melanie's revelation.

Hatley.

I grab my phone and search it on the map.

It's a small logging and mining town in northern Alberta.
Not far. Only ten hours away. Quite a difference from the
places Charlie and his dad had previously lived.

I also check *William Wolfe, Charlie Wolfe, William Charles,
Mercury Charles* in association with the town, but the hits
don't seem to be connected.

It doesn't matter, though.

If I were Charlie, maybe I'd pack and slip out into the night,
and try to hitchhike my way there. But I'm not like him, and
Mom and Dad aren't ever giving me the car again.

chapter 59

At some point, I must have fallen asleep because I wake to knocking on my bedroom door.

"Anthony, please come downstairs," Mom says on the other side.

Shit.

I guess my sentencing for bad behaviour has not been commuted. Exhausted, I drag myself out of bed and stumble downstairs.

"Happy birthday!"

Crap! With everything else going on, I'd completely forgotten what day it was.

They drag me into a hug, and I'm caught off guard.

"Would you like birthday waffles or your gift first?" Dad asks.

I think I need a pinch or something. It all feels vaguely dream-like. None of it makes sense. We went from an emotional reckoning to a celebration.

I shrug. With nothing to lose, I say only, "Gift?"

"You sure?" Dad's eyes twinkle. "They're pretty good waffles."

Mom brings out a small, narrow bag with sparkly blue tissue paper. By the way she holds it, it seems light.

I reach inside and pull out a gas card. I'm stunned, and look at them quizzically.

"There's enough on there to get you to Hatley and back," Dad says.

"Huh?"

Mom puts an arm around Dad. "We had a long talk last night after Melanie left."

"And despite wanting to ground you, we can't," Dad adds.

"You're eighteen," Mom sighs. "And maybe we overreacted by making you come home—though we certainly don't appreciate being lied to." Her face goes stern with those last words, then she glances up at Dad, and it softens a bit. "Still, we need to let you make your own decisions—"

"And let you sometimes make mistakes," Dad puts in.

"But talking with Melanie put a bit of a different slant on things, and the truth is, she's right. What you and Charlie do *is* special—"

"You've done things that amaze us," Dad interjects.

"And even though it terrifies us, your bravery in the face of danger makes us proud," Mom finishes.

I get a lump in my throat and fight back the tears. The weight of this moment is not lost on me. I pull them in for a big hug to thank them.

That's when Mom whispers, "Now, go find your friend."

chapter 60

It feels like a repeat of only a few days ago. I've re-packed my bag and loaded it, along with Charlie's backpack, into my car. But this time, my parents know all about it.

Mom calls me into the kitchen. "I made this before we decided to send you off." She holds a plate of chocolate buttercream cupcakes—there's a single red candle stuck into each one.

Dad belts out a super-bad operatic version of "Happy Birthday," prompting Ollie to howl along with him.

"Stop it, you two, before the neighbours complain," Mom yells.

Dad does, but Ollie lets out one last yodel before settling down.

"Make a wish," Mom smiles.

I blow out the candle and, following tradition, don't share the wish with anyone. I'm pretty sure we all know what I wished for, though.

chapter 61

We finish the cupcakes, and they walk me to the car.

Dad flips into advice mode. "You have money. Manage it wisely—like you always do. If you happen to run out, we're only a phone call away."

"Thanks."

Mom crowds him out. "Anthony, promise me to stay safe."

"I'll do my absolute best." It's not what she wants to hear but anything else would be a lie. "I promise to call regularly."

She raises an eyebrow.

"Hey, for real this time."

Dad pats me on the back, and it's time to go.

I jump in the driver's seat and pull out of the driveway. I look in the rear-view mirror to see Mom, Dad, and Ollie all on the street. A thick, heavy feeling churns in my gut. Even though I hope to be gone for only a few days, it suddenly feels like I won't see them for a while.

I choke back the lump in my throat, and turn on the stereo as a distraction. Dad must've taken the car to get the gas card because Tom Petty's "You Don't Know How It Feels" blares out of the speakers.

If Charlie were here, he'd be rocking out to it, so instead of turning it off, I let it play.

I turn onto the highway and head north.

chapter 62

Eleven hours later, I'm near the outskirts of Hatley.

The whole region is northern forests, winding roads, and foothills. It's absolutely beautiful.

Then the trees disappear—stripped clear away—and big box stores and bland-looking hotels appear. It's all concrete and pavement, and none of the natural splendour I passed through minutes ago. If I wasn't surrounded by mountains, I'd think I had somehow looped backed to the desolate suburbs of my hometown.

Following the GPS, I continue on and slip into a river valley at the base of a large mountain peak, and am shocked to discover a whole other part of town. Here, the trees return, and historic red brick buildings line quaint streets. I'm betting some of these building were built two hundred years ago.

But as I drive down the street, I notice the cracks in the foundations, the peeling paint, and the dust-covered windows. This town was picturesque at one time, but now everything has a touch of grime and age staining it.

I turn down a narrow side street towards a hotel that I swear could've come right out of the Klondike days. I half expect to see the ghosts of prospectors staking their claim before rushing off to pan for gold. The buildings are jammed tight together, with the occasional awning or wrought-iron balcony, and the streetlights hold old-style glass globes that hang down like glowing bubbles.

My hotel is a flat-faced three-storey brick building. The place probably bustled with people at one time, maybe back in the 1950s, but now it's quiet and forgotten. I park out front and walk inside.

The lobby is narrow and long, and there's knotty pine panelling and cowboy artwork everywhere. The worn carpeting—probably installed when the place opened—is printed in a patchwork of old ranch brands.

The main route through the lobby leads to a set of stairs at the far end. On the right, behind a series of pillars, is a lounge, which likely started out as a saloon back in the day. A dark fireplace waits forlornly in the middle of two big bookcases filled with dusty paperbacks—mostly westerns and romances. An old black Labrador retriever lies on the carpet between a pair of leather chairs.

"Her name's Juno."

I look over my shoulder.

A young man with a dark beard and a pleasant expression is sitting behind the counter. "And I'm Gabe."

I approach the desk. "I'm Tony Shepherd. I have a room."

"Ah, my last-minute check-in. Don't get too many of those anymore."

"Really? Why's that?"

Judging by the place, I'm surprised he has *any* guests.

"The Trans-Canada. This used to be the northern gateway, but now it's faster to go a couple of hours south than take this old winding highway. So, what brings you here? You taking the scenic route or just lost your way?"

I blink.

Although Gabe seems nice enough, I'm not comfortable sharing. I keep it vague.

"Neither. Came to check out the sights."

"Intriguing. You seemed a little too clean for hookers and blow—"

"Yikes! Is that what this town has to offer?"

"Well, that and drunken shotguns and four-wheelers at sunset."

"Yikes!" I say again.

"Meh. Eventually, most folks try it at least once."

"I'm hoping not to stay here *that* long."

"That's what we all say," he chuckles ruefully. "And then five years later, we find ourselves working the front desk at a hotel past its prime."

He hands over my key, a brass one. A big plastic diamond hangs off it; the room number's stamped onto it in gold. "Up the stairs, second floor, on your right."

"Cool. Thank you, Gabe."

"Continental breakfast starts at seven. If you need anything, I'm here all night."

chapter 63

I walk upstairs, and the western theme continues; the railings are made of stripped trees that have been lacquered and polished, and the upstairs hallway is trimmed in hacienda-style arches and stucco. It doesn't work anymore, but I'm sure it did once upon a time.

In spite of the deserted lobby, the second floor is surprisingly busy. Kids play hockey with mini sticks, screaming as they knock a ball up and down its length, and the blare of televisions and loud conversations can be heard through open doors. The whole floor is being treated like one big space with people moving back and forth between rooms.

As I arrive at my room halfway down, the door next to me opens, and a young woman pops her head out. She's maybe in her twenties, not much older than me, wrapped in a blanket.

"You're not our delivery guy!"

"Nope."

A guy yells from the room, "Maisie, just give him the cash and come back to bed."

"It's not our delivery guy!" she yells back.

She looks at me and flashes a big gaudy wedding ring. "Me and Stanley just got married. Didn't tell our folks or nothing."

Stanley appears then, wrapping his arms around her.

I'm pretty sure he's butt-naked, but thankfully Maisie's blanket obscures all.

"Did you show him the ring?"

"She did," I say, nonplussed.

"She shows it to everyone."

"Congratulations to you both," I add, struggling to get into my room and out of this conversation.

"Let's get back to celebrating," Stanley whispers loudly.

Maisie winks. "We promise we'll keep it down."

The two of them giggle as they shut their door.

I get the door unlocked and step into a room that literally hasn't changed since the hotel was built. It's all exposed wood beams and drab, pukey-pink walls. The whole room is stale and warm, and I try the A/C, but the cord is lying on the floor, and the only outlet is a metre away.

Right.

I dump my bag on the bed, and it lands without a bounce—although I wouldn't've been surprised if it'd been a waterbed or one that takes coins and vibrates. A striped orange, red, yellow, and black blanket that seems to be attempting a sunset motif covers it. The whole thing smells dusty and pungent, like it was just pulled out of storage.

I check the bathroom, but it's not much better. There's a wooden toilet seat with a fluffy knitted cover, a shower curtain of a cowboy riding into the sunset, and horseshoes hammered up as hangers.

And that's when Stanley and Maisie break their promise.

I rush for the TV to drown out the noise, but it won't turn on, and I discover a severed collection of wires hanging from its back.

It's only going to get worse before it gets better, so I grab my keys and wallet and bust out of there.

chapter 64

As I come down the stairs, Juno rises from her mat and wanders over to me, nudging her head under my hand.

"Looks like you pass inspection," Gabe says.

I give the dog a good pat. "How long have you had her?"

"Since she was a pup. I found her in Alaska when I was hitchhiking across the country. Saw those big brown eyes, and knew I couldn't leave her behind."

"Hitchhiking?"

"Yeah. I finished my English degree and decided I needed a little more life behind me. Once I can afford it, we'll get back on the road till I get the vibe telling me it's time to go home."

Gabe's a true wandering spirit. Maybe even more than Charlie.

I shuffle towards the desk. Juno stays close. "Um ... about the TV in my room ... ?"

"Yeah, sorry. The last guy who stayed there tried to get free cable, and it didn't quite work out."

"And the honeymooners? Is there maybe another room—?"

"Not one that I'd feel comfortable putting you in. I could call around, find you another place to stay?"

Right then, Juno plops down on my feet, just like Ollie. Her tail beats happily against my leg.

"Seems like someone wants you to stick around."

I sigh. This isn't what I was hoping for, and I feel the burgeoning pressure of a stress headache. I'm not a fan of the room, but I'm not really interested in finding new accommodations either. Also it's late, and I'd rather just make something of the day. "Drinking age is eighteen here, right?"

"Uh-huh…"

"So where would I go for a drink?"

"Depends on what you want."

"Today's my birthday, so preferably not some dingy lounge."

"Well, then steer clear of Bernie's," he laughs. "That's where old drunks go to die."

"Good to know," I say.

"Now Envelopes, 'Lopes, as its known, is an indie microbrewery. Great beer—I go there all the time—but it's filled with middle-aged dudes acting like wannabe hipsters."

"And if I want to avoid the older crowd?"

"That'd leave you with the Prickly Cactus—AKA Pricks. The food is top-notch, but the youth can sometimes get a little sloppy drunk and relive their high school dramas."

"That's it? Doesn't sound so bad."

"Yeah. Just as long as Large Marge doesn't come out from the kitchen."

"Who?"

Gabe grins. "Oh, I'm gonna let you discover that all on your own."

chapter 65

Pricks is a converted two-storey warehouse nearby in the old part of town. The parking lot is packed, so whatever I'm about to walk into, I'm going to get the full meal deal.

I crack open the door, and the last of the setting sun blasts into the bar. I might as well have thrown a spotlight on myself. People turn and glare, and I shut the door as quickly as I can.

This place is a throwback to the Wild West, too, and honky-tonk music blasts from the speakers. It's big and open—bar on one side of the room, tables on the other, and pool tables and pinball at the back. Also at the back are stairs leading to a second level overlooking the main space.

Like Gabe warned me, it's rowdy in here; a fight could break out any minute. Most of the people are my age, although some do kind of look like they'd finished high school and decided never to leave town.

A fair share of them wear rigger hats and cowboy boots, which makes me stand out like a sore thumb. I'm city and mocha, and a complete outsider, so I cross quickly to an open table near the bar and take a seat.

A waitress whose name tag reads BETHANY approaches. She's in her early thirties, tight jeans, black T-shirt with the bar's logo written in white letters across her chest. Her hair is long and red and so are her nails. She's grumpy as hell.

"Whaddya want?"

"What's good?"

She rolls her eyes, grabs a laminated menu, and dumps it on the table in front of me, not offering any suggestions.

I scan it quickly. "Can I get your signature burger, and an Envelopes IPA."

Again, this just annoys her. "ID?"

I hand it over, and she scrutinizes it, raising an eyebrow. "Says it's your birthday."

"It is."

Doesn't seem to matter to her. She tosses my ID on the table and stomps away. Hopefully she won't spit in my meal before she serves it.

Now that I've got a minute to take it all in, the Prickly Cactus starts to seem a bit sketchy. Not everyone is being carded, and the bartenders are playing free and loose with how much they're serving. They're also giving free drinks to pretty women, while making sure to charge every guy. There's two dudes in the corner who are obviously dealing, and no one's batting an eye, and one of the floor servers—not Bethany—is skimming the register, slipping a few bills into her pocket when she thinks no one's looking.

I put my head down and focus on my phone, pretending to be clueless about the hornet's nest I've stepped into. If I bail now, I likely won't make it past the parking lot before some good ol' boys ask why I'm leaving so soon.

Hopefully, Bethany will be back with the food right away. I'll take it whether she's spit in it or not.

"Screw you, Kyle!" someone yells.

I don't look up; that's just asking for trouble.

"Let go of me, you asshole!"

Dammit. I peek.

A young woman standing by the bar is pushing away a guy—Kyle—who's got a tight hold on her.

"Look, you little bitch—"

Shit, this is going south fast.

The woman keeps yelling and yanking her arm away from him, but he only gets rougher.

She kicks, pissing him off more, and I don't want to pull any white-knight bullshit—not here, not now—but my instincts ignore common sense, and I'm out of my seat.

As he raises a hand to smack her, I'm there, wedging myself between them. "Hey there."

"Get outta my way," Kyle screams in my face. He stinks like booze and oil.

I square up, and we're chest to chest. "Why should I?"

"Thish is a convershashion between my lady and me," he slurs. "Hash nothing to do with you, douchebag!" He tries to push me, but I stay solid.

Without taking my eyes off Kyle, I ask the woman behind me what her name is.

"Audrey," she says.

"And is Kyle here telling the truth? Are you his lady?"

"He only wishes I still was," she scoffs, moving away.

"You hear that? She says she isn't—"

I don't get a chance to finish. The drunk doofus cold-cocks me in the head, and I stumble backwards, bouncing off a table. People shout as their drinks splash everywhere.

"Sorry!" I say to the room in general.

I come back quickly with a tight swing that clips Kyle in the chin. I strike again, a solid punch to the gut. After a couple of years around Charlie, I've learned how to deal with these assholes.

Kyle staggers, but comes back with a couple of jabs at my face.

I block, but this leaves me exposed, and he sucker-punches me in the side, winding me. As I reel, he catches me again, this time in the eye.

Shaken, I throw a wild roundhouse, and luckily it lands on his face, giving me a chance to recover.

We're both dazed and huffing, and I hope that's it, but suddenly he pulls a knife, and I don't know what the hell to do.

I try to push into the crowd—they're not having it and shove me back. Kyle comes at me again, swiping savagely, and I arch my torso away, hoping it's enough. He over-pivots and stumbles into a table of beer bottles, and that seems to be enough for my waitress, Bethany.

"Goddammit, Randy!" she yells somewhere over my left shoulder. "Grab Large Marge!"

One of the cooks storms out of the kitchen, a big shotgun in his meaty hands.

"Sit down," says Bethany, "or Randy'll unload rock salt in all your asses."

Everyone scatters. Everyone except for Kyle and me.

He's still swaying from the fight and the booze, but he's still twisting the knife in his hand, like maybe he's ready to go after Bethany.

Randy isn't having any of it. He walks right up to him, sticking the barrel into Kyle's chest. "It's about time you leave."

"Fine!" Kyle spits. "Screw you and this piece-of-shit stink-hole." He storms off, pushing over an abandoned table, food and booze flying everywhere.

My muscles begin to unclench as he leaves, but Bethany points at me. "You too, birthday boy. Get the hell out."

"But I was just trying to help." I look around for Audrey to back me up, but she's nowhere to be seen.

"Yeah, well, we don't need your kind of help around here."

"I never even got my food!"

"Yeah, and you never paid for anything either, so we're all square. Now, as I said, get the hell out."

Well, shit.

Happy birthday to me.

chapter 66

I wander out of the bar, knowing better than to argue with Bethany, Randy, and Large Marge.

Thankfully, there's no sign of Kyle. But before he gets any ideas and comes back with a couple of friends, I climb into my car and leave.

Even though I'm pretty sure I won the fight, my body doesn't feel like it. As the adrenaline drains away, my face starts to hurt like hell, and my knuckles begin to swell, and I know I need to treat my injuries.

I pull into a convenience store on the way back to the hotel. The door *dings* as I enter, and the cashier looks up from his phone and sees my face. "I don't want any trouble," he says.

"Neither do I."

I wander over to the cooler and look for ice. All they have are five-pound bags—not what I want—so I grab a container of Ben and Jerry's that I can eat while I mend.

My stomach aches at the thought of food, so I gaze at the warming oven and take a taquito and nachos drizzled with cheese sauce. None of it looks great, but it's exactly what I want right now. And since it's my birthday, I might as well have refreshments and a cake, so I grab a six-pack of beer and a Twinkie.

I dump it all on the counter, and the cashier stares at me.

I stare back. "What can I say. It's my birthday."

chapter 67

Juno greets me when I walk into the hotel. Although I feel like crap, I give her some scratches behind the ears.

Gabe sees me and whistles. "Well, *you* certainly know how to make friends. You okay?"

I lift my bag of supplies. "I am now."

I'm in no mood to chat and trudge up the stairs, leaving the two of them behind. Upstairs, kids are no longer running in the hallway, but a room at the far end is hosting a raucous party.

Inside my room, I discover that Maisie and Stanley have added vocal accompaniment to the rhythm of the headboard.

Seriously, do they ever give it a rest?

I sit on the bed and slip on my headphones to drown out the sound, soothing my sore knuckles with the ice cream while eating the taquito and nachos. I wash it all down with a beer.

None of this is how I imagined my eighteenth birthday. I'd thought I'd be surrounded by Mom, Dad, my sisters, and

Charlie, before the two of us went to hang out with Elaina and our friends.

I text Mom and Dad, letting them know I'm safe. No other details are necessary, I figure.

It doesn't take long for Mom to respond.

All safe?

Of course, I'm not going to tell her the truth:

**Yup. Arrived late.
Hotel is good.
Had some food and
my first (legal) beer.**

Dad chimes in:

What'd you eat?

If I tell him I'm eating an over-cooked chewy convenience store taquito, he'll disown me.

Burger.

Any good?

**Not bad.
You make better.**

Nice! Have a good bday!

Mom's back:

Love you. Miss you.
Happy birthday.

I drop the phone on the bed and switch the ice cream to my face for a bit, lying on my back, staring at the ceiling.

Maisie and Stanley hit a crescendo, overwhelming any attempt to drown out their sounds, then suddenly—finally!—it's quiet next door.

Is it intermission, or was that the finale? Either way, I'm enjoying the reprieve.

I send a quick note to Elaina to let her know that I haven't found out anything new. Although I'm in a new town with a new lead, nothing much has changed, and I don't want to get her hopes up.

In the silence, my mind wanders to Lakshmi. Her card is in my wallet. She's just a text away, but I check my watch. It's late, and she's an hour behind. She's probably working or walking Spirit along the beach.

What's it matter anyway? Even if she were interested, we live two provinces apart. And at some point, she's going back on the road or travelling the world again, and I'm going to stay in my city and go to school.

I should just let the idea of her go.

If Charlie were here, he'd say not to be a pussy and call her.

Maybe, but not tonight.

I dump the phone and grab a beer. Tonight, I only want to drown my sorrows. I raise the beer bottle. "To the truly shittiest birthday ever," I say to the empty room.

chapter 68

The next morning, I wake in a pile of crushed nacho chips and melted ice cream. Yuck.

I check the time. 10:38.

Ugh.

I heave myself out of bed and towards the bathroom, wincing all the way. My whole body aches, and my head doesn't feel so hot either.

I catch a glimpse of myself in the mirror, and I'm surprised by how poorly I fared in last night's fight. My cheek is bruised, and my left eye is bloodshot. I squeeze my fingers into fists, and my knuckles ache. I've been in worse scraps—but if Bethany, Randy, and Large Marge hadn't put an end to it, I might not be standing here.

I turn on the shower and soak for a long while. But although the hot water feels good on my muscles, I'm running behind. I decide to grab breakfast downstairs before searching Hatley's public records for what they may have on Charlie and his dad.

When I get downstairs, Gabe's no longer at the front desk; an older woman has replaced him. She turns to greet me, but when she sees my face, she scowls.

I ignore it. "Which way to breakfast?"

"I'm sorry. It's all done."

"What?"

She points to the table in the lounge, empty except for the coffee carafe.

"We clean up at eleven."

I check my watch. 11:13. Damn, did I really take that long?

Whatever. I pour the last little drizzle into a to-go cup.

"It's probably cold by now," she calls out.

I sigh. About par for the day.

"Where's the closest breakfast place?" I ask.

"There's a doughnut shop three blocks down on Main."

At this point, I'll take what I can get.

chapter 69

The place she sends me to is a twenty-four-hour national chain shop, and it's slammed. I stand in line for way too long. I wouldn't usually care, but I'm stiff and sore, and I keep getting dirty looks from people around me. Even though I've cleaned myself up, I'm pretty sure they're making judgments about the teenager with a beaten, swollen face.

I ignore everyone and check the hours of the public records archives to make sure they don't close over the noon hour. Thankfully, they don't—the first positive news this morning.

I order a coffee and a breakfast biscuit before noticing a stack of newspapers on a table. I flip through the first few pages: no mention of a shaggy-haired teenager causing trouble, though the front page goes into glorious detail about a splashy new country club and golf course.

An old guy shuffles up behind me and grumbles, "This ain't no library. Leave 'em alone."

It obviously wasn't his newspaper—he'd been nowhere near while I was in line—but I'm in no mood to deal with him. I don't know why half of this place acts like a pile of garbage, but the sooner I'm done with this town, the happier I'll be.

Thankfully, my order is called, so I toss the papers back on the table, grab my food, and get out of there.

Unfortunately, any enthusiasm for my breakfast is quickly squashed. The coffee tastes weird, like it's flavoured by the dust of every building I've ever been in. My sandwich is no better. The biscuit has crumbled away down one side, the cheese is only halfway in, and instead of sausage, they gave me ham. I try to talk myself into eating it by conjuring the taste of Dad's chipotle chicken wraps, and take a bite, but the whole thing is dry.

I accept my fate that I'll starve before ever getting a decent meal in this town, toss all of it in the garbage, and climb back into the car.

chapter 70

The public record archives are stored in the library, on the north side of town. The homes around here are in much better shape. Lots of older places, well-built and cared for, with plenty of trees and landscaped yards. Whoever lives in this area cares about their community. As I drive closer to the edge of town, the houses get newer and the evergreens and conifers smaller. The homes also shrink in square footage, but are well maintained just the same.

Kids bike in the streets, play in the front yards, race to playgrounds attached to schoolyards. Whatever initial negative feelings I had of Hatley are slowly being swayed in the opposite direction.

When I pull up to the library, I'm surprised. The building is new and absolutely beautiful. Its exterior is a combination of concrete, wood, and mountain shale, and the inside is bright and sunny with large windows and white stones that pattern its walls. At the centre of the lobby is an impressive reflecting pool.

And the place is packed! I've never seen a library so busy. People fill the tables and workstations, reading magazines and newspapers, hunting for books. Staff buzz around, serving customers and guiding folks through the stacks. A deep, hearty laugh catches my attention, and I turn to see a tall dude behind the desk who looks more like a football player than a librarian talking to a bunch of teens.

I'm on a mission, so I manoeuvre past all of this and find a computer. Unfortunately, I'm locked out without an account.

"Hey there. How's it going?"

The football librarian has suddenly appeared beside me.

"I...uh...can't seem to search the records."

"Yeah, that's a formality. Too many people come in here to look up porn."

"I just wanted to check out your local archives."

"Ah, a fellow genealogist?"

"Uh, yeah..."

The fewer questions, the better.

"Then let's set you up with an account."

"Actually, I'm not from around here—I only need it for the day."

"Oh..." He studies me.

I raise a hand, palm out. "I swear I'm not here for the porn."

Another boisterous laugh, and it's so inviting, I smile too.

"Let's do you a favour, then, friend, and get you guest access." He taps away at the keyboard. "Is there anything else I can help you with?"

"No, I think that's it."

He offers a hand, and I shake it. "If you need anything else, ask for Gavin."

I thank him as he saunters off to help a mother whose kid has wandered into the reflecting pool.

I type in my list of searches:

Charlie Wolfe

No results.

William Wolfe

No results.

William Charles

No results.

Mercury Charles

No results.

Dammit, what the hell? Nothing?

Not even a tiny *hint* that they were here? Have I travelled all this way for nothing?

Maybe the depressing truth is that this whole trip has just been the sad end to a pointless wild-goose chase.

I think it's time to go home.

chapter 71

I plod across the parking lot to the car.

I'm not happy, but at least I tried my best. And on the upside, I'll soon be on the highway, and it'll be the last I'll ever have to deal with this sewage puddle.

I wonder if Charlie would've done something else if he were looking for me—something *more*? What lengths would he have gone to that I haven't considered? What rules would he have bent? What laws would he have broken?

What am I not thinking of?

Maybe when I get home, I can track down someone who can somehow break into Charlie's phone records and find out who actually called him. Or figure out some sort of surveillance and dig deeper into Charlie's connections. Or break into Gekas's office and read her file on him.

My phone buzzes, interrupting these thoughts. I don't recognize the number.

Is this Tony?

Who is this?

Audrey

What the fu—? The girl from the bar last night? Why is *she* contacting me? But more importantly:

How'd you get this number?

Charlie gave it to me.

chapter 72

Is she joking?

Where did you see him?
And when?
And who was he with?
And are you with him now?

The typing indicator bubbles for a while, until it finally says:

Wally's Diner in ten.

In my car, I Google the place, and get there in three minutes. It isn't far from the library, close to the river. There are two cop cars and an ambulance sitting out front, along with a couple of pickup trucks.

Of course, this *is* the sort of place Charlie would pick. He might not be a fan of cops, but he understands the safety they provide, as well as the source of information they can be. A wave of something like comfort washes over me.

I step through the entrance, and a bell chimes in welcome. It's small but homey, and the place smells like baked buns, pancakes, and bacon.

Officers and paramedics fill a couple of booths along the windows, while the counter is occupied by two older men enjoying their coffee. I try not to draw attention to my face as I move to the far end and slide onto the last stool. Hopefully the purple bruises don't show too badly on my skin.

The owner comes out of the kitchen, grabs a coffee carafe, and pours me a cup. "What can I get you?"

"I'm just waiting for someone."

"Well, then, let me feed you while you wait."

"No, it's okay. I really shouldn't—"

The elderly man next to me interrupts. "Son, we've been coming here long enough to know that Wally's not going to stop until you're fed."

His buddy adds, "Besides, you're not going to get a better meal anywhere in town."

I can see none of them is going to let it go. "Uh, sure. I'll have, um..." I struggle to find a list of options.

"Nope, let me handle it," Wally says. "Any allergies?"

I shake my head.

"Excellent." He wanders to the kitchen and returns shortly with a small plate of mini pancakes dusted with icing sugar. "Blueberry pancake bites. Good on their own, but if you really have a sweet tooth, drown them in syrup."

I take one. It's still warm from the oven and smells like breakfast at the cabin. I take a bite and appreciate the burst of flavours. I pop the rest of it into my mouth before taking another. I don't realize until that moment how little I've eaten and how hungry I actually am.

"I think he likes it," says the man who's furthest away.

Wally smiles and slaps a menu down. "I'll be back to feed you some more." He proceeds to the officers, ready to settle their bill.

"What's your name?" asks the man closest to me.

"Tony."

"I'm Nick, and this is Jerome. What brings you to Hatley?"

"I'm looking for a friend," I say. I don't know why I'm so forthcoming. Maybe it's the smells and the good food—the comfort of a safe place.

Jerome nods. "Hopefully he's not the one who gave you that shiner."

"Nope. Picked that up last night."

Nick frowns. "Did you go looking for it?"

He sounds like my mom.

"Not intentionally."

"Well then, it sounds like the town rolled out the red carpet for you," Jerome says.

"Should I feel honoured?" I chuckle.

"This place has always been a little tough." Jerome holds up a hand to show the nub of a missing thumb. "Lost it working as a lumberjack north of here."

"Fell out of a tree, plumb near twenty feet—" says Nick.

"Then the damn saw followed and took the finger—"

"Lucky it wasn't his arm—"

"Or my nuts," says Jerome.

They both cackle.

I try to hide my shock, but I don't do well.

"Aww, don't give him too much sympathy," Nick smirks. "The nurse that stitched him up is now his wife."

Jerome adds, "And I tell my grandson that's what happens when you suck your thumb too much. Great way to get him to stop."

"You both work in logging?" I ask, making conversation.

"Jerome retired last fall, and I'm on my way out this year."

"How long did you work there?"

"I'm doing a full forty, but he got out early at thirty-five."

I can't even imagine being at a job that long, let alone one as dangerous as that.

"Has Hatley always been this friendly to strangers?"

Both Nick and Jerome laugh.

"Never," Nick says.

"Tourism's a new thing here. No one used to stick around."

"They'd stop here at night but get the heck outta Dodge as fast as they could."

With the reception I'd had, I didn't blame them.

"But the last couple years has seen a real uptick in people hanging around a few more days."

"Why's that?"

Jerome clicks his tongue. "Land development on the other side of the mountain." He doesn't seem too impressed.

"Oh?"

"Houses," Nick adds.

"*Pshh*," says Jerome. "Try mansions."

"Fine. And with mansions come people with the money to buy them. Though they do have a hard time if they try to sell."

"So, there's lots of building going on then." I can just about imagine the reception that anyone new in town gets.

Nick and Jerome cackle again.

"Yup. Seems to be quite a bit of new money around here lately. Serious money," Nick says. "And all I got is what's stuck to my shoe!"

I'm about to ask why anyone would build a big home here if they're so expensive and hard to sell, but that's when the entrance bell rings again, and Audrey walks in.

chapter 73

I excuse myself to sit at a booth with Audrey.

Since I'm not in the middle of a fight, I actually get a look at her. She's about my age, petite, with strawberry blonde hair and a pink complexion. She's got a nice smile, but there are bags under her eyes, and I wonder if she kept partying after Pricks.

She notices my eyes too.

"Oof. Is that cuz of Kyle? Sorry."

"It was my fault," I say. "I should've left it alone."

"Well, I appreciated it. He can be such an asshole."

I want to be polite, but I'm here for answers. "Where did you see Charlie?"

"Whoa. Let a girl get a cup of coffee first."

"But—"

It's too late, though. Wally arrives and fills her cup. "Hello, Audrey." His voice is terse, and he glances over at me. "Haven't seen you or your dad around much lately."

"Oh, you know. Work's got him busy," she says sweetly.

He heads back to the kitchen, and she rolls her eyes at me.

Over her shoulder, I notice both Nick and Jerome giving me a look. What is this?

I turn back to Audrey. "Okay, you got your coffee. Where's Charlie?"

She doesn't answer immediately, getting a few sips of coffee in before saying, "That, I don't know."

"But you said you saw him."

"Geez, what's the rush?" She half turns away and focuses on the drink.

I take a deep breath and do my damnedest to be patient. "Listen, he might be in trouble. Wherever he is, I need to know."

"Sure didn't seem like he was in trouble last night."

She gloats a little, savouring the power of her intel along with her Colombian roast. "We met at a party."

"A party?" It's not what I expected to hear. Actually, I don't even know what I expected to hear.

"Uh-huh," she says coyly. "The kind of party you don't tell your daddy about."

I frown.

Were Mom and Gekas right? Did Charlie send me on some kind of scavenger hunt across the country? Was he even really missing? Or did he take off of his own free will?

I shake my head. No, he had asked for help. He would never do that, even as a joke.

She eyes my pancake bites, then picks one out and scarfs it down. "Oh, and he told me to give you a message."

"Yeah? And what's that?"

She takes a big swig of coffee to wash down my breakfast. "It was something like, tell him to leave it alone, and go home."

I stare at her. "What?"

"*What* what? That's what he said." She snags another blueberry bite.

I lean back in my seat. It doesn't make sense. If Charlie's in trouble, he needs my help. But if he isn't, why send me away?

"No, I'm not going anywhere."

"He figured you wouldn't listen. He also said you'd try and smooth-talk me."

"Then let's skip that step, and you tell me what else he said."

"Ugh. The way he talked you up, I figured you'd be a little more fun."

I sigh and move to stand up. "I really don't have time—"

"Listen," Audrey says, holding my arm, "I'd tell you where he is, but I owe him. He got me a sweet deal on some weed."

What is she looking for—a bribe? Has she forgotten that *I* took a black eye from Kyle? All right then, whatever—if that's what it takes. "What if I buy you that coffee and some pancake bites of your own?"

"There ya go!" She grabs her purse and rises. "Do that, then let's roll."

"What? No."

"Tony," she chides, "you're never going to find the place on your own. I'll show you."

Like it or not, I'm stuck with her.

chapter 74

After her food arrives and I pay, we climb into my car and she points me west towards the mountain.

"Thanks again for stepping in last night. Kyle was being a dickwad," Audrey says. She directs us north at the end of the street, and we travel along a highway beside the river.

Might as well be friendly. "You guys were a couple?"

"What can I say? In this town, options are limited."

She cracks open the styrofoam container of food and quickly polishes off two pancake bites soaked in icing sugar and maple syrup.

I'm not thrilled that she's eating in Dad's car, but she's supposedly taking me to Charlie. As long as she keeps the interior clean, I'll keep my opinions to myself.

"Were you together long?"

"Yeah. I dumped him a year ago. But some people have a hard time letting go of the past."

She licks her fingers after finishing another, and we drive over an old steel bridge that crosses the river and up a well-built mountain road.

"So, what was going on back there at the restaurant?"

"What? With Wally and his guys? They don't like Daddy working with the new developers."

Oh geez, she's your typical daddy's girl, but I need her help. "So, the developers building these big houses—"

"And the hotels and stores and restaurants," she interrupts.

"Right. So, what's it matter who your dad works with?"

"Daddy says the locals don't want them here."

"Why not?"

"Cuz it's new money from out of town. Hatley people get suspicious. Where's it all coming from? Why here?" She giggles. "But Daddy says people in Hatley wouldn't know a good thing if it bit them in the ass."

Obviously, I'm missing something.

We wind around the bend, and the trees open up to reveal a crystal blue mountain lake. A stretch of large homes lines the waterfront. Not quite the palatial estates that Nick and Jerome described, but definitely much bigger than anything else around here.

On the far side, I can see what looks like a golf course under construction. Must be the new one that was featured in the newspaper.

Audrey knows all about it. "A big chunk of this area was cleared by the mill years ago. Daddy said some folks from the city saw the potential and built it up. Now we've got millionaires coming here to retire."

We descend into the hidden valley, and I can see why people would want to live here. It's quiet and beautiful and a welcome break from urban life.

"You saw Charlie out here?"

She nods. "Like I said, he didn't seem to be suffering any."

"What happened? Where was this party?"

"After Pricks, my friend Bethany texted us something was going on in the hills. Parties out there are always a mixed bag. I mean, the parties are good, but the guys can be creeps sometimes."

"What do you mean?"

"Oh, there's just a lot of rich assholes who try to get away with whatever shit they want, so you have to be careful."

"And Charlie was there?"

"I didn't see him when we first got there, but the guys he was with were there already."

"Guys? What guys?" This is news.

She shrugs. "Never met them before, but they were seriously a couple of chotches."

"Chotches? What the hell's that?"

"Slimy. Dressed like businessmen—suits and ties—but seemed like they were trying too hard."

After what Kosmos had told me, I wouldn't be surprised if they were a part of the Family. "But Charlie wasn't with them to start with? When did he show up?"

"I was downstairs looking for a bathroom, and he just suddenly got up in my face, asking me questions."

"About what?"

"You."

"Me?"

She nods. "Said he heard me telling Kaitlyn what had happened at Pricks. Started quizzing me, asking what you looked like. Asked me if you looked like a mocha all-star."

I laugh. Definitely sounded like Charlie. "Then what?"

"Then he told me to meet you at Wally's and do my best to send you packing."

"He told you to take me to Wally's?"

"Uh-huh. Said you'd need a decent meal after being around this shithole."

Even when he's trying to get rid of me, he still worries about food.

Still—why is he trying to get rid of me at all?

"You said there were a couple of guys with him? Who were they?"

"First guy's name was Cal...no—Cass. Total d-bag. Totally handsy. The other guy was nicer. Not good-looking, but kinder."

"And what was his name?"

"Red."

Neither name means anything to me. Whoever they are, they're no one I know.

"Those two are the only ones? There wasn't a woman with them?"

She shakes her head.

Why the hell are they here? What the hell is Charlie up to? Is he in trouble—or is he working with this Cass and Red? There's no sign of Cousin Rachel yet, but that doesn't mean she isn't lurking somewhere.

Audrey indicates a tree-lined driveway—and I note the address—but drive past it a ways, do a u-turn, then park.

"What are we doing?" she asks.

"I need you on lookout while I go in and scout around. You see anything, you text me."

"Why not just drive in?"

"If we do that, we could get boxed in and exposed."

She stares at me. "Are you like a secret agent or something?"

"Nope. Just a guy who's done this way too many times."

chapter 75

I cut through the forest towards the house. The ground is uneven, and the rough rocks dig into my shoes.

The house is big and ugly—an unhappy mix of stucco and brick—the kind that has no clue what it wants to be. There are columns, turrets, different-sized windows, multiple rooflines, and a three-car garage. I've seen these kinds of places in the newer subdivisions of the city, but out here, on its own, it's the architectural epitome of trying too hard.

I skulk along the treeline until I'm at the edge of the garage, where I peek around the corner, hoping no one's around.

The backyard is large and manicured, containing a deck and a gazebo. It would probably look pretty nice, normally, but right now, the place is trashed.

Beer cans and whiskey, gin, and vodka bottles are strewn everywhere. The wicker patio furniture has been smashed to pieces with an ax, and the cushions have been burned in a makeshift bonfire in the middle of the yard. Our prairie farm and bush parties seem civilized next to these remains.

I skirt along the house to a covered outdoor room with a hot tub and fireplace inside. Again, it would look nice—if someone hadn't yakked in the water.

I turn away, crossing to a set of double doors that lead down to the basement. Unfortunately, they're locked, so I move on.

I go up a set of stairs that takes me to a second covered deck with a dining area beside a large four-grill barbecue. Again, garbage everywhere.

Whoever owns this monstrosity is going to be pissed.

Another set of double doors looks into the main dining room. One of these is open, so I go inside.

Beyond the table, the room opens up to a living room with a fireplace and a high vaulted ceiling. On the left is a kitchen and a staircase that will take me either up or down. I choose down, since that's where Audrey said she saw Charlie.

The basement is an entertainment space; there's a television over the fireplace, and the big double-door walkout looks out onto the patio with the puke-filled hot tub.

There's a bar area too, a wine room behind a glass door, and a big projection screen complete with comfy couches. It's all trashed, and wine and booze and burn marks mar the furniture and carpets. I move through it until I locate the hallway that leads to the bathroom.

No sign of Charlie.

I head back to the stairs.

A loud *bang* from above startles me. It's clanky and metal, like an air hammer, but I know it's not.

It's a gunshot.

chapter 76

I do exactly what my parents hate: I run towards the sound.

I do, however, stay close to the edge of the wall, peering through the railing to see if there's any movement on the main floor.

Nothing. No blood. No body.

Who got shot? Happily—at least for the moment—it's not me. I just hope it's not Charlie either.

The noise must've come from the second floor, which is good because there's currently some distance between me and the gun—and I hope the shooter is already gone by now—but if they're still here, it also means that going to investigate could very well prompt them to shoot again. Like any animal, if they feel threatened, they might strike.

The stairs twist in a wide arc to an open gallery on the second floor. There's no cover. I pause, assessing the options.

There are none.

As quickly and stealthily as I can, I move towards the stairs. If the shooter sees me coming, maybe I won't get shot by accident. I push aside the thought that I could get shot deliberately. The climb up is terrifying.

I poke my head cautiously above the top step, feeling like a gopher about to dart across the highway. But all is silent on the second floor.

Several doors branch off the bright hallway. To my direct left is a bedroom with a gas fireplace—one more excess of this place. I know winters can get cold around here, but do you really need a fireplace in every room? Above it is a television, and it occurs to me that whoever built this house really wasn't interested in hanging out with the rest of their family.

Past this is another bedroom—and yet another fireplace and television—as well as a sitting room built into the turret in the front corner of the house.

I step out and cross the corridor to a family room with a huge seventy-inch screen and couches. The electronics and space in this house is too much, even for me. I can only imagine what Charlie thinks of it all.

I find a space intended to be a huge gym. There's no equipment installed yet, but there are mirrors everywhere, weight racks, a pull-up bar, and what must be an indoor golf simulator with an Astroturf mat and a hitting mesh. No one's in here, so I walk to the final set of doors.

If the shooter is still here, they're waiting for me.

I enter slowly. A curtain blows in the corner of what has to be the master bedroom.

I move towards the sitting area—this place is unreal, even the bedrooms have living rooms—staying alert. There's a balcony that looks out on the front lawn, but it's empty.

If someone *had* been here, they'd heard my warning and bailed. And if they're that cautious, I doubt Audrey will even see them. I study the rest of the room, looking for clues.

My breath catches.

A bare leg is stretched out at an odd angle on the white tile of the ensuite bathroom.

Shit.

I should probably get the hell out of here.

But my friend … I need to know that it's not him.

I cross to the bathroom entrance and step inside.

A towel-wrapped man is slumped against the wall of the walk-in shower. His eyes are open, his mouth too. Broken glass from the shattered shower door litters the floor around him.

It's not Charlie.

My phone buzzes. A message from Audrey.

Someone's here.

chapter 77

I rush to the balcony window and push aside the heavy curtains to look out. A sleek car is approaching, but I can't get a better look without revealing myself. Maybe they're the owners of the house, or they know the dude in the shower. Either way, I need to get out of here. Now.

I can't go out the front, so I double back into the hallway. I check every room, every window, to see if there's a way down without giving away my position to the new arrivals, but my best option takes me out onto the sharp, sloping roof that I am sure I'll fall off of and break my leg.

People enter through the front door. I have only seconds to duck into the bedroom with the turret before I'm seen.

"Boss? You here?" yells some guy.

"Winston?" says another.

I need to hide. Moving as silently as I can, I quickly slide behind the opaque curtain, pressing my back into the curved wall, leaving a sliver of visibility.

They continue to call out for Winston, and by the sound of their voices, they've split up to cover more ground. One has gone downstairs, while the other searches the main floor.

"Hey, check upstairs."

Dammit. I wish I could melt into the walls. Anything other than being here.

There's a shift of shadow and light on the wall of the stair-well, and I pull the curtain closed all the way.

The fabric muffles anything quieter than a shout, so I'm standing here, blind and deaf. I hold my breath, trying my best to limit any chance of exposure.

Suddenly, there are footsteps on the wood floor nearby.

The tread is slow and deliberate. They're probably study-ing the space. I squeeze my eyes shut in case that helps, and hope they move on. I'm not that lucky.

The footsteps move closer.

I'm screwed. There's no escape.

Blood pounds in my head, and I feel a mad rush of adren-aline as I prepare to attack.

I push my foot back into the wall, ready to spring, tensing for the attack. I'll only get one chance—I'll have to give it everything I have.

The curtain is pulled back.

My friend stands before me.

"*Charlie*?!"

Joy fills me, and I reach out to give him a big hug, but he pushes me away, hard.

"Shepherd," he hisses, "what the hell!? You need to get out of here!"

part 4

Charlie pushes Tony towards the door. "I'll distract them so you can climb out the window."

"What? No! What the hell is going on? And why the hell are you wearing Crocs with your suit?"

He winces. "Long story. I'll explain everything later, but right now you've got to be anywhere but here."

"I'm not going anywhere. *We* are getting out of here."

"I can't."

"What? Why not?"

"Charlie?" Cass calls up the stairs.

"Enough with the questions. You've got to hide." Charlie pushes him back into the curtains.

"Wait!" Tony grabs his arm. "Who's out there?"

Charlie shakes him off. There isn't time for this. "Just shut your doughnut hole until we're gone."

"But there's a dead guy next door—" Tony whispers fiercely.

"Yeah, don't worry about him. I'll distract these guys, and you get the hell out of here."

"Charlie, you've got to tell me what's going on!"

"No."

"Goddammit," Tony says. "I put everything on the line to get to you."

Charlie can hear all the frustration of the last seven days in his friend's voice. But the clock's ticking. If he can't shut Tony up, they'll both be toast.

"Fine. Did you bring my backpack?"

"Yeah."

"In the bottom is a hidden pocket. There's a burner phone inside. Stick it in the toilet tank at the restaurant Audrey took you to. I'll grab it when I can. Now, *be quiet*."

He yanks the curtain back into place, checking it briefly before going out of the room and over to the stairwell.

"I found Winston," he calls down.

Cass takes the stairs two at a time, gun drawn, Red right behind. "Show me."

Charlie points towards the master bedroom. "Sorry—he's dead, like all the others."

Cass pushes past him into the room, Red on his heels. Charlie follows. It doesn't take them long to find Winston.

Cass is down on his hands and knees, the gun clattering against the tile.

"Don't touch him," Charlie warns.

"I'm not going to goddamn touch him." Suddenly, he's up, angry. "Who the *hell* did this?"

"I'd have to take some time to look around—"

"Then *do* it!" Cass yells.

He hovers over Charlie's shoulder, staring at the body. Suddenly he spins and punches the mirror. The glass fractures across its surface. "We're searching every goddamn room in this house," he snaps before storming out.

Charlie peers out of the bathroom. The bedroom curtain isn't quite closed anymore. No sign of Tony, but he can't have gotten too far yet.

If Charlie doesn't slow this idiot down, shit could still go sideways. "Uh, Cass?" he calls.

"What?" Cass barks from the hallway.

"Where do you want me to start? Downstairs?"

"No. See what you can make of things up here."

"Cool. I'll check the other rooms—"

"No, Red'll do that. You check out Winston."

"Check what? He's dead." Charlie slides a thumb across his neck.

"Just tell me who murdered him!" Cass hollers, putting a hole in the wall with his fist before pounding down the stairs.

Red glares at him. "What's *with* you, kid?" he says, then goes down the hall, presumably to check the other rooms, leaving Charlie alone with Winston.

He can only hope that Tony's long gone.

Charlie turns back to Winston's half-naked body in the shower. It's twisted in a heap against the white tile and broken glass, a towel still wrapped around his waist.

His glazed eyes are red. His neck is swollen and bruised. His fingers are blue, and he's pissed himself.

All the signs of strangulation.

But that shattered door and the scratches on his neck suggest that he didn't go down without a fight. If this was their mystery woman, Winston should've been able to put up a pretty good struggle.

Charlie returns to the bedroom and finds a half-empty bottle on the side table. He pours out a few drops on his palm, then sticks a finger in to taste it. There's a hint of salt. Winston had most likely been roofied.

So she'd been here, got close, let him know who she was. Then incapacitated and killed him.

He'd been a bad dude—but not enough of an asshole to deserve this. Besides, his death really screws things up for Charlie.

Charlie still has a rendezvous with Robert—he has no doubt Cass will make sure of it—but without Winston's protection, he's hooped. Shit out of luck. A day late and a dollar short.

What the hell is he going to do now?

chapter 79

I'm not leaving my friend.

I've scuttled into a mudroom off the kitchen. The lights are off, so it's kind of dark, but I don't know if that'll help much.

The guy Charlie called Cass is in the dining room, muttering expletives under his breath. The kitchen island is the only thing that prevents him from seeing me. If he comes around the corner, it's all over.

Across from me is a short hallway that leads to a back set of stairs down to the walkout basement and up to the second floor, as well as to the laundry room. There's also another door that I'm guessing goes out to the garage. I could duck out right now and escape into the trees. But I don't. Not yet.

My phone buzzes. Audrey.

Another car pulled in.

Shit. Who can it be now?

Uh-oh. Cass has come into the kitchen, and he's moving around the island. He pauses, and I hear the door to the butler's pantry slide all the way open. After he's done searching there, this room will be next.

I duck down the hall to the back stairs. Cass would undoubtedly hear the garage door if I opened it, but maybe I could make it downstairs and hide by the hot tub?

Thankfully—perhaps—the front door opens and someone enters.

"Okay," says a woman's voice, "tell me what's happening?"

chapter 80

There's a mirror in the mudroom, and I move back over, staying low, barely in time to catch a tall, slim brunette—maybe forty—walk across the reflection. Her black blazer is all sharp lines, and she moves like a shark.

"Someone got to Winston," Cass tells her.

"What do you mean, 'got to'?"

"He's dead. Upstairs."

No one says anything for a moment, so I have no clue as to her reaction. I don't dare stick my head out to look.

"Show me."

There's a shuffle of feet up the stairs, and as soon as I think I'm the only one down here, I slide back into the kitchen to hear better.

"What the hell is *he* doing here?" the woman shouts.

Shit! I immediately shrink back, then realize she must be talking about Charlie.

"This is the kid Winston brought along."

"I *know* that," she snaps. "But what would possess you to bring him here?"

"He's got a talent—" Cass fumbles.

"For what? Making my life difficult?"

"No, he's some kind of teen detective."

"I don't care if he's freakin' Sherlock Holmes. Get him the hell out of here!"

Just then Charlie's shaggy head pops out from the stairwell. He spots me right away and shoots me a hard glare, jerking his head at the garage door.

I shake my head.

He gives an exaggerated, though silent, sigh, and gestures with his thumb and pinkie at his ear, mouthing, "I'll call."

"Charlie!" one of the goons yells, and he turns away.

I can't convince him to leave, but I can't let myself get caught either.

I resign myself to the inevitable and slip back into the mudroom to exit through the side door, leaving him behind.

chapter 81

The garage is vacant. A long, concrete room with nowhere to hide. If anyone comes looking, I'll be seen—and probably die—very quickly. Everyone is amped up and angry, and I'm sure they'll shoot first and ask questions later.

On the far side is a metal door, and I sprint to open it. It's only a short dash across the yard to the trees. I dive between them at full speed, moving as fast as I can, trying to be careful—don't need to twist an ankle—but wanting as much distance between me and the modern-day chateau as possible.

Having disappeared among the leaves and brush, I slow down and work my way back to Audrey and the car.

She's standing beside it, nonchalantly having a smoke. "Shit, I thought you were screwed for sure when that second car showed up."

"Thanks for your help."

"Did they see you?"

"I think we'd know already if they had."

"So, what happened up there?"

I skip mention of the body and focus on the arrival of the two cars.

"You were right. Seemed like Charlie didn't really need me. Did you recognize the woman?"

She shakes her head. "She didn't look too pleased to be here."

I nod. None of us is really pleased to be here.

chapter 82

I drop Audrey off at the restaurant.

As soon as she drives away in her own car, I open Charlie's backpack and find the hidden pocket. Inside is a burner phone, a fake ID, a few hundred bucks, and…a *police badge*?! I fish it out and study it. Damn, I think it's actually real! He never ceases to amaze me.

I stuff it back inside with everything else, but keep the phone, dropping it into one of the cleaner sandwich bags from Dad's lunch wraps, and duct tape it tightly shut.

The restaurant is empty except for Wally and a couple of EMT workers sitting in a booth.

"Can I get a coffee to go?"

Wally nods, but he's not as friendly as before. Whatever stained his opinion of Audrey's father seems to have rubbed off on me. Still, it seems to be the only good diner in Hatley, so I'm not about to be run off.

"Mind if I add a club sandwich and apple pie?"

While he boxes everything up, I wander into the bathroom.

It's your standard commercial bathroom. Not a lot of hiding places. But the back of the toilet tank is fairly close to the wall, and when I lift the lid, I can see that it will both weigh down and conceal the zippered edge of the baggie that holds the phone inside.

I close it up and flush, making sure I didn't accidentally jam things up in the process. Convinced, I wash my hands and go back out.

chapter 83

My meal is on the counter when I step out of the bathroom. I leave an extra-generous tip, grab the to-go bag, and walk to the car.

I drive to the far side of the street and tuck behind a truck, hoping to remain inconspicuous. I dig out a pair of binoculars from Charlie's backpack, adjust the focus, then lean back and wait.

There's a good chance Charlie and the thugs will never show up. He might not be able to convince them to stop here. And even if he does, who knows when they'll finally come. I try to push it out of my mind.

My stomach gurgles. Other than the coffee and the pancake bites, I haven't had much of anything since last night's crappy birthday dinner. I pull out half of the clubhouse and take a bite.

It's delicious. Turkey with a hint of avocado and mustard. Everything is fresh and made to perfection—just like Dad would make. The bacon is crunchy, but not crispy, and I'm pretty sure Wally bakes his own bread. I devour it quickly, but leave the second half in the container.

I pick away at the pie while sipping my coffee. I don't want to be a glutton, but it's pretty damn hard, considering how good everything is.

In the silence, I go through everything I've learned. None of it makes sense.

If Charlie is under lock and key, how is it that they're letting him walk around so freely? And why wouldn't he escape when I did? They'd even made it sound like the dead guy—Winston?—had brought him along to help. Why would he possibly be helping them?

More importantly, why isn't he letting me help *him*?

What could they have on him?

Something from his past, no doubt. After all I've learned, it wouldn't surprise me. Whatever it is, he's scared enough to cooperate.

All my questions are pushed aside when a sleek-looking vehicle drives into the lot. A Maserati? No one gets out right away, and I grab the binoculars. I can see the driver—a big hulk of a dude, but it's hard to make out anyone else.

Then Charlie hops out of the back seat on the far side. He leans into the passenger window, but someone waves him away.

He's way too damn friendly with these guys. I don't like it.

He goes inside, and I can see him at the till through the window. Shortly afterward, he crosses over to the bathroom, disappearing behind the door.

I pan back to the car. A smaller guy—the one I saw briefly at the house—climbs out of the passenger side.

He seems worked up, walking partway to the restaurant, then returning to the car. The driver signals him to get back in the car, but it isn't until Charlie reappears that the passenger calms down.

Charlie offers him one of the coffees he's purchased, but the dude bats it out of his hand, and impatiently motions for him to get in the car. Charlie shrugs and climbs back in, and I chuckle. Even when things seem bad, he's still willing to piss people off. They pull away in the opposite direction.

Only after I'm sure they're gone do I drive to the hotel to wait for Charlie's call.

chapter 84

When I get back, Gabe has already returned for his next shift. Juno rises from her spot in the lounge to greet me.

"How are you doing, my friend?" he asks.

At first, his greeting sounds odd. I only met him last night, after all. But considering all I've had to deal with, I have to admit he's currently my closest ally besides Charlie.

"Better."

"I'm sorry for sending you to Pricks."

I guess my Jamaican skin isn't doing much anymore to camouflage the darkening bruises I've acquired. "It's all right. I should've known better than to stick my nose where it didn't belong."

"Still, to make amends, some folks checked out, so I've upgraded you to one of our newly-renovated executive suites."

"Gabe, I can't. I'm on a budget."

"Don't worry. No extra charge."

"Really, it's too much."

"No worries, Tony. It's the least I can do."

He hands me the new key—still on a big plastic diamond—telling me to leave the old one in the room before sending me on my way.

I pack up my things, happy to be done with this crap room. Kids are running up and down the hallway again, televisions blare, and Maisie and Stanley are going at it next door. I hope they've come up for air, at least to eat lunch. They'll need their strength.

As I haul my bag to the third floor, the noises fade away. I'm actually shocked—and pleased—by how quiet it is. My new room is at the end of the hall, and I unlock the door and enter.

Holy shit! Gabe's been holding out on me.

No more western-themed decor. The room's been stripped down to the original hardwood floors, and the walls have a beautiful fresh paint job. I hop onto the bed and sink into cushioned softness. Fresh sheets, a new blanket, and a quality mattress. No more mothballs and dust!

Even the TV is an upgrade; when I turn on the fifty-inch display, I actually get a picture. I flip through the channels mindlessly, pleased by the image quality. A documentary pops up about two high school students from Chicago with dreams of playing professional basketball.

I check my watch. Less than fifteen minutes have passed since Charlie grabbed the phone from the diner. He's not calling right away. Might as well watch something until he does.

I stretch out on the bed, grab the last of Wally's pie, and enjoy the show, amazed at how easy it is to relax when you know your best friend is alive.

chapter 85

Something buzzes in the distance.

Ugh.

Another buzz. I groggily regain awareness and struggle to get my bearings.

Another buzz.

Shit, it's my phone.

I drag myself off the bed, half dazed, half lost in the new space, stumbling across the floor towards the noise.

"Hello? Hello?"

Nothing. I was too slow and they hung up.

Dammit.

I search for missed calls, but the phone rings again before I find it.

Caller ID says my parents' house. I answer it.

"Anthony?" It's Mom.

"Hey, Mom."

"Are you okay?"

"Yeah, I just..." My brain is still playing catch-up, and the TV is still on and distracting me, so I turn it off. "Sorry, just waking up."

"Why are you sleeping? It's still afternoon."

"Yeah, it is. It's... I was relaxing and must've fallen asleep."

"You aren't staying up too late, are you?"

"Mo-o-om..." I say, with a playful scold.

"I know, I know." She clears her throat. "What have you been up to? Have you found out anything about Charlie?"

My next words surprise me. "I haven't."

I'm hesitant to tell the truth. Charlie's mixed up in something far worse than I would've expected. For now, I need to be patient and trust him and—how had he put it?—keep my doughnut hole shut.

"So are you coming home, then?"

I need to stall at least another day. "Uh. I want to check the archives here a bit more."

"And then you'll be coming home?"

"Yes."

"Okay." I can hear the hesitancy in Mom's voice. "But you're safe?"

"Yeah," I answer, maybe a little too quickly. "It's all pretty boring. Going through old newspapers and asking a few of the locals if they might've known Charlie or his dad."

"Okay." The phone goes muffled, and I can hear her calling Dad. She returns. "Your dad is busy cooking but says hi."

"Is he concocting something good?"

"He won't tell me, but it smells spicy."

"Tell him to save me some."

"Okay..."

"I'm okay, Mom."

"Okay. If you don't find anything soon, we want you to come home."

"Sounds good."

"We love you."

"Love you too."

I turn off the call and fall back onto the bed.

It never feels right lying to my folks, but for the time being, it's a necessity. At least until I figure out what the hell is going on.

chapter 86

Now that I'm awake, I check through my phone, just to make sure I didn't miss any calls.

Elaina has messaged with her regular check-in, as did Laura, making sure I'm not keeping anything from her friend. I reply to them both, telling them nothing except that I'm still searching. I'm not interested in explaining that I've seen Charlie, but that he isn't with me or why we aren't on our way home—because I don't really know.

I search through my messages, but there's no anonymous texts or calls.

My phone rings again, but it's not Charlie.

It's Lakshmi.

I scramble to answer. "Hello—?"

"Tony?"

I can hear the smile in her voice, and it lifts me up.

"Lakshmi,"—okay, be cool—"I didn't expect you to call."

"Oh?" She sounds disappointed. "I can let you go—"

"No! No," I shout. "It's all good. For real."

Shit! I smack my forehead. What is *happening* to me? "I'm glad you called."

"Well, I *did* wait a while."

"What do you mean?"

"Oh, you know the rule: Let at least three days pass so the other person has had time to think about the last time they saw you."

"Ah." I smile knowledgeably, even though she can't see me. "And here I thought it was so you didn't seem desperate."

"Well, that too. Did I give you enough time?"

"Oh, absolutely."

"Good."

I feel my heart leap again like it did the day I met her.

"So, where have your journeys taken you?" she asks. "Did you find your friend?"

"I did." Somehow, I feel safe telling her the truth.

"And is he through his storm?"

"Nope, right in the middle of it," I sigh.

"Which means you are too?"

"Yes." No sense lying now.

She's quiet. Serious. "Do you see a way out?"

I consider it. "Not yet."

"But you don't sound worried."

Until she said it, I hadn't noticed. But she's right. A sense of calm washes over me. "Now that I've found him, I think we'll be able to fix it."

My phone buzzes again. "Rocketman" is on the display.

I don't want to say goodbye; it's selfish, I know, but even with everything going on, I want to stay on the line with her.

"You have a call?" she asks.

"Yeah."

"Your friend?"

"Yeah."

"Then go do what's right."

"Thank you," I say, and I mean it.

I'm about to hang up when I hear her say, "Don't be a stranger, Tony Shepherd."

"I promise. I won't."

"I'll hold you to it."

chapter 87

I answer the other call. "Charlie?"

"Hey, Shepherd."

"Are you okay?"

"Oh, you know—I've had better weeks."

"What the *hell's* going on?"

"Yeah, well, Red and Cass grabbed me at your graduation—"

"Red and Cass? The guys from the house?"

"Yeah, they juked me by stealing my mom's phone—"

"You mean your stepmom," I interrupt.

He barely acknowledges this. "Yeah, well, they took her phone—"

"Charlie?!"

"Yeah, Shepherd," he says, "I get it. I never told you that Melanie's my stepmom, because my birth mom is dead, but now's not the time. Sooner or later, these guys are going to come looking for me, and if they catch me, they're going to kick my ass, take the phone, and we're back to square one."

"Fine. How do I help?"

"You don't. Head home and convince your folks to go up to the cabin—"

"What are you talking about? No!"

"These guys know all about us. They've been watching us for months."

"I know. I've been doing my own digging—"

"Then stop. If they find out you're here, they'll hurt you, your family…" His voice cracks. I've never heard him this desperate. "Go home and warn Gekas there's a mole in her department, then take your parents and disappear."

"No."

"What do you mean, 'no'?! Your family's in trouble—"

"And so are you!"

"Shepherd—!"

I let him have it.

"I busted my ass to find you. I've been back and forth across this country—twice!—*and* I pissed off everyone I love doing it. So whether you like it or not, I'm sticking around until we can figure out how to get you home safe."

He breathes heavily into the receiver. He's not happy with me, but I don't really care. I can be just as stubborn as him.

"And when exactly did you grow a pair?"

I give a short chuckle. "Right after I met this girl—"

"Who *are* you?! And what have you done with the candy-ass Tony Shepherd?"

"Charlie, focus!"

"Fine, but don't think I'm forgetting that 'girl' tidbit." I can hear him shift; he's more hushed, closer to the phone. "Someone's offing these guys. But before Winston died—"

"The dude in the bathroom?"

"Yeah. He suspected the hit man—hit woman, actually—had help."

"From who?"

"Someone high up on the inside."

"*Shit.*"

"Oh, it gets worse. That someone is the brother of Tommy 'The Falcon' Sullivan, the old Mob boss, and he might be responsible for Sullivan's murder."

"Crap. So what can I do?"

Charlie talks quickly, and I listen hard. "Find out what you can about that house. Who owns it. Who knows about it. Anything and everything. I'm sure it was supposed to be a safe house, so if we can connect the woman who was there today to the guy in charge, I can maybe use it as leverage."

"Speaking of which, who *was* that woman who showed up?"

"Not sure. They seemed to know her. Called her Rachel—"

"Crap!—I heard about her. Careful, she's dangerous."

"Guess I'll try not to not piss her off then," he jokes.

"Charlie!"

"Listen, Shepherd—I can handle it. Just find out what you can about that house, okay?"

It's impossible to argue with him.

Silence falls between us. I want to tell him how worried I am, how scared I've been for him, but he cuts me off.

"Before you get all mushy, Shepherd, thank you for coming."

It throws me off. Gratitude from him is rare. "Really?"

"Of course. I'm most likely pooched, but I'm glad you're here so we can be pooched together. Talk again same time tomorrow."

And with that, he hangs up.

chapter 88

I don't delay. First up, Gekas needs to be warned. If I ask her to call, she'll probably just shrug it off, thinking I only want to pester her about Charlie. But if I offer too much, and the mole somehow finds out, it puts us all at risk. Maybe if I use something a little obscure, something only she would raise an eyebrow at, it'll catch her attention. I text:

Maggie, I got info re: Spencer.

It's risky to call Gekas by her first name, let alone bring up her ex—it wasn't the healthiest relationship—but it's vague enough that someone else might not question it.

Hopefully it gets her to call.

Next, I open up the browser on my phone and search the municipal address of the property to find its legal address. A few years ago, I wouldn't have had any clue how to do this, but since knowing Charlie, I've been surprised by all the things I've learned. Thank you, Rocketman.

The name on the property is L.K. Jonasson. I search it online, and multiple results fill the screen. I narrow it down by adding *Hatley*. Only one hit. It's a Facebook account, but it's been switched to private. Crap. All I can see is a distant, blurry image of a blonde woman on a mountain. Definitely not the one I saw at the house today.

I scroll through the results again. Plenty of garbage links for *Jonasson* that lead to machine-generated lists for social networks and genealogy websites, but none with initials L.K.

I return to the mansion's municipal info. The address listed is 1398 Pine Street. I enter it and add *Hatley*. The map appears, the pin marking a spot on the south side of Main Street, close to the river and the mill. I click it, and a picture of the street appears. Well, now, *that's* not the mansion, is it? The building on the screen looks derelict. I wouldn't be surprised if junkies were asleep in it right now.

I do a reverse look-up. Despite being rundown, multiple businesses seem to be headquartered at 1398 Pine: Grand Global Inc., Elevate Endeavours, Promise Holdings Ltd., Noris Industries. All sound professional; none seems likely to operate in the abandoned building that Street View is showing me.

And when I click on each website, they are strikingly similar—though that's not saying much. Each one is drab, using a lot of corporate-speak like "global," "synergy," and "partnership," but none really says what they do. When I try the contact us pages, I end up at a blank webform for submitting questions. They're deliberately making this difficult. Something shady is going on with that house and these companies.

Tomorrow, I'll pay them a visit and figure out what.

chapter 89

I'm up early and check my messages. Dammit. Nothing from Gekas. I try not to overthink it and walk down for breakfast—I'm not missing out a second time.

I've barely eaten anything over the past twenty-four hours, so I'm starving. I load up on hard-boiled eggs, cheese, fruit, and toast with blueberry jam. After polishing that off, I grab a coffee to go, but as soon as I start pouring, I can tell it's been sitting too long and is cold.

So before driving over to the office building, I stop in at Wally's.

Inside, Nick and Jerome call out, "He's back!"

Certainly friendlier than the cold shoulder I got when Audrey was around.

"I said you'd get hooked," Jerome tells me.

"Yup," I nod. "It's my third time here."

Wally calls out from the kitchen, "How was the club?" and I guess my continued patronage of his place means he's warming up to me again.

"Good. Can I grab two black coffees and some of those pan-cake bites to go?"

Wally nods and gets to work, leaving me alone with Nick and Jerome. They don't beat around the bush.

"Why's a nice kid like you hanging around with the Driscoll girl?"

"I helped her out the other night, so she was just thanking me." I've got nothing to hide from these veterans of coffee row.

Jerome quirks an eyebrow as he glances at my black eye.

"Careful," Nick warns. "Her and her dad have a bad reputation around town."

Hmm. There's clearly more to it, but all I say is, "Oh? Why's that?"

"Well, for one thing, Ed's never been shy about screwing over a neighbour to make a quick buck," Jerome says.

"How do you mean?"

"Those new developers? As soon as they showed up, his construction company hopped on most all of their projects."

"So?" I prod, paying for the tray of lidded coffees Wally's just set down in front of me, along with the box of baking.

"So, they're gutting this town with their big box stores," Jerome adds.

Nick picks up the thread. "We're losing our history—"

"If it's even legal," Wally mutters as he turns away.

"Wait, what do you mean?"

Wally and the other two men exchange a glance. Then Nick says, "There's a lot of cash been changing hands lately."

"Folks coming in from out of town, buying up property."

"Jacking up prices all around."

"Now folks can't get anything without paying a premium."

"Can't even get a plumber without being charged an arm or a leg," Wally adds.

"Or a thumb," says Jerome, lifting up his nub of a finger.

Wally glares and continues, "Unless you're willing to pay under the table, no one'll give you any attention."

All three shake their heads.

It seems all this new construction in Hatley has opened a big ol' can of worms. But they haven't answered my question.

"So, what does any of it have to do with being illegal?"

Jerome sighs. "A lot of anonymous money is coming into this community from people we don't know."

"And why's that a problem?"

Nick lifts a shoulder. "Just makes a guy wonder where it's all coming from. And why they've taken such an interest in a little town like ours."

chapter 90

As I drive over the bridge across town, the conversation with the three men swirls in my head.

Why would the Mob be investing in this town? Hatley sure seems past its prime, so why dump all that money into the place? Do they really think they'll make their money back? Or is there some other reason that I don't yet understand?

The questions disappear when I arrive at my destination.

The neighbourhood looks nothing like the shithole I saw online last night. The whole thing's been completely revitalized. It's a freakin' poster child for trendy urban renewal.

The former train station at the end of the street has been converted into a farmer's market, while the building beside it is Gabe's indie craft beer pub, Envelopes. Along the street are storefronts for a custom bike shop and repair place, a hip furniture store, a juice company, and a bespoke T-shirt emporium.

Number 1398 is the three-storey building on the corner of Pine and Main. The first floor has been gutted and rebuilt with plenty of glass and polished black metal, and has a new life as an outdoor goods store and co-op working space.

Getting into those offices might be a lot harder than I'd thought. I need a new plan.

I grab the box of pancake bites and hop out of the car.

Around the corner is a sandblasted glass door that leads to a small entry housing a set of mailboxes. I'm unsurprised to discover several of the companies I found online last night are neighbours on the third floor.

I climb the stairs, carrying my takeout containers of coffee and food. I hear a radio playing and the sound of workmen through the heavy metal fire door on the second floor. A sign beside it says DANGER—CONSTRUCTION AREA and, in tiny letters at the bottom: DRISCOLL CONSTRUCTION.

The door to the third floor is open to a bare yellow hallway carpeted in worn brown broadloom that doglegs around a corner. It's quiet as a tomb.

There are six unmarked doors, three on each side, built out of cheap pressed wood. Nearly every one is unmarked, the gap between it and the floor, dark. Seems like no one's been up here in years. Graveyards are busier than this place.

Wait. I turn the corner to see that the door at the far end of the hall is open, and inside is a young guy, fast asleep in a chair, head back, feet on a small wooden desk. He's got to be around my age, or maybe a year or two into university. As I move closer, I can see the folders and papers that clutter the desk. A takeout coffee cup with *Ryan* written on it leaks onto a toppled tower of unopened mail.

"Hello?" I call lightly.

He wakes, nearly falling backwards in his chair. "Holy *shit*!"

"Sorry, man. You okay?"

He shakes off the sleep and stammers, "Yeah, it's all good. Just resting my eyes for a sec."

"Pretty quiet up here," I say, indicating the general lack of anything going on.

He yawns. "What can I do for you?"

"You Ryan?"

He nods.

I hand him the takeout box and cardboard tray of coffees. "I'm supposed to drop this off."

He studies it suspiciously. "Who from?"

"Not sure." I nod towards a coffee maker in the corner that probably hasn't been touched—or cleaned—in years. "Someone must've known you needed it."

He cracks open the takeout container and sniffs the blueberry pancake bites. "Damn, those smell tasty."

"I know, right?"

He squints, shifting his gaze back to me. "Who'd you say these were from?"

I shrug. "I just do the deliveries."

He's not buying it. Not even the smell of fresh baked goods can melt his distrust. He closes the box and pushes it back towards me. "No thanks."

"What? Why not?"

"People don't like this place."

"So?"

"How do I know this food hasn't been messed with?"

"What do you mean?"

"I don't know—coughed on, spit in … maybe worse."

Jeezus, just what type of people does Ryan deal with?

"I can promise you nothing like that has happened."

"And how'm I supposed to trust you?"

He's got me there—I'm no one to him. I open the container, take one, and pop it in my mouth.

Damn, these *are* good.

I offer him the box again. He's tempted—but still not convinced. I take another—might as well not waste them—and take a gander around. The office is pretty empty, like they've just moved in. Or are just moving out. Along the back wall six clear bins sit on the floor, each filled with a few pieces of mail, each marked with the name of a country: United Kingdom, Seychelles, Denmark, Cayman Islands, Russia.

Is this a front for all the businesses I found online?

"So, what do you do here? Besides avoid being poisoned?"

He hesitates, his jaw clenched.

"Come on." I play it up a little. "Seems like a sweet gig."

"Office stuff," he finally says.

"Yeah? Like what?"

"Sorting mail." He picks up a few envelopes and starts flipping through them, pretending to work.

I wait for him to continue. He doesn't. "That's it?"

He shrugs.

"Damn. I'm working for the wrong people."

"Anything else?" Ryan asks, sifting through the rest of the pile of mail.

"Nope, I guess not." I go for the door.

"Wait, you're not leaving those here?" He nods to the carry-out container.

"No way, man. I'm not having your death on my conscience," I say, popping one last blueberry bite before exiting.

chapter 91

So, Ryan wasn't much help. He didn't trust me, and I can't blame him. Considering the amount of abuse it sounds like he puts up with, I probably wouldn't trust me either.

Hearing the radio blaring below, an idea comes to me: Maybe the Driscoll Construction workers have something to offer.

I'm pleased to find that the metal fire door to the second floor is now propped open.

The entire level has been gutted to the brick walls and wood support beams. Wires dangle above, and a series of metal studs are lined up like floor-to-ceiling fenceposts at the back of the room, where two men are fastening a bottom plate to the concrete floor. They wear dirty jeans and pit-stained T-shirts. The Driscoll Construction logo is emblazoned on the back.

And that's when I notice Kyle, the prick from Pricks who clocked me the other night, shooting the shit with the men at work.

I sidle back to the stairwell, hoping they haven't seen me. Kyle's about the last person I'm interested in dealing with this morning.

I peek again, and he's still talking to the construction workers. I can't hear anything they're saying over the music, but he turns, and I can see his black jacket has "Security" and "Noris Industries" stitched on it.

One of the businesses I found online.

When I think they're not looking, I slip down the stairs and check the mailboxes again. Nothing for Noris Industries, so I go outside and search the street. A black car with a mounted light bar and SECURITY printed in white on the side is parked down the block.

Perfect.

I jump in my car and stay low, munching the last of the blueberry bites of bliss until Kyle walks outside. He crosses to the security vehicle and gets in. As he pulls away from the curb, I drop my car into gear and follow.

chapter 92

I follow Kyle across the old steel bridge and along the highway up the side of mountain. I do my best to keep enough distance between us that he shouldn't notice me, but my earlier run-in with him has me nervous.

I'm not going on a lot, but Kyle's connection to Noris Industries is curious. Sure, he's probably innocent, but the presence of the company logo on the side of his vehicle is compelling.

He pulls into the first driveway we come across, but I don't follow. I pull to the side of road and give myself plenty of distance. I can't see anything through the trees, but I'm guessing it's another mansion. It has a similar driveway marker and mailbox at its entrance.

I don't dare get out of the car to confirm. I don't need to be accidentally seen, or be too far from my car when Kyle comes out and possibly lose him as he drives away.

While I wait, I search *Noris Industries* again, adding *security* this time. A few results, but nothing local. Then I add

Hatley and this wipes out most of the results, except for the company webpage I found earlier. I open and review it a second time, but there's nothing to suggest it's even a security company. Whoever designed Noris's website definitely never intended it to be useful.

After about fifteen minutes, Kyle pulls back onto the highway. A few minutes later, he pulls into another driveway, but this time I drive past and peer down the lane. Definitely a big house, though not as large as the one I found Charlie in the other day. Must be his security route, checking on all these big shacks. I do a u-turn and drive back to where I'd been before he went onto the property.

It takes me a moment to realize that I'm near the mansion where I found Charlie—or rather, he found me—yesterday. The trees are familiar, and I'm sure it's just around the bend.

Kyle squeals back onto the road, kicking up dust and burning rubber. He zips up around the bend, and I follow.

Sure enough, the next place up is the house Audrey took me to, but instead of pulling in, Kyle drives on, which is a surprise. Where the hell are you going, Kyle?

Maybe he's been told not to go there, which makes him seem even more suspicious. Now I *absolutely* have to see where he'll lead me. He does turn down the next driveway. Like clockwork, he reappears after another fifteen minutes, but this time, instead of turning right at the end of the driveway, he turns left, doubling back towards me.

I slump down in my seat, hoping he doesn't see me, and after I hear his car drive by, I poke up again to make sure he's past.

He's already winding back down the mountain, so I start the car and spin around to chase after him. Looks like he's heading back to town. Then, just before the last wide corner at the iron bridge, he turns down a dirt road that runs low by the lake.

There are no signs indicating a driveway or house, but this close to the lake, it doesn't seem like a road that can go very far.

Best to play it safe.

I pull over halfway onto the shoulder behind a tangle of ragged scrub brush that partly screens the car from view and grab Charlie's backpack. Time to hike the rest of the way.

chapter 93

I creep down the narrow lane, evergreens towering high above me. The road is all but overgrown, except for a set of rutted tire tracks. Wherever Kyle has gone, it's certain he's one of only a few people who have driven this way in a very long time.

My senses are on high alert for the slightest noise. The last thing I need is to be surprised by him coming around a corner and running me over.

Another trail of tire tracks branches off into the woods and towards the lake and, considering how grown in the path I'm following is, this new direction seems like the better option.

The further in I go, the darker and creepier it gets. The trees get even taller, and the shadows grow longer. Even the birds seem to have abandoned the place. I would not be surprised if Jason Voorhees popped out of the woods with a machete to take off my head.

Halfway down the lane, I come across an iron gate hanging from two stone pillars. They're buried in overgrown weeds and trees, but I can just make out the faded sign on one: JONASSON.

The name listed on the other property.

I climb over the gate and keep following the winding tire tracks as they curve through the woods, and round a corner to find a weatherbeaten cottage waiting in a clearing.

Kyle's cruiser is parked in the flattened grass in front of it, so I'm not going to risk getting closer this way. I backtrack a bit, then step off the road to push through the thick bramble for a better view.

A small porch wraps around the cottage's left side; there's a garage on the right. It sort of seems like no one's been here for ages, and yet there's a sense that the place has been maintained. No windows are broken, no graffiti on the outside. The fact that Kyle is even here checking on it makes me think that someone wants to keep it safe.

Kyle comes out from a pathway that stretches around behind the cottage and climbs back into his car. His radio squawks as he checks in with his office. When he drives back down the lane, I crouch down low in the brush, getting poked in the back and ribs by twigs and branches.

I wait a little longer, just in case he's forgotten something or notices my car parked out on the highway, but the moment never comes.

Time to find out about L.K. Jonasson.

chapter 94

I walk up the stone steps to the front door and knock—might as well play it safe—but no one answers.

I look through the glass. Empty plant hooks hang from the ceiling of the small porch, and a large full-length mirror leans against the wall. From what I can see, the front of the house holds a living room with an old leather sofa and chairs in front of a fireplace on the left, and a staircase and another room on the right. The decor is rustic: dark-stained wood floors and wood-panelled ceilings paired with antique sofa tables, a china cabinet, and bookshelves. Seems homey, like a summer retreat for a professor.

I pop the lock with Charlie's handy-dandy lock-picks, enter, and immediately see the flash of an alarm sensor at the top of the door frame.

Crap.

I probably have only a few minutes before Kyle returns. I could bail now and hide in the trees, but I'll have the same problem if I try again. Now that I'm in, I might as well do a quick sweep and find out what I can. I set the timer on my phone to go off in five minutes and get my ass in gear.

The bookshelves are filled with paperbacks, knick-knacks and trinkets, and a thick layer of dust coating it all. A stack of magazines sprawls across a basket behind the couch, at least ten years old, based on the celebrities on the covers. A thick, warm-looking blanket hangs over a chair, but mustiness hovers over it. There's an aura of neglect about it all.

There aren't any personal mementos or photos. None. Not even a picture of a pet. This place doesn't seem to have a heart.

I move past a set of double doors that lead to the back patio and enter the eat-in kitchen. The fridge is unplugged and open. The cupboards hold plates, bowls, and mugs, as well as some very old canned food and dusty spices, sugar, and salt. It's like someone closed the place up at the end of the season, then forgot to come back.

Past the foot of the staircase is a large master bedroom—it's nice too, even has an ensuite bathroom. The bed is made, towels are on the hangers, but the walk-in closet is empty.

No basement, so I take the stairs two at a time to the second floor, wary of the passing seconds. Two more bedrooms and a bathroom, but they're even more sparse than the one downstairs. The whole vibe is that of a guest house that's never hosted a guest.

In the middle of the hallway ceiling dangles an attic door drawstring. Hmm. Given that the rest of the place is so impersonal, I doubt there's anything to find, but I'm not about to leave a stone unturned.

I leap, pull down the ladder, and up I go.

At first, I think it's a waste of time. It's unfinished up here, all rough plywood and angled walls. The air is hot and dry and smells like mouse poop. Then my eyes adjust to the dim interior, and I make out a pile of stuff in the back corner: boxes, fishing rods, skis, a standing mirror, a guitar. Most of the boxes are unmarked, so I open one and find it filled with VHS tapes and CDs. Another is packed with a snarl of electrical cords.

And then... *jackpot.*

What seems like hundreds of photos, all dumped loose into a box with neither care nor order. I paw through them quickly. Many are of a tall, long-haired blonde woman and a girl. No names on the back, no dates. Only photo after photo of these two people: in the cottage, on a dock, in a restaurant. Many show the girl alone, growing older, looking more like her mother with each passing year—playing on a swing set, swimming in a pool, standing on a stage, playing lacrosse. Finally, I find one of her blowing out the candles on her eighteenth birthday cake. Based on that, it's likely one of the most recent photos the box holds.

I pull it out and set it aside, and open another box. Old books and ugly kid art. At the bottom, a couple of yearbooks. I page through the most recent: 2004. In the back are plenty of signatures from friends and classmates—many of them addressed to someone named Kat.

Something else catches my eye.

In the bottom right corner of the page, someone has scrawled "I know what you did," pressing so hard that the ink has left an imprint in the paper. It's unsigned, but the letters are messy, and the loops are round and full, especially the D's.

I page through the grades, scanning as fast as I can for "Kat Jonasson," but don't find anything.

Bzzz.

Shit! The alarm. I'm out of time.

I grab the photo of the birthday girl, shove it inside the yearbook and toss them both into Charlie's backpack, hoping maybe I can cross-reference the image with a class photo later. I nearly slide down the ladder and fling the trap door shut.

Pounding down the stairs, I flick off the irritating phone alarm, swipe open a web browser and two-thumb the name into the search bar, not looking up once. Multiple hits. At the bottom of the stairs, I narrow it down to Hatley, but nothing comes up, so I try *Kat Jonasson Canada*. A few links, but suddenly it occurs to me to try the images tab. One stands out: a tall, blonde woman with sharp features.

Just like her mother.

I'm feeling pretty good about sussing out a lead on the owner of these properties—but it doesn't last long. Because someone is coming up the front steps, and it's not Kyle.

It's Rachel.

She's got a gun. And she's looking right at me.

chapter 95

I race out the double doors, leaping off the patio towards the treeline behind the cottage. There's the barest hint of a stone pathway in the grass that leads into the trees, and I follow it.

The trail disappears immediately, engulfed by a mix of fallen trees and sprouting saplings. But through the trees, water glitters, so I stumble my way down.

Branches slash at my face, and I nearly trip on gnarled roots sticking out of the ground. I hope to hell I don't twist an ankle.

The forest comes to an abrupt end at a rocky drop, and I jam on the breaks to avoid a literal pitfall. A rickety set of stairs leads to a decrepit dock, and I beeline for them.

The treads are weathered, and some steps barely hang on with a nail or two. I don't have time to evaluate and simply hope they hold.

I'm right to worry. The second one breaks, and I pitch forward, grabbing the rail just in time to prevent plummeting to my death on the jagged rocks below.

I drag myself up, shift my weight to the edges, and scuttle down as fast as I can.

The dock is steadier, but I don't stick around to appreciate it—and slide over the edge into the water.

My body convulses. Crap, it's cold!

Charlie's bag fills with water, pulling me down.

I struggle to keep the splashing to a minimum, and drag myself under the broken dock, closer to shore.

I've done what I can so she won't find me.

All I can do now is wait.

chapter 96

I strain to listen for her, my whole body shivering.

Why is the water like ice? Isn't this summer? I pull my legs to my chest, hoping to stay warm, hoping to stay hidden.

The water laps against the rocks on the shoreline, and the wind hisses in the trees. It's too noisy to hear anything.

At least she won't hear my teeth chattering.

Maybe she *didn't* actually see me.

Or thought I was smart enough to run deeper into the trees. Or looked over the edge, saw nothing, and went back up the hill.

But that all washes away when I hear her call out, "Tony?"

I seize up, barely breathing.

She calls out again before trying the stairs. "To-o-ny!"

Maybe I'll catch a break, and she'll fall and snap her neck.

No such luck.

She steps out onto the wood above me, the old boards bending and creaking under the weight of each footfall.

"Tony? I know you came this way."

I tense as she passes over me down the broken dock.

"I want to talk."

Yeah, right!

Her footsteps echo through the wood, reverberating in my ears beneath the surface. Her shadow moves in jagged edges on the restless water.

I tuck myself close to the slime-covered piling, seeking shelter in the darkness.

She's coming back from the end but stops midway, dropping down quickly at the edge to look underneath.

There's only a moment to take a big gulp of air and sink beneath the surface. Did she see me?

The light refracts in weird ways, so there's no sense of where she is or what she's doing, even with my eyes open. All I can do is stare up at the light spilling between the slats above to know whether she's moving off the dock.

My chest is full of air and floats me to the top, and I scramble to hold onto something. Everything is slippery, so I exhale a little out of my lungs to counter the buoyancy, praying the bubbles aren't noticeable among the waves.

Dammit, *leave* already! She's taking forever.

Or maybe she left, and I didn't see her go? Maybe my mind wandered as I struggled to distract myself from the pounding pressure in my chest.

A shadow moves above me.

I fight for a moment more, a moment that would allow distance between me and her, before I let my body rise to the surface. I breathe out and gulp in air to clear my lungs.

But I don't move from my spot. Not yet. Not until I'm certain she's gone.

chapter 97

Water plugs my ears and everything is muffled, so I can't hear a thing. If she's still on the shore or the stairs or looking over the rocky edge, I have no clue. I have no way of knowing anything.

I check my phone—thank god it's waterproof—and see that fifteen minutes has gone by.

She can't be that patient, can she?

I pull myself carefully out of my hiding spot to search the rocky shoreline.

Nothing. No sign of her.

Not that I can see, anyway.

I drag my freezing ass back onto the dock, and the cool air only makes me shiver more. I want to curl into a ball to keep warm, but I need to move. I pull myself to my feet and carefully climb the stairs, water pouring out of my shoes and making everything slippery.

I peek over the top, scanning for any sign of her.

Again, nothing.

Maybe she's searching the trees or sitting up at the cottage, waiting to strike.

Doesn't matter. I need to get out of here.

I scuttle along the stairs to the top. My legs protest with each step, my jeans are cold and stiff, and *so* uncomfortable, but I tell myself that it's just like a winter morning during basketball season. I just have to do the work—especially now, when my life depends on it.

I work my way through the trees until I can see the house.

No Rachel.

I rush to the wall and nearly hug it, then scoot around to the front corner, and peer out.

Nada. Not even a car.

I'm not taking my chances. I break for the driveway, running hard, legs like frozen jelly, chest bursting. I pass the gate but don't stop, not until I come to the main road and scramble into the car. Staying low, I start the engine, shift into gear. Then I'm spinning the car around, and speeding back towards the highway, blasting the heater as high as it will go in the middle of summer.

It isn't until I'm over the bridge that I finally start to breathe again.

chapter 98

I get back to the hotel and slog inside.

I'm no longer leaving trails of lake water behind me, but every stride squelches. The woman behind the desk gives me a cautious eye, but I ignore her. I don't have the energy to explain myself.

I climb to the third floor—each step a cold, wet reminder of my ordeal—and strip out of my clothes. The hot water of the shower is a balm on my chilled skin.

Why the hell was Rachel there? What was she after? Me or the house? Or does she know L.K. Jonasson? Maybe *she* is L.K. Jonasson?

I run circles in my head but come up with nothing solid.

If only I could bounce things off Charlie. Maybe we'd come up with answers.

I check the time. Still a while until he calls, so I change into a dry pair of jeans and T-shirt. My shoes are soaked—and they're the only pair I've got—so I shove towels in them to sop up the excess before turning the blow dryer on them.

Charlie's bag is a dripping mess. I unpack everything, spreading it on the floor by the open window to let the sun and the gentle breeze reach it.

The photo I grabbed from the cottage is stuck in the water-logged pages of the yearbook. Its pages are warped and wavy, grey with water. Shit. I'm not going to able to search through it yet. I prop it open on a towel, hoping the pages will fan apart as they dry.

I open my phone and return to the online search for Kat Jonasson. Clicking on the image I found leads to a company called Fallynx Trust in Toronto. She's apparently the CEO. Although there's not an about page telling me what they do, there *is* a long list of press releases announcing investments in construction and tech.

One project catches my eye: the Hatley Public Library.

I can't find any further info, but that's all right. I'm pretty sure Gavin, my friendly neighbourhood librarian, will be able to help me out.

chapter 99

As soon as my shoes are remotely dry, I drive over to the library. It's as busy as ever.

I head right for the archives and do a local search. Only one *Hatley News* article comes up, and it contains only a single pertinent line: "Funding for the library provided by Fallynx Trust."

That's it. Nothing else.

I log out and track down Gavin. He's with a group of seniors, praising the patchwork quilt they're working on. When he sees me, he excuses himself and comes over.

"You've returned! Hopefully you're not here for the . . . *you know?*"

"Yikes, no," I laugh. "I'm wondering what, if anything, you could tell me about Fallynx Trust?"

His eyes go cold. "I thought you were here for genealogy?"

"Well," I hesitate. "Not exactly."

"Please tell me you aren't here to stir up trouble? All the new construction has been a real boon to this town."

I'm guessing Gavin and the boys down at the café don't see eye to eye.

"No," I improvise, "I was passing through Hatley and saw that it was thriving. Thought it might be a good place to look for work."

"And what does that have to do with Fallynx Trust?"

"Just figured I should find out more about them before moving across the country to a job that might disappear."

He nods. "All right, I get that."

"Can you tell me why they invested in the library?"

"The owner grew up around here."

"Really? Who's that?"

"Kat Jonasson." He guides me over to a wall of donors beside the reflecting pool. "If it weren't for her, we wouldn't have any of these benefactors."

"None of these people are local?"

"No. Not at all."

It's a long list. "So, who are they all?"

He shrugs. "Philanthropists. People from around the world who support the arts and culture."

Anonymous donors from parts unknown? Yeah, it doesn't sound fishy at all.

"And she convinced them to invest here? That's quite a feat."

"She was determined to leave a legacy for her mother." Gavin points to a special dedication at the bottom of the wall: LYNN KATHERINE JONASSON. "She used to be a librarian here. We offered to name a room after her, but Kat thought that would be too ostentatious."

I try to figure out how to get to what I want to know. "Did you know her mother at all?"

"Not really. She was before my time."

"How about the daughter...Kat?"

"Well, she was several years older than me, so we never really crossed paths."

"But you knew who she was?"

"Sure. She was pretty much the opposite of her mother."

"Oh?"

He smiles ruefully. "From my teenage point of view, she was the pretty, popular girl who was confident in everything she did."

"Was she in sports or clubs?"

"She was in everything: lacrosse, Key Club, Young Entrepreneurs. Nothing seemed to intimidate her." He smiles. "She scared the heck out of most of the guys."

"You said the library was meant as a legacy for her mother? I take it that she died?"

He glances around at the patrons of the library before turning his attention back to me. "They said it was an 'accident,' but..." He clears his throat, leaving me to fill in the rest. "After that, Kat went out east to university and never returned."

I'm getting closer. I can feel it. "How long ago was that?"

"Oh, about fifteen years ago.... This is a lot of questions for someone just interested in a job."

"What can I say? I'm intrigued."

He smiles again. "If you say so."

"Any idea why she came back?"

Again, the glance around.

"Most say it was her father's death."

The mention of her father is a surprise, though maybe it shouldn't have been. There'd been no sign of a father-type figure in that box of photos in the attic. Had I stopped to consider it, I'd've assumed he'd left them long before. But I was beginning to think that perhaps he was conspicuous by his absence.

"She and her dad were close, then."

He laughs outright—the first one I've heard since we started talking. "Let's just say he wasn't exactly the paternal type."

I raise an eyebrow.

"You don't know?"

I've got no clue what he's going to say. "Know what?"

"Her father. He was Tommy 'The Falcon' Sullivan."

chapter 100

Although I knew very little about the Mob—really only what Kosmos and Charlie had told me—it doesn't take me long to discover Sullivan's atrocities.

There was nothing The Falcon hadn't been part of. Drugs, extortion, corruption, human trafficking—if it was illegal or reprehensible in any way, he got the Family involved. But what made him so ruthless was his absolute hunger for power. He destroyed anyone who stood in his way.

But despite these moral failings—indeed, maybe because of them—some newspapers loved him. They printed articles with headlines like: "Falcon finds prey," "Falcon's feud," and "Falcon feeds Feds crow," and filled them with splashy, sensationalized photos of police tape and crime scenes.

Every image is like a mugshot—a tough-looking man with slicked back hair, cold eyes, and a hard jawline. If I saw him on the street, I'd run the other way.

He'd met his end in the restaurant he owned. Shot in the back in what the police called retribution from a rival gang by an unknown assailant. Based on what Charlie had said, the killer had to be a woman—my bet's on Cousin Rachel.

More tabloid articles about The Falcon's funeral, with images of men and women in gaudy suits and dresses, climbing out of flashy cars at a cemetery. I zoom in and search for Kat, but don't see her.

I do, however, see several photos of his brother, Robert Sullivan. He looks like Tommy—sharp features, slicked back hair. But he's younger and somehow seems more educated, though I can definitely see how someone might not trust him. He's like one of those scammy stock market moguls that pop up in YouTube ads telling me how I can make a six- to seven-figure income just like them. But he's also softer, not as battle-hardened. If he had gone to war against his brother, he'd never have survived a frontal attack. He would have had to flank The Falcon when he wasn't looking.

Enter the hit woman.

The weird thing is that Robert didn't get control of his brother's assets. One article says it all went to Kat, and she immediately invested in a bunch of philanthropic projects, like the Hatley Library. But she didn't stop there. She'd also made a deal with the authorities, handed over evidence from her father's estate. The Family's businesses had been raided, its members arrested. She was her uncle's worst enemy.

So why hadn't they taken her out? Isn't that the sort of thing the Mob is known for? Something else is going on.

But I'm done. After staring at the screen for an hour, my eyes are sore and my head spins with too much information. I need a break.

I have all I need, so I log out and drive back to the hotel.

chapter 101

Gabe hasn't started his shift yet; the older woman is still behind the counter. I walk right past her, but she barely acknowledges my existence.

I still have time before Charlie calls, so back in my room, I look up a pizza place. If I were at home, my folks would probably get something like arugula prosciutto pesto, but on my own, I keep it basic and order a double pepperoni.

While I wait for the food to arrive, I check my phone. No new messages from Elaina or my folks, but there's one from Gekas an hour ago.

I know what you're doing.
Leave Charlie to us.

It immediately pisses me off. Is that all she's going to say? Doesn't she think it's a little weird I'm using her first name and texting about her ex? And besides, if she really gave two shits, I wouldn't even be here to begin with.

I respond with a short:

No.

My phone rings immediately.

"Anthony, you need to leave it alone."

My back's up. "Why? Charlie needs my help."

"And we're working on it."

"Really? Because from what I've seen, you've been sitting on your ass this whole time and meanwhile, he's in serious trouble."

"Anthony, I understand you're emotional—"

"Don't do that." My voice has gone flat. "Don't talk down to me. I'm not a kid anymore."

"I understand that, but there's procedure—"

"*Screw* procedure," I fume. "You've got bigger problems." I'm heated—more than I want to be—but after such a long wait, I don't want to be told by anyone what to do, especially when she can't even get her own house in order.

"What are you talking about?"

"You've got a *mole* in your department," I burst out. "And they're threatening you, me, and my family!"

"Wait—? What?! What do you mean?"

"The guys that have Charlie?—and oh, yeah, by the way, someone *did* take Charlie—they've gotten to your guys, too."

She's speechless. "How… How do you know this?"

"Charlie told me."

"You've spoken to him?! You know where he is?"

Shit, I shouldn't have told her. But I'm not backing down now. "Would it matter if I did?"

"Of course it does!" she exclaims. "If you know something, you have to tell me—"

"Really? Why? So their goons can come after us all?"

"Anthony, we can deal with this together—you just have to be patient—"

"I'm *done* waiting around!"

"If these are people who can get to someone in the police department, you have no idea what they're capable of—"

"Which is why I don't trust the cops not to mess it up."

"Anthony—!"

"No, we're done," I yell, and before she says another word, I end the call.

chapter 102

I immediately block Gekas's number so she can't call me back. Texting her was useless. I'm pissed off and need to cool down. I pace the room, running over the conversation—running the whole damn day over in my head—until there's a knock at the door.

Pizza's here.

I dig in, and the meaty, greasy goodness goes a long way to soothing my anger. I wolf down three slices in quick succession, and chug down the last remaining can of beer.

I glance at Charlie's backpack. Most of the stuff looks dry. Well, less wet, anyway. I pack it up before turning my attention to the yearbook. Although it looks in bad shape, the pages are no longer soaked and fragile.

I search for Kat again, carefully peeling apart the pages, this time with the last name "Sullivan."

Bingo. There's her grad photo. She's beautiful, striking, even if it's weird that she's a generation older than me.

Her senior quote reads: "Few will have the greatness to bend history itself. —Robert Kennedy." Below it is her signature, larger and more slanted than the others on the page, the K and S far bigger than the rest of the letters in her name.

I flip further and find a photo of her standing beside a guy who looks ready to take over the world. Good-looking, well-dressed. He's got to be from money.

I turn back and search for him in the grad photos.

Todd Savage.

He's got long, windswept hair, sunglasses propped atop blond highlights, and sports a pair of layered polo shirts, collars double-popped. His choice of a memorable quote? "Great men aren't born great, they grow great."

What a douche.

But it's his signature that catches my attention. There's something familiar about it, and I suddenly realize why.

I turn to the back of the book, to the unsigned message in the bottom corner: "I know what you did."

Messy. Full, round loops—especially the D's.

I type *Todd Savage* into the search bar, and one result pops up in the province: the owner and operator of Savage Video in Edmonton. When I click on the link, the website looks like it hasn't been updated since Magic Johnson played for the Lakers.

It can't be the same guy, but when I click on the contact link, sure enough, there he is—except time hasn't been that kind to him. He's older, fatter, and balder.

I want to dig deeper, but the phone rings, interrupting me.

Charlie.

Looks like Todd is going to have to wait.

chapter 103

"Where are you?"

"Not even a hello, Shepherd?"

I ignore it. "Are you still at the house?"

"Wow, who pissed in your corn flakes?"

"Charlie!"

"Fine, no, they moved me, and I'm not telling you where."

"Why not?"

"Because I need you focused, not showing up here."

God, he can be annoying. Especially when he's right.

"Did you find out who owns the other place?"

"Yeah." I fill him in on my day, beginning with the house's connections to the different companies.

"Totally sounds like a setup for shell corporations."

"To do what?"

"Launder money and avoid taxes, mostly. If someone tries to make a connection between them and a shady deal or illegal payment, the paper trail disappears in some country on the other side of the world."

That's why they've come to Hatley. They're using the whole town to clean their dirty money. Worse, seems like they've sucked half the citizens into their rotten scheme.

But Charlie and I are on the clock; I don't have time to feel sorry for them.

"There's something else," I say. "I found a connection to another place in town that belongs to Kat Sullivan, daughter of The Falcon."

"That asshole has a daughter?"

"Yeah, and after her father's death, she went on a redemption tour, turning his people in to the cops and spending all his money on charities. She even built a new library."

"Good for her. Better than those douchebags using it."

But I've been thinking it over, and something else has occurred to me. "I don't buy the Mary Poppins routine, though. If she really had gutted their organization, how are they still in operation?"

Charlie's quiet on the other end. If he were with me right now, he'd be pacing, walking through the scenario.

"It wouldn't take a big organization to grab me."

"No, but they're rolling in enough money to be building big box stores and mansions in the mountains to launder their money."

"Then they've got a regular illegal cash flow to clean..."

"They must have. But from what?"

"Well, The Falcon was all about drugs, prostitution, extortion, human trafficking—" Charlie rhymes it all off.

"So they're still at it."

"Sounds like it."

"So they're bankrolling their organization with laundered money that's been funnelled through all these property developments and shell corporations."

Charlie thinks for a minute. "Right. And maybe the money never left. We know the daughter took it and invested it in at least one project in town."

"The library," I say.

We can't prove it—yet—but what if Fallynx Trust owns the shell corporation that owns the property developer that owns the construction company that had been given the contract to build it?

"Maybe she *didn't* eliminate her Mob ties," Charlie goes on. "She just eliminated her competition and rebranded."

"The question is," I put in, "are she and Robert working together? Who's actually in control?"

"From everything you've told me, she's running the show."

"So why keep Robert around?"

"Because he's the fall guy."

"Or worse. Once she's got full control, she gets rid of him."

Charlie's quiet. Then he says, "I can work with that."

"What do you mean?"

"If I can convince Robert that she's going to whack him when the time is right, maybe I can buy my freedom."

I groan. "But if you're planning on convincing him that his niece is out to kill him, you'd better have some serious proof—"

There's a loud crash on Charlie's end. A deep voice growls, "Who the hell are you talking to?"

"No one!" Charlie shouts. And the line goes dead.

chapter 104

Red busts through the bathroom door, reaching for the phone. "Who the hell are you talking to?"

"No one!" Charlie shouts, mashing his fingers against the keypad, hoping it'll end the call.

Red bearhugs him from behind and lifts him off the ground, shaking him, hard, until the phone falls from Charlie's hands.

He can't let these guys hit redial. Or learn that Tony's here.

He needs to destroy that phone.

Charlie plants his feet against the sink and drives his legs hard. He and Red both fly backwards, slamming into the wall and breaking the towel rack off its mount. Red holds tight, so Charlie kicks off again. This time they crack the drywall.

Red's grip loosens, and Charlie squirms free.

He drops to the ground and scoops up the phone. He slams it hard against the edge of the counter, cracking it in half, and tosses the pieces in the toilet for good measure.

Cass shouts from the other room, "What the hell's going on down there?"

"He was on the phone!" Red sputters.

"How could he be on a phone?"

Red drags Charlie out of the bathroom and slams shattered chunks of wet phone on the coffee table.

"Eww, gross," Charlie says. "And that's now *two* phones and a pair of kicks you owe me."

Red punches him, sending him to the ground, but Cass is not deterred. "What. The. Hell—? Where'd he get a *phone*?"

"Don't know, but he was talking to *some*one."

Cass is in Charlie's face. "Who'd you call?"

"I was ordering take-out."

Cass grabs his gun and cracks the side of Charlie's head with it. Charlie falls forward. There's the sting of air on an open wound, and the warm tickle of blood running down his neck.

"Oww—!"

"Start talking."

"No."

Cass nods to Red to hit him again, but before he can, Charlie hooks an arm behind his knee and sweeps it. Red lurches forward and crashes to the ground.

"Goddammit, that's it!" Cass shouts, shoving his gun against Charlie's temple.

"Wait! You aren't done with me yet—"

"Oh, yes I am."

"Fine, okay! I'll do it. I'll talk!" Charlie shouts, waving his hands in surrender.

The gun doesn't move. "Then start yapping."

"Okay, okay. It was a contact I have in town."

"Who?"

"Doesn't matter."

"It sure as hell does."

"No," Charlie says, "it doesn't, because what they told me is more important than who they are."

"And what's that?"

"Who's killing your people."

"Keep going."

Charlie shakes his head. "No. I'm not saying anything else until you take me to Robert."

"You really want me to take you to Robert?" Cass sneers.

"It's my only guarantee that you won't kill me."

"You're not in much of a position to bargain."

Charlie stands and squares his shoulders. "Pretty sure I am. Your guys are getting bumped off, and your boss would probably like to know who's responsible—especially since he's next on the list."

Cass glares at him, then glances at Red.

And Charlie knows he has them.

Cass lowers the gun. "Fine, we'll take you to him. But I swear to god, if you screw us in *any* sort of way, I'm going to kill you, and after that, I'm going to hunt down your contact and kill them too. Understood?"

"Yeah, I got it." Charlie offers a handshake to seal the deal, but Cass just turns his back.

It doesn't matter.

Getting to Robert is all he wants now.

It will buy him time. Not a lot, but a little. And he needs all he can get. With the new information Shepherd's just given him, he's certain he knows what's going on: Robert doesn't want him—Kat Sullivan does. He even thinks he knows why.

And once Robert delivers him to Kat, he's pretty sure shit will go sideways fast.

What really worries him is that Tony will play boy scout and do something stupid—like come looking for him. It's a good thing he doesn't know where Charlie is, so that will take a while.

But if Tony figures it out and does show up...

Well, *that* scares him.

Because he's pretty sure people are going to die. A lot of them. And he's not certain his friend will escape unscathed.

part 5

chapter 105

Shit!

My brain is in overdrive. They got to Charlie, which means I've got to save him, but it also probably means that it won't take long until they decide to pay a visit to Mom, Dad, Gekas—

I grab my phone and call my parents first. Dad answers.

"How are you doing, son?"

"Dad, you need to listen—"

He's distracted, not listening. "Not sure where your mom is … She was—"

"Dad!"

He goes quiet; he's not used to me shouting at him.

"You need to get Mom and get out of the house. Now."

"What are you talking about?"

"Some … very bad people are coming …" I stumble on the next words, "I–I don't know what they might do to you."

Again, he doesn't speak for a moment, trying to comprehend what I've just said.

"Okay…does this have something to do with Charlie?"

"Yes—but it's not his fault. He didn't ask for this."

"Okay," Dad repeats. He sounds eerily calm. "And how much time do we have?"

"I don't know."

He's quiet again, but I know he's shifted into crisis mode, trying to work out what he needs to do, what he needs to take, how to figure out where the hell Mom is—

"Son, are you all right?"

The question surprises me. I'm supposed to be worrying about *him*. "Yeah," I say, then add more honestly, "I think so."

"And you know where Charlie is?"

"Yeah."

"Then you grab him and get the hell out of there." Dad's not mincing words.

"Okay." That's not going to be easy, but I won't bore Dad with the details.

"We'll call you once we're on the road."

"Okay, be safe." Thank god Dad's taking this seriously.

I hit *end*, and dial Gekas, unblocking her number.

She answers on the first ring. "Where are you?" she says.

I don't mince words either. "You need to get out of there. The guys that have Charlie are coming for you."

She doesn't pause or flinch. "Got it. How about you? Is your family safe?"

"Yes, I called Dad already."

"I'll get a patrol car over there immediately—"

"Make sure it's someone you trust."

"Absolutely."

But that's not good enough. "Detective, this is my *family* we're talking about."

"And they're my friends. I promise I'll keep them safe."

I believe her. I have to. "You be careful too."

"I will." She pauses, and I know what's coming. "You need to tell me where you are."

"I can't."

"Anthony—"

"Not yet. But I will—soon."

She doesn't like it. I don't like it either. The whole world is burning around me, and I'm in the middle of the inferno without even a cup of water.

"Okay. Be careful," she says, and all at once my earlier anger and frustration is gone, and I'm glad she's on our side.

"You too."

I turn off the call.

Now to save my friend.

chapter 106

I don't know where Charlie is—they've probably moved him anyways—so I'm not going to waste time trying to track him down. Hopefully, he'll be able to reach out to me when he can, so I need to ready when he does.

Kat Sullivan is his best way out of this, and Todd Savage is my only lead to her.

I search Savage Video again and call the phone number. It rings three times before an answering machine picks up:

'This is Savage Video, the marquee destination for the hottest releases, the cheapest prices, and the most ferocious return policy'—a lion's roar punctuates the point—'We're busy helping customers right now, so come on down and check us out! We're open 'til midnight!'

Outkast cuts in, with Andre 3000 counting "One, two, three, oh" before belting out the first verse.

I end the call without leaving a message.

I sit on the edge of the bed staring at the yearbook, the page still open to the Grade 12 grad photos. Kat's poised and permed portrait is two rows above Todd's douchebag face. I glance over to where Charlie's backpack leans against the wall.

I can't sit here doing nothing.

I open the map and check how long it'd take to get to Edmonton. Two and half hours. If I leave now, I can be back sometime after midnight.

It's all I've got. I grab the bag and yearbook and race for the door.

chapter 107

"Tony?" Gabe calls from his desk.

"Hey, I'm kind of in a hurry—"

"I thought you'd like to know that some woman stopped in not too long ago looking for you."

"What? Really?" Must've been Rachel.

"Yeah. She didn't leave a name, but Juno didn't seem too impressed, so I followed her lead."

On cue, Juno wanders over and sits on my feet. Her furry warmth pressed against me is a comfort.

"What did you tell her?" I ask.

"That I didn't have anyone on the register under your name. In fact, when she said he was a young black man who'd only been in town a couple days, I added that I hadn't seen any-one fitting that description in the hotel."

I lean down and scratch Juno behind the ears. "Looks like I owe you one, girl. How can I thank you both?"

"Aw, I don't need anything, but Juno there has got a soft spot for Old Dutch ketchup chips."

"I think I can make that happen," I say, giving Juno a final pat before heading out the door.

As soon as I step outside, I realize my mistake.

If Rachel is as smart as I've been told, she wouldn't have given up that easily. She's probably waiting for me.

Unfortunately, my car is parked halfway down the street, shrouded in darkness, so if she's out here, there's no way I'll see her.

But waiting around makes me a sitting duck.

I shuffle down the street, pull up my hoodie, senses alert for any noise or movement.

Shit.

There's a shadowy figure across the street, walking in sync with me. I don't take a second look, but listen to their quiet footsteps, keeping them in my peripheral vision.

Shit shit.

There's another figure ahead of me, leaning in the recessed entrance of a storefront, close to my car.

I quickly deke down the alleyway beside the hotel, and as soon as I'm in the shadows, I sprint.

The lane splits into a T halfway down, and I take the right arm, running for the exit. That's when I see another silhouette step out from behind a dumpster at the end. There are buildings all around. I'm boxed in.

Shit shit shit.

chapter 108

The ripe smell of rotting food floats up from a trash bin, and the nearest back door says FOOD DELIVERIES ONLY, so I hammer on it, hoping it's a restaurant.

A young guy in a cook's apron opens up, and I push past him. I'm in the middle of a small, steamy kitchen, and an older man in white yells, "Get the hell out of here."

Dude, I'm trying!

"Sorry," I shout as I race past the server who's just come in the swinging doors that open onto the dining area. The place is bustling, and I dodge wait staff and patrons and shoot for the front door.

This road looks quieter, but I don't take the risk. I run across it into the alleyway opposite, putting more distance between me and my pursuers, slipping into the darkness. I race straight to the end, then stop short, squatting low to peer up and down the next street. No sign of anyone—until a running figure appears down at the corner on the left.

Dammit.

I pull back, catching my breath, and that's when I see another silhouette emerge from the shadows behind me.

There's no choice.

I shoot out of the alley, veering right, racing away from my pursuers down the sidewalk to the end of the road. I duck around the corner and don't look back until I'm at the end of the next block. My senses are on red alert, and I check all four directions. These people could be anywhere, and the closer I get to making it back to where I'm parked, the more likely I'll run into them. Fortunately, the coast now looks clear, and I pull my keys out of my pocket. Now or never.

I rush down the street towards my car. No going back now. I hear a shout and see someone pop out of the alley beside the hotel, almost as close to my car as I am, then I'm balls-to-the-wall, giving it everything I've got to beat them there.

I click the unlock, grab the handle, yank it open, and dive inside. I slam the door shut, locking it just as a goon slams on the driver's side window with his fist.

I start the car, drop it into gear, and peel out, nearly hitting the truck parked in front of me. The tires squeal around the corner, and I feel a hint of relief, but it doesn't last long. In the rear-view, bright headlights swing around the corner, following.

I cross Main Street and take the next left, pressing on the gas. I'm halfway down the block when another car appears.

I'm no longer cautious. I take the next turn and, with barely a glance, cross the intersection and squeeze down a back alley. I hit the next road, turn left and right, randomly zig-zagging my way down various streets.

Suddenly, I pull between two cars parallel-parked in front of a furniture store and kill the engine. I slide deep into my seat, nervously stretching my neck to check the mirrors, fingers crossed that I'll blend into the rest of the shadows.

No car appears, but I'm not chancing it.

I stay low, fingers on the key, foot on the gas.

I should give it more time to be certain, but the clock is ticking, and the people I love are in trouble. I can't waste another moment.

So after five minutes, I start the car and pull out, praying I've left the danger behind.

chapter 109

I drive through the night, checking the rear-view mirror. There's a long, unbroken line of headlights behind me, winding along the highway to Edmonton. There's no way to tell if anyone is following, and I can't help but feel the night closing in.

Unsettled and needing a break from my thoughts, I dig into Dad's music collection in the glove compartment. I choose *Brothers in Arms* and slip it into the CD player. The soft, lingering electric guitar of Dire Straits fills the quiet car. It's not my music, but it connects me to home, to my folks, to safety and comfort. I turn up the volume and relax into the gentle sounds, trying to forge a sense of security away from the darkness outside the car.

I voice-text my folks, asking if they are safe, and my phone rings right away.

"Hello?"

"Anthony."

"Hi, Mom."

"Are you all right?"

"Yes." Not a lie. I'm okay right now—at least as much as I can be.

"Your dad told me everything—at least everything he knows."

"As long as you two are safe."

"Yeah," she says, and I hear her voice waver a bit. "We packed up a few things, grabbed Ollie, and made it to—"

"No, don't tell me! It's better if you don't say a word."

Silence on the other end as she composes herself.

"You lied to us."

"I know." No use denying it. I *haven't* been honest. I've been stubbornly doing what I believed needed to be done—without their permission or Gekas's. And now their lives have been turned upside down and they're hiding from whatever hornet's nest has been stirred up.

"Anthony, don't take any unnecessary risks."

"I won't." At least, I hope not.

"Stop lying to me." Her voice has an edge. She's not yelling, but she's certainly not happy.

"But Mom, it's so easy—"

"Anthony—!"

"Joking!" I knew it would piss her off but the heaviness of this call is nearly choking me. "I can't make that promise," I say finally. "I need to get Charlie safe, and these people aren't going to make it easy."

"Do you know what you're going to do?"

"Yes, but I can't tell you because there's no way of knowing if someone is listening."

She's quiet on the other end. I'm sure she's got a whole lot to say, but she's restraining herself. I'm sure if we were at home and having a warm pot of chai, she'd definitely let me have it.

"Well," she says eventually, and I think the waver is back, "we've done everything we can, and you've been a good kid—but now you need to make that call. Are you confident in your decision?"

"Yes." To save Charlie? No question.

"Okay. Be safe. We love you."

"Love you too, Mom."

Two hours later, I'm driving into the city. Savage Video is on the far southeast side, and it won't take me long to get there. Although the website says it's open late, I'm not confident anyone will be there. I try the phone number once more but get the answering machine again.

Whatever. I'm not turning back now.

On the freeway, I keep checking my rear-view mirror. Even though I'm two hours away from Hatley, I can't shake the feeling that I'm being followed. I push the thought out of my mind and focus on the road ahead.

Google tells me to take the off-ramp to Wayne Gretzky Drive. I pass through a neighbourhood of smaller homes, then over the North Saskatchewan River, and then through another neighbourhood, older still, judging by the tall trees that hang over the streets.

I eventually arrive at my destination, a strip mall that houses a mini-mart, a dry cleaner, a liquor store, and a yoga studio. I don't even notice Savage Video until I drive around the corner and find it tucked in at the end beside an Ethiopian restaurant.

Well, not *tucked*. More like shoved or half-swallowed by the other businesses.

The front of the place looks the same as its online image—same brick, same windows—but the awning has been painted over, and the ridges of the stencilled pattern of the old sign peek through. I'm betting the video store once probably took up half the building, but over time lost the battle for square footage.

A neon OPEN sign flashes in the window.

Phew. I grab the yearbook and head inside.

chapter 111

I enter the store, and an electronic bell chimes somewhere in the back. The interior is painted a pastel-pink rose, and the gaudy geometric patterns on the worn carpet hurt my sense of style. It's a little like going back in time.

The shelves are lined with DVDs, but even in this small space, there are large empty gaps between the rows. The new releases are at the front, and the selection is pretty dismal. Nothing but the top blockbusters from last year, and a few one-off films that look like they were filmed on someone's smartphone. This place has seen better days. If Todd Savage still owns it, he can't be doing too well financially.

No one's behind the till, and no one answered the bell, so I call out, "Hello?"

Nothing.

At the back of the store is a doorway shrouded by a bead curtain, so I wander over.

I regret this decision immediately.

As soon as I enter, I'm faced with rows upon rows of xxx-rated videos crammed into the small room. But beyond it is another open door to a glorified closet with an industrial-sized sink, and a clutter of brooms, mops, and other tools. The plastic shelving unit beside it is filled with cleaning supplies, plus several stacks of hand-labelled DVDs in clear plastic cases. I can just see the corner of a desk.

"What're you looking for?" someone calls out.

I can't see who's talking, so I take another step. "Uh, I'm just wondering if the owner is around?"

"Maybe. Who's asking?"

The shelves of porn are really throwing me off, and I feel like a pervert standing among them, so I edge closer to the open door, only to catch a whiff of the unpleasant combo of pine-scented cleaner and B.O.

Through the crack between the door and the frame, I see a balding, heavyset guy in his forties, lit by the glow of two security monitors. He's in a zip-up hoodie and sweats, feet up on the desk, reading a cheap detective novel.

"Are you Todd Savage?"

"Listen, buddy, unless you're here to rent a couple of movies, I've got better things to do than play twenty questions."

I edge deeper into the room so I can see his face clearly. He's way rougher looking than his grad picture. Like time and stress beat the crap out of him for the full twelve rounds.

Screw it. I'm just going to launch right in.

"I'm wondering what you can tell me about Kat Sullivan."

He looks at me over the rim of his glasses. "Who wants to know?"

"My name's Tony Shepherd—"

"Well, Tony Shepherd, it's time you go," he says, rising and moving towards me.

I backpedal, and my voice comes out louder than I intend. "Were you the one who wrote in her yearbook?"

That stops him. "What are you on about? I wrote in a lot of yearbooks back in the day."

Oh geez. I hope Mr. Popular here isn't about to regale me with the conquests of his glory days. I yank the damp yearbook out of Charlie's backpack and turn to the message at the back. "You wrote this, didn't you?"

He barely gives it a glance. "Doesn't matter. I've kept my mouth shut, just like you wanted."

This catches me off guard. "What are you talking about?"

And I'm not the only one who's confused.

"What are *you* talking about?"

"Did you or did you not date Kat Sullivan?"

He doesn't respond, just glares at me, trying to figure me out.

"If you wrote it, I just need you to tell me what you know," I persist.

He squints and rubs his brow. "Exactly *who* are you again?"

I shrug. "No one. I'm a nobody."

"A nobody isn't likely to come around asking about Kat."

I've got to lay all my cards on the table. "Look, a friend of mine is in trouble, and I think Kat might be the reason."

Todd looks back at his book, then back at me, then sighs. "Fine, but I'm gonna need a drink."

"Because?"

"Because she was one of the worst mistakes of my life."

chapter 112

Todd shuffles past me to the front of the store. I follow him, thankful to be out of there.

He flips the lock on the front door and turns off the neon sign, then slides behind the counter to grab a couple of dirty coffee cups and a nearly empty bottle of whiskey from beneath the till. He pours the last dregs into both cups and offers me one, but I wave it off.

"Is it the cup?" he asks. "I can wash it in the sink."

"I just want answers."

He shrugs. "Your loss," he says, downing the contents of one cup in a single gulp before picking up the other.

"Earlier, you said you'd kept your mouth shut, just like I wanted. Who did you think I was?"

"One of his thugs."

"Whose thugs?"

"Robert Sullivan's. He sent them my way a couple of years back. They busted up my store, then they busted up me."

"Why would they do that?"

He sighs again. "Back in the day, this place used to be the premier destination for movie rentals in the city. We had over a dozen stores. Then Netflix happened, and we didn't pivot fast enough. We lost it all—found ourselves up to our asses in debt." He points at the yearbook. "So, I did what I could to keep my parents' legacy alive."

I realize what had happened. "You tried to blackmail her."

He shrugs. "Desperate times. Seemed like a good idea then."

No wonder he was so cautious about talking to me. Still, one question remains.

"But what did you have on her? Did it have anything to do with what you wrote in her yearbook?"

He drinks the last of the booze, swishing it around a bit before swallowing. Even then, it takes him a moment before he decides to share.

"Her mother. I knew Kat killed her."

chapter 113

I try to process this.

"People in Hatley told me that her mother killed herself."

He looks at me, smug. "That's what they wanted everyone to think."

"Who? Robert Sullivan's guys?"

"And her dad—Tommy. He protected her until he died."

"But I thought she didn't get along with her father."

Man, if this is true, it changes everything I thought I knew about Kat.

"You kidding? Let's just say the apple didn't fall far from the tree."

"But didn't she try to shut down his business right after he died?"

Todd ignores the question, and instead grabs the bottle to pour himself another drink, forgetting that it's empty. "Do you want more booze? I could really use more booze."

I try to get him to focus. "If she got along with her dad, then why'd she shut down his operation?"

"You know, this would be easier if I just showed you the book." He searches the drawers, slamming each one shut when he doesn't find what he's after.

"What book?"

"You know..." he says, gesturing vaguely. "My scrapbook."

"What's that got to do with anything? What's in it?"

He grins. "Everything you'd need to bring that bitch down."

chapter 114

I wait in the car while Todd locks up. I am unsurprised to learn that he lost his driver's license because of a DUI a while back, so I offer him a ride home.

He climbs in, pulls a small pistol from the waistband of his sweatpants, and sets it on his lap.

He catches the look on my face. "This? Don't sweat it. I keep it tucked in my undies in case of emergency. Never know these days."

"Well," I finally muster, "do you mind pointing it away from me?"

"Sure thing." He twists around, studying Dad's car. "Man, a couple of mine were a lot nicer than this, back in the day."

"A couple?"

"Oh, yeah. My folks bought me a new ride almost every birthday." He points. "Turn here."

The houses are a lot nicer than I might have expected. Grand heritage homes of brick and stone—they kind of remind me of the older houses around my neighbourhood.

We pull into the driveway of a three-storey residence veiled in vines. I park beside the shrubbery lining the front, and we hop out, but he doesn't take me to the door.

Instead, he directs me along the side of the house towards a garage that's seen better days. The door has about three padlocks, but he completely ignores it. Instead, he tries to lift the overhead door; it jams with a heavy thud a quarter of the way up.

"Dammit, something must've fallen on the rail," he says. "Never mind. We'll just scooch underneath."

He pockets the gun in his underwear and drops down next to the opening. The pavement is dirty and littered with leaves and an old fast food wrapper.

After a lot of grunting, he wriggles through like a dying slug on a hot sidewalk.

I kneel down on the dirty ground and follow—a little more smoothly than Todd—unsure what I'll find on the other side.

chapter 115

I dust myself off in the cramped and dark garage. From somewhere in the back, Todd calls out, "You got a flashlight?"

"Isn't there power in here?"

"Nah. Turned it off a long time ago to save on the electric bill."

I use my phone to illuminate the place and am stunned to see how much crap Todd has been hoarding. Dusty boxes are stacked high here and there against the walls, along with saggy furniture, and an old Cadillac covered by a large red-and-white striped sheet.

Todd shuffles over to a corner where a velour recliner crouches beside a cooler. He opens it up, and a rancid smell wafts my way. I almost gag, but it doesn't seem to bother him. He pulls out a beer and cracks it to take a couple of gulps.

"Now where the hell did I put that book?" He wanders to the back, but I don't follow. "You wanna help me here?"

I squeeze past the car and find him balancing four boxes in his arms.

"Grab that one on the ground."

I quickly pull the box he indicates out of the way, and he drops his pile into the corner, spilling them everywhere. I'm not sure why he even asked for my help.

He lifts the one I moved and dumps it onto the hood of the car. "Give me your light."

I shine it on top, and he lifts the flaps and digs to the bottom. "Ah, here it is," he announces, and yanks out a thick three-ring binder.

"Aw, baby! How I've missed you."

He opens it and the dried plastic spine crackles with age. It's filled with clippings and photos glued to loose-leaf paper. He licks his finger and thumbs through it, searching sticky notes that act as bookmarks.

Stuck in the middle of the book—apparently with no rhyme or reason—is a large, folded sheet of paper. He pulls it out and unfurls it until its nearly as big as me. He lays it out on the hood of the car.

"There we go!"

I shine my light on it, and all I see at first are drawings of boxes, lines, and scribbles. I lean in and realize it's a giant mind map about Kat. A timeline runs diagonally through it, dates branching out along its spine, which break out into further notes, all tied together with colour-coded symbols.

"This has everything I discovered to build my case."

"To blackmail her?"

He nods, stroking an absent hand across its surface. "It's a shame they shut me down before I could share it."

My feeling is that if he showed this to anyone, they'd have laughed him out of the meeting. The whole thing looks more like the scribblings of a possessed kid in a horror movie than actual proof that Kat was up to something.

Still. I'm here now. "Explain it to me," I say.

He spins it around, jabbing a finger at a box close to the middle. "Here! This is where it begins."

I examine it. *May 5, 2004: Lynn Jonasson found dead.*

I ask, "If you're saying it wasn't suicide, then how did she die?"

"In her bed with a straight razor, like the kind you'd see in an old western."

I cringe at the thought. "And you're saying Kat did that?"

He nods. He points to another box: *Sex/Dock.*

My face screws up like I just swallowed a lemon. "What's that even mean?"

"Back when we were dating, we'd go down to the dock, smoke weed, and fool around." He gives me a lurid wink, like we're buddies now. I don't acknowledge it. "Anyways," he adds, "sometimes afterward, she'd let me do some fishing—"

"What's this got to do with her mother's death?"

"I'm getting to it." He finds his beer and takes another slug. "Like I was saying, she liked me fishing because she liked gutting them. And at some point, she quit using a filleting knife and started using a straight razor—"

I swallow hard. "Like the kind that killed her mother."

He nods.

"It's not enough," I say. "There's no guarantee it was Kat—"

He sputters. "It *was*, though. 'Cause one day while I was fishing, and she was filleting, she stopped and asked, 'How much d'you think it'd hurt to slit your own throat?' And then she held it to my throat and asked, 'Should we find out?'"

Jeezus. "No wonder you dumped her."

"You kidding? I laughed it off and stayed with her for almost a year after—I thought she was edgy and cool." He points to another point on the timeline: *Broke up w/ Kat.*

I notice the date. "Wait, you were with her after her mom died?"

He shrugs. "How do you end it with someone you're pretty sure is a murderer?"

"But if you knew that, why didn't you tell someone?"

"Tried to," he says, taking another swallow; the beer's gone. "But the cops didn't listen. Paid off by her dad, I bet." He pushes the mind map aside and flips through the scrapbook until he opens it to a newspaper clipping circled in red marker. "Here's the police report. Says that Kat was travelling from her father's the day her mother died."

"Okay. So?"

He grunts, frustrated by my lack of understanding, and turns to another page, this one filled with grainy 4 × 6 photos. Most of them are of a bunch of teens wearing too much plaid, crop tops, and low-rise jeans standing around a grungy basement.

"What am I looking at?"

"Darren Ognoski's party. May 4, 2004. Day before her mother died. Now look right there." He points to a group of people sitting on a couch. Behind a red-headed guy taking a hit off a bong is what looks like a woman with blonde hair.

"That's Kat?"

He nods. "I'm thinking Kat came home early from her father's, snuck in and used the razor, and made it look like Lynn did it herself, then went to the party after." He slaps the scrapbook triumphantly like he's proven aliens built the pyramids.

My chest tightens. If what he's saying is true, Kat's definitely got some issues, but there is also a lot of circumstancial evidence, supposition, and wild guesswork. Not to mention that Todd doesn't seem to be playing with a full deck, either.

Besides that, none of it gets me anywhere. I'm hours away from all the people I love who are in danger, stuck in a dingy garage with some dude full of wild conspiracy theories.

He senses my unease. "Okay, okay, listen. Maybe I'm not completely explaining it properly...." He flips the pages of the scrapbook. "You go through it, look at all the articles, all my notes. It'll make better sense if you get the whole picture."

He keeps flipping page after page, and headlines and photos flash before my eyes—

"Stop," I shout. "Go back."

He freezes, and I yank the book away from him. I thumb back through the pages, searching for what I'd seen.

"Easy! Don't rip it," he cautions.

I pause and shine my flashlight closer on the page, unsure. It's a picture of a young couple: a curly-haired woman I don't recognize—but the man is definitely the spitting image of Charlie's dad.

And written above it in dark bold letters are four words that barely make any sense in my brain: SOPHIE CHARLES STILL MISSING.

chapter 116

I read the article, trying to understand what the hell I'm looking at.

Almost fifteen years ago, the thirteen-year-old daughter of William Wolfe and Irene Charles went missing from a party, along with her friend. The article goes on to say that after a fruitless, months-long interprovincial search, thousands of tips, and countless dead ends, investigators were scaling back their efforts.

The detective-in-charge was quoted as saying, "We'll keep the file open, but we can no longer continue to invest the resources into such a prolonged search for these two individuals." An unnamed source within the department added that the likelihood of finding the teenagers alive is "grim."

I scan it again, hoping that somewhere between the lines I'll find the answer to the question that hammers like a heartbeat in my head: Does Charlie have a *sister*?

I turn on Todd. "What is this?"

He pulls off his glasses and leans into the light to get a closer look. "Oh, that."

"What do you mean 'Oh, that'!?"

"It's about those missing teenagers from Calgary from a while back."

"Yeah, I get that. Why is it in here?"

He spins the book around, checking his notes on the side. He turns a few pages before shoving it back to me. Another headline: DOUBLE HOMICIDE IN EAST SIDE HOME.

"Here it is. Back in 2006, cops were called to a home after multiple gunshots were reported. Two bodies were discovered—a man and a woman. As well as...something else."

I can barely breathe. "What?"

"In the basement, they found rooms. With padlocks on the outside."

"Why?" I ask, although I'm not sure I want to know the answer.

"The house was part of a human-trafficking operation."

"And the teenagers?"

"When the investigators swarmed the place, they found the DNA of dozens of victims—including the two girls."

"Oh god."

It's a gut punch. All this time, I never knew. Charlie holding onto it while he helped me—and I never knew. I clear my throat, trying to push my feelings away so I can focus.

"So why do you have it in here?"

"Turns out they were associates of The Falcon."

My mind reels. There *was* a connection.... But—why had they come for Charlie now, so long after the fact?

It hits me like a thunderbolt. Maybe now that he was old enough to try to do something about these scumbags, to avenge his sister, Charlie had begun poking around in their business. And if so, no wonder they were after him.

"Was Sullivan ever charged?" I ask.

"Never. Wasn't enough evidence to make it stick."

"So what does all of this have to do with Kat?"

He gawks at me, stunned that I can't keep up. He pulls his timeline back towards us. "Here's where her mother died. Since Kat was eighteen, she stayed in the house on her own until she graduated. But right after, she moved away to live with her father." He runs his finger forward on the timeline. "And here is where those two girls went missing."

No—when Charlie's sister, Sophie, went missing.

"What are you getting at, Todd?"

"Well, Kat was hanging out with her father through all of it. If he was responsible, she probably saw something. Maybe she's not just guilty of murder, but other stuff too."

My frustration and sadness boil over. "Stop. Enough of the theories—"

"But she had to be part of it in some way—" he sputters.

"Is there any tangible evidence of that?"

He trips over his words. "My scrapbook. The timeline—"

"Screw the timeline! Do you have *proof*?"

"Yes, it's all here!"

"No, it isn't." I've wasted enough time.

I push past him towards the door, fighting to lift it up, but the clutter on the garage door rail gets in the way, and I'm about ready to scream.

I drop down and roll under, not giving a shit about the dust and garbage. The cool night air is a welcome relief from the stuffiness—but sadness and pain still swirl around me. I stagger towards my car, trying to comprehend everything, struggling to sort out the facts from Todd's paranoid fiction.

I pop the lock and nearly tumble into the driver's seat.

I start the car and am about to put it into reverse when out of the corner of my eye, a dark shadow separates itself from the depths of the back seat.

"Easy, Tony. I've got a gun, so don't do anything stupid."

I recognize her voice from a few days ago, so I'm not surprised when she leans forward, and I see her reflection in the rear-view mirror. The gun is aimed at the back of my head.

"The name's Rachel. It's about time we have a chat."

chapter 117

I've spent all this time fearing her, but now that Cousin Rachel's right behind me, I discover I don't really care. After finding out about Charlie and his sister, all I want to do is get back to him.

"What do you want?"

"You're a hard man to track down."

"Well, you haven't exactly been the friendliest," I mutter.

"Why are you here?" she sneers.

"In the city?"

"No. Hatley."

Seriously? "What do you think? To help Charlie."

She pushes herself further forward, talking right in my ear, enunciating every word. "Help him do what?"

It's my turn to sneer. "To escape *you* weirdos—"

Suddenly, the front passenger window pops, like someone tossed a rock at it. It spiderwebs into a thousand cracks. In the centre is a small hole. Another *bang* and a *pop*, and I suddenly realize what's happening.

Someone's shooting.

Through the shattered glass, a drunken figure trundles towards us, a revolver waving our way.

Todd.

"I see you, you crazy bitch!" he shouts. "Get out of the car!"

Rachel raises her gun towards him, and I act on instinct. I drop the car in reverse and hit the gas. She tumbles forward, and I careen onto the street. Before she can collect herself, I twist the wheel, and the front end spins ninety degrees.

"Stop!" she shouts, but I ignore her, shifting into drive.

"Stop!" Todd yells somewhere behind me.

I ignore him too and hit the gas, putting distance between us and his wild aim.

"Go back. He saw me."

"So?"

"He knows who I am."

"What do I care."

She swings around to point the weapon at me. "Pull this goddamn car around."

"No," I say, leaning on the gas. "As long as I'm driving, I'm in control."

"You so sure about that, cowboy?" she asks, gesturing forward with the gun.

The stoplights ahead flash from yellow to red.

Shit.

If I stop, I'm done for. If I keep going, I'll likely crash. But I can't slow down.

Momentum is my only bargaining chip.

My stomach clenches as I grip the wheel and plunge into the intersection.

A big three-quarter-ton truck appears out of the dark, lights glaring, horn blaring. I gasp as the bumper misses us by millimetres.

We come out the other end without a scratch, and I barely process what's just happened.

Rachel leans forward. "All right, now that you've proved your point, stop."

I ignore her and pull a hard right up a cloverleaf. She realizes what I'm up to and pushes the muzzle of the gun into my side, hard. I can already tell it's going to leave a bruise.

"Pull over."

"No!"

I merge onto the freeway, sliding between a semi and a sports car that refuses to move for me. I cut into the next lane and find myself bumper-to-bumper in traffic. But I don't care. We're all going highway speed, with no chance of stopping, and I can finally breathe.

It doesn't last long.

Rachel hisses in my ear. "You got some nice moves there, but if you don't pull over, I'm shooting."

"You won't—we'll crash."

"*Pff.* I can shoot you without killing you, Tony. And trust me, I'll make it hurt like a son of a bitch."

I swallow hard. "What do you want from me?"

"Pull over first."

"No. Tell me what you want."

She fires the gun at my feet, deliberately missing. I flinch at the sound, my eardrums ringing, the car swerving over the rumble strip.

"I told you! I'm here to help Charlie," I cry out.

"Sure. But why are you *really* here?"

"What the hell do you mean?"

She fires another warning shot, and the sound is deafening.

"Seriously, I don't understand—"

She jabs the gun into my leg. "Just how are you helping Charlie Wolfe?"

"I'm looking for answers!"

"Quit bullshitting me, Tony. How are you two planning to kill Robert?"

"*Kill* him? If anything, we're trying to save his ass."

"Really? How's that exactly?"

"The one guy—Winston?—thought Robert was behind all this. But Charlie and I think it's Kat!"

"Kat? Why would you think that?"

"Because—because she's like her father." In the absence of proof, it's the strongest rationale I can come up with.

"What's that mean?"

"She's ruthless and ambitious. She'd kill anyone who got in her way."

"But why kill her uncle? He raised her."

"Well, so did her mother, and look where that got *her*. Once Robert's gone, Kat regains control of her father's legacy."

Rachel falls silent, and I glance in the mirror. Her lips are pursed, and she looks pissed. I'm scared what will come next.

Slowly, the pressure of the barrel eases off.

"If that's true, then we've got a problem."

"What's that?"

"Right now, Robert's on his way to meet Kat. And he's taking Charlie with him."

chapter 119

Before leaving the city, I pull into a gas station, confident that Rachel's no longer going to kill me. At least, not yet.

I fill up and pay, and when I return, she's sitting in the passenger seat. I toss her a pack of kale chips. "I wasn't sure if you wanted anything, so I grabbed these."

She quirks an eyebrow.

"My dad seems to like them," I add.

She tears it open and gives it a sniff. "Smells like dirt." She digs into the bag and tries one. "Salty, but not bad."

I rip open my own bag of Doritos and stuff a few in my mouth.

She glares. "You serious?"

I shrug and offer her some.

"Just drive."

chapter 120

We speed back towards Hatley. The sun hasn't risen, but I can see a glow on the horizon in the rear-view mirror.

"So," I ask, "how long have you worked for the Mob?"

"Long enough," she says curtly, popping one of my Doritos in her mouth.

Now that my life's not in imminent danger, curiosity has taken over. "And how'd you start working for them?"

She glares at me. "We're not spending this drive playing twenty questions."

"Why not? We've got a couple of hours to kill."

"Then we'll drive in silence."

I ignore the request. "Why did you think Charlie was trying to kill Robert?"

"Remember, I have *you* on that list too." But then she shrugs. "Process of elimination. William Wolfe, and later Charlie, are the only two of my leads that never had a good alibi."

"But if you thought Charlie was guilty, why didn't you off him when you had the chance?"

"Because taking him out wasn't my instructions. I was only supposed to track the killer down, then send them to Robert."

"But Winston beat you to it."

She grimaces. "No, not him. His two goons, Red and Cass, picked Charlie up."

"But if it wasn't Winston, then who gave them the order?"

"Not Robert."

I look over at her. "Kat?"

She nods.

"What does she want with Charlie?"

"That's the trouble. I'm not sure."

chapter 121

After the Doritos and kale chips are gone, we fall into silence.

Rachel stares at the bullet hole in the cracked passenger window for most of the trip. She's stuffed a napkin from the glove compartment into it so it doesn't whistle on the highway. I can't even begin to think what I'll tell Dad about the bullet holes in his car. So I don't.

I don't really know what to say to her, either, or if there's anything else I really want to know. Too much information is a dangerous thing with these people. Plus, it's not like we have a lot in common. If she hadn't suspected me of working with Charlie to kill her boss, we probably would never have crossed paths.

She surprises me when she speaks. "You know, we almost met each other once."

"At the Jonasson house."

"No, before that. In Estoria. We were both dealing with Terry Butler, that poor son of a bitch."

"You were *there*?"

She smirks. "In the area. I've been keeping an eye on you ever since."

I feel a flash of anger. "Like busting into my house? Yeah, I heard about that."

"Who told you? Kosmos?" She glances over at me and smiles. "Of course he did."

I stay quiet, worried about the punishment Kosmos might get for sharing this information.

"Still. Considering everything you faced these past couple of years, I'm impressed," she adds.

The compliment surprises me.

"Even Charlie—if he really isn't out to get Robert—seems intent on doing some good." She looks down at the gun in her hand. "All I've done.... Well, it would've been nice to have made some different choices."

She falls silent again and doesn't say anything else until we're fifteen minutes outside of Hatley.

"The meet-up is at the country club on the far side of the lake." She pulls out her pistol and checks the chamber. "When we get there, they'll be looking for us. We'll have to pull off-road, and I'll hike in."

"What about me?"

"You stay in the car and keep the engine running."

Nuh-uh. "No way—my friend is in there."

"And you getting killed isn't going to help him. That place'll be swarming. I'll be able to get close enough to Robert to warn him."

"And what about Charlie?"

She pauses. "If you two are legit, and this is all Kat's doing, then I'll send him your way when I can."

We enter town, and she points at an exit by the big box stores. "Turn here."

The road takes us along a ridge around the far side of the lake. The sun is just breaking on the horizon, and the mountainside is bathed in its golden orange light. At the bottom of its slopes is a large building of wood and stone that looks like something out of a national park. Between it and us is the golf course, eighteen holes of finely groomed fairways.

Ah, yes. The new country club and golf course. Exclusive. Private. Built by the Mob.

We drop down the hill towards it, and I steel myself for the fight to come. It happens sooner than I expect.

We crest a ridge, and a lone figure stands in the middle of the road in the distance.

Whoever it is, they're barely discernible, in jeans and a leather jacket, and at first I think they're holding a pair of binoculars, but Rachel swears, and I immediately know I'm wrong.

I see the muzzle flash, and Dad's car pulls hard left. I fight it, trying not to oversteer, but it resists, and we're heading for the ditch.

"Stop!" Rachel yells, but it all happens too quick, and we slide off the road.

The front end drops, the steering wheel rips out of my hand. My body slams heavy against the door, my world is spinning, flailing, and screeching, and I tumble into darkness.

chapter 123

"Tony!"

A stinging slap yanks me back to awareness. My whole body hurts, inside and out. The seatbelt is digging into my side, and my face feels like it's been punched by a brick wall. I'm smothered by airbags, barely able to comprehend that they are likely what's kept me alive.

"We've gotta go."

Rachel's kneeling beside me—upside down—and all at once I realize *I'm* the one who's inverted. She's got a knife, and she stabs the airbags to get them out of the way.

She moves to the seatbelt and says, "Sorry I can't do this any nicer," and before I understand what she means, I fall out of my seat into shattered glass and cracked CDs.

"Anything broken?" she asks.

I groan. "Everything—?"

"Can you move?"

"I think so."

"Good." She climbs over me, gripping the steering wheel with one hand while she kicks at my door. I try not to pass out again. On the fourth attempt, it springs loose with a loud shriek, and she pulls herself across me and out.

"If you don't get your ass out of there, we're dead," she says.

I'm still trying to flip the world rightside up in my head when she gestures over my shoulder through the back passenger window.

The lone figure is walking steadily towards us, rifle raised.

I drag myself through the door, suddenly unconcerned about cutting my hands on the jagged metal and glass, but my right arm hangs numb and limp.

"Shit, my shoulder."

She barely glances at me. "Probably dislocated. On your back."

Before I'm even settled, she grabs my hand and slowly tugs my whole arm at a ninety-degree angle.

I wince as everything *thunks* back into place.

"Better?"

I rotate it. It still hurts like hell, but it's a lot better than it was. I nod.

"Think you can make it to the woods?" Rachel asks.

"They've got a gun," I say, stating the obvious.

"So do I."

I check the distance. It's a long run, and out in the open the whole way. But the shooter will be on us shortly anyway, and there'll be nowhere to hide. Except—

"What about you?"

"Don't worry about it."

That's when I notice the bloody slice in her leg.

"Just get out of here."

I want to stay and help, but that'll only get both of us killed.

She grins. "Keep our people alive until I get there."

I nod, and before I give myself a chance to rethink it, bolt for the trees. The crack of a rifle ricochets off the mountainside, immediately followed by three rapid higher-pitched shots.

I thrash my way into the pines and don't look back.

But I hear the short, sharp *pops* of Rachel's revolver until a final, echoing *bang!* cuts them short.

I know what it means, but I don't turn around. I can't.

If I do, Rachel's sacrifice will be in vain.

I keep running, hoping I can make it to Charlie in time.

chapter 124

The woods are thick, and I'm running blind. If I keep going straight, I'm hoping I'll end up at the golf course.

Every sense is on edge. Every rustle of leaves or flash of sunlight through the canopy feels like the shooter closing in.

But I can't stop.

I push through the dense bush, ignoring the scratches and the scrapes, doing my best not to clothesline myself on low-hanging branches or trip on gnarled roots.

At the edge of the woods is a barbwire fence with NO TRES-PASSING signs marking every twenty feet. I struggle over it and stumble out of the trees—my bare arms bleeding, my body aching—onto the lush fairway. Sprinklers *tchk tchk tchk* around me.

The clubhouse rises above the trees in the distance, and I jog towards it, staying close to the treeline. If the mystery shooter makes an appearance, I'd like the chance to duck into the woods and hide.

I approach the closest green. A flag for the eighth hole waves in the light morning breeze. At the end of the ninth hole, I spot two men strolling along the wide, stone-lined deck of the clubhouse's immense patio, and I crouch-run towards a scattering of bushes near the first tee box.

As best as I can tell in the morning sun, they look like security guards, booted and suited in all black, and armed with semi-automatic rifles. It flashes in my brain that their whole SWAT team vibe is a lot different than the casually stealthy sniper I've been struggling to avoid, but I don't have time to ponder it.

A third man steps outside through a patio door and speaks to them, and I wonder how many more of them there are. One thing's for sure: there's no way to sneak past them.

There's only one option.

But first I need to make a phone call.

"Detective Gekas? It's time…"

part 6

After Red and Cass agreed to take Charlie to Robert, they bound, gagged, and bagged him with duct tape and a pillowcase, and tossed him in a closet. And there he waited, fighting to keep the fear of dark memories from engulfing him.

At some point, he fell asleep and was woken by Red kicking the bottom of his Crocs.

"Time to go."

They'd marched him out to the car. Blinded by the pillowcase, he did his best to track where they went. He felt the gentle rock of the car, the lightness in his stomach, the pressure of his back against the seat. He was certain they had travelled down the mountain, through the town, and up the other side, but then they took a left turn and went down another hill.

This threw him off.

He suspected that they were now on the other side of the lake, but back when he'd lived in Hatley, there hadn't been much over there except sawmills and clear-cut forest.

The car rolled to a stop and he was dragged out. The crunch and feel of gravel under his feet became hard and even like cement, which pretty much guaranteed they'd taken him inside a building. He was forced into a chair and then...nothing.

They didn't take off the pillowcase or talk to him. They sat in silence, and when Charlie tried to mumble through the tape to ask what was going on, he was ignored.

Now, after what seemed like fifteen minutes, other men had arrived. They speak quietly, but one dominates the rest, his voice reedy and pretentious. When they finally unbag Charlie's head, he isn't surprised that it's Robert.

He is exactly how Tony described him: slick like The Falcon, but weaker. He isn't built to fight, and if it were just the two of them, Charlie figures he could take him.

Robert also looks like shit, with dark bags under his eyes and grey hair breaking through the once jet-black hair. The man probably hasn't slept for a month, and his nervous eyes tell Charlie he trusts no one.

He has his own team of four security guards patrolling the perimeter of what will be the clubhouse's huge restaurant/banquet room, armed with AR-15s and built for war. Definitely not the goons Charlie's been driving around with for the past week.

Probably hired mercenaries.

The cavernous banquet room boasts an aesthetic straight out of *The Shining*—an ugly mix of rustic lodge and gaudy country club, with enough stone and wood to have wiped out an entire coastal rainforest. At one end of the room is a stage, and on the other, a long bar and a set of swinging doors.

Robert drags a chair over and sits across from Charlie. He's uncomfortably close. The man doesn't speak at first, only studies him, then takes a sip from a hip flask. Yet his breath is minty, not boozy—probably from an antacid for an ulcer.

"The boys say you got something to tell me. That true?"

Charlie nods.

"Interesting, interesting..."

Robert doesn't pull the duct tape off Charlie's mouth right away, and Charlie knows something is wrong.

Robert continues. "Lemme ask you a question: Have we ever met before?"

Charlie shakes his head slowly, unsure if the mobster is aware of his shared past with Robert's brother.

"No. Didn't think so. But that doesn't mean I don't know all about *you*."

Charlie's chest tightens.

"Of course, you're nothing but a street rat. But I can tell you *exactly* what's going on in that head of yours."

Charlie swallows hard.

"You figured you'd come here to tell me that my dear niece Kat plans on killing me. And you hoped that'd be enough for me to let you go free. But if you haven't noticed"—he points to the armed men surrounding them—"I kind of figured that out already. And what you may not have realized, at least until now, is that you're *my* bait to get her here, so I can finish her off." He pauses for another sip from the flask. "And once I'm done with that, I won't need you anymore, either."

Charlie struggles to rip the tape off his hands.

"Oh, and one more thing..." Robert snaps his fingers, and the door opens.

His chest caves as Tony is led through the door.

"*Mhhrrhuhrr*!" Charlie screams through the duct tape, but no one pays attention.

His friend looks like hell—hands bound behind his back, face bloodied and scraped. Did they beat the shit out of him before they hauled him in here?

Tony shoots him a wide-eyed look and shrugs as if to say "Oh well, no big deal." But, yeah it is a big deal.

"Put them in the back until she gets here."

Red and Cass grab him and Tony and shove them out into the lobby. A grand fireplace takes up one wall next to a winding wooden staircase that leads to the upper level. They're pushed down a hallway, past a pro shop and a gym, before being prodded into a locker room. Of course it has a sauna.

Red shoves Tony inside, and he falls hard into a wooden bench.

Charlie turns on Red, ready to kick-box, hands or no hands, but Cass is way ahead of him and draws his gun—pointing it at Tony.

"You come an inch closer to either of us, and I'm shooting your buddy here. Now, get in there."

Before Charlie can take a step, Red yanks him by the lapels of his once-new suit jacket and tosses him inside. His head slams hard against the wall, and he nearly loses his balance. Red punches him in the gut, and Charlie struggles to stand, twisting his wrists in the duct tape, letting it burn as he tries to break free.

But that's as far as he gets, because Cass cold-cocks him, hard, and Charlie tumbles into blackness.

chapter 126

"Charlie, you okay?" I shuffle over to check on him, stupidly grateful for the small window in the sauna's door that lets me see that he's still breathing, at least.

He opens his eyes and tries to speak, but it comes out a mumble through the tape over his mouth.

"Two seconds. Let me get out of these."

I drag myself up, my side hurting from where I collided with the bench. I bend over, make a space between my zip-tied hands, and hit them hard against my tailbone. It takes three hits, but the binding breaks.

I yank off Charlie's gag.

"We need to tell these guys about the long-term effects of repeated concussions," he says groggily.

"How are you doing?" I prod. "They hurt you?"

"Nothing that time won't heal."

I help him up, and he catches me off guard by pulling me into a hug.

"You shouldn't be here. But it's really good to see you."

We're about to be slaughtered, but I know what he means. He fills me in about what he's learned of Robert's plan, and I update him on what Todd told me about Kat.

"Of *course* she murdered her mother!" he exclaims. "It wouldn't be a Shepherd and Wolfe adventure unless we're dealing with the worst of humanity."

"Hey, don't blame me!" I protest. "My life was boring until I met you."

He cracks a small, crooked smile. "And normally I'd say that you're better for it, but on a scale of one to 'our usual shit,' this one's pretty well a thousand."

And much as I hate being in it up to our necks, I'm glad we're in it together. And that we can finally talk—what I know about his past weighs heavy.

"Charlie, there's something else."

"Oh damn, you've got those puppy-dog eyes. What is it?"

Now that the moment is here, I'm hesitant, but I just need to say it. "I found out about your sister." I let this statement sit with him for a second before adding quietly, "Why didn't you ever tell me about her?"

He closes his eyes.

"I was four when it happened, so I didn't really understand. She was playing with me one day, and then she was just…gone…the next. I didn't get it." He looks away, shaking his head. "Every day, I asked my parents when she was coming home. Must've broken them every time."

"Aw, man. You didn't know…"

"I know, but old regrets, right?" He shrugs and takes a seat on one of the change-room benches. I take a spot across from him. "Her disappearance broke my family. Shit got ugly, and my parents separated. Dad took me to keep me safe…."

I'm not going to make Charlie dwell on the tragedy of his mom, so I hurry on. "I tracked you through your past, you know. Went to Snowberry, Penticton. Met Mr. Whitaker. Found out about Mercury Charles—"

He goes a bit red. It's kind of fun to watch.

"Yeah, yeah. We don't need to go *there*—"

"I also met your dad."

His face softens. "How's he and Julie doing?"

"They're okay. She's good with him."

"Yeah, he's pretty lucky."

"There's one thing, though, Charlie, that I don't understand. You guys moved around a *lot*—why?"

He glances at me, and suddenly I get it.

There's something else I don't know. Something more. One final secret he hasn't told me, and he's about to speak when we hear the distant sound of a helicopter.

Cass appears at the sauna door, gun in hand, pointed at us. "All right, boys. Let's go."

chapter 127

Robert stands by the doors that open to the deck. In the distance, swooping down low over the lake, is a small, sleek, black helicopter.

He points at us. "Put them in the middle of the room where she can see them." Red and Cass grab two dining room chairs and shove us into them.

"Shepherd—" Charlie whispers, but Cass elbows him.

"Quiet."

The helicopter descends and settles on a makeshift landing pad on the flagstones of the patio. The door slides open, and a woman steps out. She's wearing big sunglasses, a white suit jacket and pencil skirt, and a chic bag slung over one shoulder. Although her long blonde hair is scraped back in a tight bun, I've seen enough photos to know Kat when I see her.

She's like a statue. Perfectly poised, but stone cold. She smiles, or at least it seems like she does, but I can't tell. It's enigmatic. Like she's amused by something only she knows.

As she walks across the deck, high heels tapping a staccato beat, Robert steps out to greet her. He gives her a hug and she reciprocates, though with minimal effort—merely a hand tossed over his shoulder and a short peck on the cheek. They stand there for a moment; the thick, triple-paned glass windows and slowing whir of the chopper blades drown out their words.

He flashes a grin like a car salesman and gestures our way. With her sunglasses on, it's hard to tell if she's looking at us. He takes a step towards us; she doesn't follow.

That's when I notice the hired guns positioned out of sight in the corners of the room, AR-15s tucked into their shoulders. Robert's trying to convince her to come inside so she'll be surrounded. If she makes the slightest move against him, she's done.

There's an awkward distance between Robert and Kat now, and he beckons her to accompany him. She doesn't respond, so he returns to her. He puts a hand on her back, urging her forward, but she stands her ground. She takes his other hand in hers and pulls him in to whisper in his ear, motioning with her head first at us and then at her bag.

Whatever she says wipes the smile off his face. She steps back and waits as he deliberates his next move. Reluctantly, he accepts whatever she's offered and walks back towards the restaurant doors.

Only then does she follow.

He opens the door and waves at the team of hit men to stand down. They comply, lowering their semi-automatics.

"Seems like you prepared quite the welcoming party, Uncle," Kat says as she finally walks inside.

His smile returns, but this time it's strained. "You can never be too safe these days. There's a killer on the loose."

Ha ha. You have to admire the audacity.

"No, I don't suppose you can," she says. She takes off her glasses and slips them into her bag and sets it on a nearby table. Not once does she look our way.

Instead, she checks her watch.

She turns to her uncle. "I don't suppose you have anything around here to celebrate with? Champagne or wine, perhaps? Today will be a momentous one for us all."

Robert glances at Red and Cass, who shrug.

"Ah, well. Not a concern." She pulls out her phone and calls someone. "Please pick up a case of the '90." And just like that, the helicopter lifts off to fulfill Kat's request.

Charlie shakes his head at the brashness.

She turns back to her uncle. "Now, I'm aware you had other plans for me, but I promise that what I'm about to offer is worth your patience."

Robert raises his hands, all innocence. "I'm not sure what you're suggesting—"

"Oh, I'm sure."

Kat reaches into her bag and everyone in the room tenses. Slowly, she pulls out a thick folder and passes it to Robert.

"What's this?" he asks.

"A peace offering."

Cautiously, he opens it and peers inside. "It's a contract."

She nods. "To bring you into the business."

He laughs. "I'm head of the Family. I *am* the business."

"Oh, absolutely," she coos, "and I'm grateful for all you've done. But this—" she taps the tips of her manicured fingers on the pages he's pulled out, "this is an offer to be a part of *my* business."

"What? Commercial investments?"

She smirks. "Among other things." She reaches into her bag, pulling out a pen and a pad of paper, and writes something on it. "I'd like to offer you a percentage." She shows him the pad.

He frowns. "What is this? It's not even one percent—"

"No, but this..." she writes another number on the page, "is how much it's worth."

Any semblance of scorn drains from his face.

"That should cover the Family's expenses for a few generations, correct?"

"*How*...?"

She smirks again. "The best lesson Dad ever taught me was never to let someone else draw the lines that define me."

Robert gives her an incredulous look. "But why would you offer me this?"

She lifts an elegant shoulder. "Oh, because I felt it was time that you received your due." She glances at her watch again. "But please, review it. I don't want you to think I'm trying to swindle you."

"Yeah, yeah..." he mutters, still distracted by whatever large number she'd written on the page.

Cass clears his throat. "Uh, boss?"

"Yeah...?"

"What should we do with these two?"

Kat turns our way, and I realize it's the first time she's even noticed us. Robert waits for her to respond, and that's enough to drive home the fact that *she's* the boss Cass means.

Her hand slips into her purse, this time pulling out a polished pearl object that looks like a long, thin vape. I know what it is, and my stomach drops. She unfolds the blade of the straight razor and saunters towards us.

She studies Charlie. "You were a lot of effort to acquire. But you"—she points at me—"you are inconsequential." She pulls back the blade—

Shit! She's about to slash my throat!

But Robert calls out, "Maybe don't make a mess on the carpets."

The zeal in her eyes fades into disappointment.

He nods at Red and Cass. "Get one of your boys to find a place to dispose of him."

She gestures at Charlie. "Hold on to him for now, but get rid of the other one."

The words are sudden and quick; I don't have time to react.

Red grabs me and hauls me up. Charlie lurches towards us, but Cass restrains him.

I feel a gun jab into the tender spot on my side. "Move."

There's nothing to be done. Charlie and I can't take on this room full of guns and muscle alone. I stare at my friend, and the terror in his eyes says it all.

This might be the last time we ever see each other.

chapter 128

Red marches me out of the restaurant and down a set of stairs, his gun shoved into my back. Only now do I realize how close I am to my death. I've faced it before, but never with such executionary flair.

He pushes me into a large garage space, currently filled with boxes and building supplies. There's a set of roll-up doors at the far end.

"Grab that." Red points to a large roll of poly.

I don't argue—why don't I argue?—and pick it up. It's heavy and slippery, and I heft it awkwardly into the crook of my arms.

"Keep moving," he orders.

He leads me past a workbench of greasy tools and a filthy sink, until we arrive in a back corner, small and cramped.

There's no way out.

Red's next words are so clinical, they chill me to the bone. "Spread the plastic on the ground."

I stand there, hesitating, and the world devolves into slow motion. I'm suddenly outside myself, staring down at the two of us.

I know that as soon as I do what he says, this asshole is going to shoot me in the back of the head in this half-built pretentious country club in this shithole town.

I can't let it happen. I've got to fight back. And I've got to do it now.

In one quick motion, I back-step and slam the heavy roll of plastic into his chest. He stumbles backwards, and before he can lift the gun, I swing again, this time striking his forearm. The weapon flies out of his hand and slides somewhere out of sight amidst the packing crates.

I throw myself at him, scooping him up to fling him down onto the cement.

Red lands hard, plastic roll still on top of him, but he tosses it aside, jumps to his feet faster than I anticipated, and throws a punch, catching me hard in the jaw.

He might as well have hit me with a fist of rocks. Every bone in my head vibrates, and all I see is black and red.

But it doesn't matter, because if I don't get out of this, I'm dead.

I start swinging, whether I see him or not, aiming where I think his head might be. The first punch misses, but the next doesn't, and I don't stop. I zero in on his face with ground-and-pounds.

He pulls his arms up for cover, and before I realize it, he's got me in a bear hug and throws me off. A millisecond later, he's raining down his own punches, and I'll be out in a blink if too many connect.

Thank god I've spent enough time hanging around with Charlie that I've learned to fight, and I quickly wrap my legs around him and deflect his jabs with my own. I catch his arm and slam my elbow several times into his head, and he pulls away.

It's all I need. With enough space between us, I bring up my knee, then use my foot to push him off.

I scramble up and get behind him so I can wrap my arms around his neck in a headlock. He tries to shake me, lifting me off my feet and slamming me against the wall, but I tighten my grip, cutting off his blood flow.

He crumples to the ground, and only when I'm certain he's knocked out do I let go.

I grab some duct tape and bind Red's arms and legs. Mouth too. Let's see how you like it, buddy.

I pat him down but find only an ammo clip and his cell phone, which I pocket. I search for the dropped gun, lost somewhere under the crates, but can't find it anywhere. I could spend more time looking, but someone is going to come for Red if he doesn't return soon.

I need to get moving.

There is an exit to the outside beside the roll-up door. Maybe if I sprint for the trees, none of the hired guns will notice, and I can lay low until Gekas's reinforcements show up.

But I don't know what Kat's plan for Charlie is. And even though she didn't send him to the same fate as me, that doesn't mean she won't change her mind and bring out her pearl-handled razor.

It's simple: I can't leave without him.

chapter 129

I check the hallway outside the storage area. It's empty, and I move down it swiftly and back up the stairs. At the top is another door, and I'm about to open it a crack to make sure the coast is clear when a radio squawks on the other side.

I step back into the stairwell, back down the steps, ducking out of sight. This has to be the worst high-stakes game of hide-and-seek I've ever played.

"West hallway clear," a deep voice reports.

I hold my breath, hoping no one comes through the door. When no one does, I risk it and sneak back into position at the top of the stairs. I listen for a moment, then open the door.

No one's around, except for a hired gun plodding down the hall away from me. There's another door across from me, and before I psych myself out, I step across and test the handle.

It's unlocked.

chapter 130

Inside is an industrial kitchen filled with appliances big enough to feed a thousand. Stainless steel cabinets line the walls, and in the centre are several polished metal prep islands. At the far end is a set of swinging doors. I scuttle across the floor, staying low, and peer through the crack between them.

Robert sits at a table, paging through the contract. All of his hired guns await further instruction out on the deck. Kat stands at the far end by the windows, scrolling through her phone, occasionally checking her watch. Charlie hasn't moved from his chair, but Cass hovers behind him, binding his hands once more.

What's going on? Kat hasn't killed Charlie or Robert, and Robert hasn't killed her. They're all standing around . . . and just waiting? Was her grand plan to get them all together in one room, just so they could *hang out*?

No. Something else is going on, probably connected to what Charlie was trying to tell me.

I need to do something, create a diversion, and get him out of there, but I don't know what. Drive a golf cart through the halls? Drop a chandelier on Kat's head? Why is raising hell always easier for Charlie?

I look over at him for inspiration and realize he's looking my way. Does he see me? As soon as our eyes lock, he motions at me—unnoticed by everyone else, thank god—to get out of here.

I shake my head.

Unfortunately, he's got other plans.

chapter 131

He clears his throat, but no one looks. He speaks anyway. "So, when things go south—and they will—what's your contingency plan?" he asks.

Kat looks at him. "And what makes you think things will fall apart?"

"No, not you. I'm talking to him." He gestures at Robert, who looks up from the contract.

"Hmm...?" he mumbles.

"I said, what's your plan for getting out of this alive when she tries to kill you?"

He shakes his head. "Whatever, kid." And he goes back to reading.

Charlie shrugs and looks at Kat. "He's forgotten he doesn't trust you. Guess greed can do that to a person."

She puts her phone away and studies him, really noticing him for the first time. "You think I'm going to kill him?"

Charlie nods. "Of course I do. Me, him, all of us...." He glances my way and scowls when he sees I haven't moved.

"But I came with an offering of good will. I'm sharing my profits with him," she protests.

Charlie laughs. "Oh, that's just a diversion."

She smiles. "Oh, is it?"

"Yeah, it's buying you time."

"For what?"

"For the arrival of the real killer."

"What's he on about?" Robert asks. He's got a confused look, and he's no longer reading.

Kat glares at Charlie, annoyed. "*Tch*. You really know how to ruin a surprise."

The distant sound of the helicopter returns.

Robert rises, drawing his gun. "Wait! Who's coming?" He turns to Cass. "Get out and secure that thing before it gets too close."

Cass rushes outside, and I reposition myself to see what's happening. He's yelling, and the hired guns fan out, taking cover behind the stone wall that lines the deck.

Robert points the gun at Kat. "Who's on the helicopter?"

"No one," she shrugs. "Just the pilot and our champagne."

Robert swings the gun around to Charlie. "Then what's he talking about?"

She nods to Charlie. "Go on. I'm curious to see how much you think you know."

Reluctantly, he answers, "I don't know exactly how, but I think Kat's been working with the person who killed her father."

"Working with—? Did *you*—?"

"No, of *course* I didn't kill my father—" she snaps.

"But," Charlie interjects, "you *did* use the moment to your advantage."

"Oh, you *are* clever," she sneers.

Clever? What exactly does Charlie know?

He leans in, genuinely curious, I can tell. "How?"

She grins. "It's amazing how people will voluntarily let themselves just be...used." She smirks. "The real question is do *you* know who it is?"

"I do." Charlie answers, and his voice cracks.

Gunfire erupts outside, and my attention shifts. Robert's men are firing—but not at the helicopter. They're aiming for the treeline.

Robert rises from his chair. "What the hell—?!" but he's cut off as a large flame bursts from the machine.

The aircraft drops fast, bouncing hard off the deck, the tail swinging wildly. Men scream, scattering as the whole thing tilts sideways, the rotor blades crumpling against the stone with an ear-piercing mechanical whine. It jerks and rolls and slams into the windows, and I have only moments to retreat before the whole thing bursts into a ball of flames.

chapter 132

It's pure pandemonium. Smoke and fire fill the banquet room, and gunfire and shouts erupt outside.

"Cover, cover, cover—!"

"Watch your position—!"

"Moving to flank—!"

Robert's men are dropping quickly—picked off by a faceless assassin out in the trees. Soon, the killer will have worked their way through Robert's men and come looking for the rest of us.

I need to move.

I look to where Charlie has been sitting, but there's no sign of him. Or Kat. Robert, however, lies in a twisted heap on the floor.

I stay low, choking on the noxious fusion of oil and paint, and rush to him. He's bleeding badly from the gut—looks like a knife slash. There's probably not much I can do for him, but I can't just leave him here to be burned alive.

I grab him by his shirt and drag him into the lobby. He screams in pain every step of the way. The fire is raging, and it won't be long until it spreads throughout the whole place.

"I can't—" he struggles to say, but I ignore him and grab him under his armpits and haul him out the front doors. Every step is a struggle as I drag him across the driveway and into the grass. I lower him down slowly and put pressure on the wound, hoping he's still breathing.

"Wh—?" he mumbles, then someone yells out, "Get away from him!"

A figure stumbles towards us, gun aimed at my head in what has become an all-too-frequent occurrence, and I lift my hands in surrender.

It's Red.

"You little son of a bitch—"

"Put it…down…." Robert sputters.

"This asshole knocked me out!"

Red sees the blood.

"Not his…fault…."

"Kat did it," I tell him.

He stumbles closer but doesn't lower the gun.

"She used you…to get to me…."

Unfortunately, this is all the help I get from Robert before he passes out.

Red looks around. No Cass. No Kat. No one to tell him what to do. It's clear he's at a loss.

I guess that's where I come in. "Let me go; you stay with him. Besides, I *think* I know what she's planning," I add, hoping that he knows nothing.

"What if I just shoot you and go myself?"

"He bleeds out."

Red glares at me, still weighing his odds.

I decide to push my luck. "Pretty sure Robert isn't too pleased that you've been helping the woman who stabbed him."

"Hey," he grunts defensively, "I just do what I'm told."

"Exactly, and saving Robert's life might just help him forget about your part in Kat's little coup."

Red stares at the unconscious Robert, then at the black plume of smoke rising from the fireball that had once been a helicopter.

"Emergency crews will be on their way," I persist. "Get him out of here."

Red knows he's got no choice.

I move to let him take over, then figure I might as well ask. "Hey, give me your gun?"

He scowls. No way he's handing it over. Fine, I'll do this with only my good looks and charm.

I leave them and stumble back into the fire and mayhem.

chapter 133

As soon as I open the front doors, smoke billows out towards me. Who the hell goes back into a burning building? Since this is the second time in my life I've done this, I guess I know the answer.

On my left are heat and flames, but the right seems safer. I duck low and crawl towards a set of double doors on the ground level. On the other side is smoke, but it's not dense—yet—so I cover my nose and mouth with my T-shirt and rush down the hallway.

Logic tells me that Kat's getting out of here as quickly as she can—though not by chopper—and my gut says her plan still somehow involves Charlie. I don't waste time checking any of these rooms and keep my eyes open for anything that hints at where they've gone. I pass a tipped-over cleaning cart, toilet paper and shampoo scattered everywhere, and wonder if in the chaos of their departure, Charlie or Kat had collided with it.

There's a second set of doors and another long hallway. A sign says TENNIS COURT at the end of the hall, and a second reads SWIMMING POOL over the set of doors to my left.

I hesitate: which way would Kat go? I'm losing time.

That's when I notice a small chunk of soap by the doors close to me. It's one of those sample sizes that you'd find in a hotel, broken off from the main piece, a ripped piece of paper wrapped around it. Sure, it could maybe have fallen off the cart, but there's a good chance that Charlie's marked his trail. Faked a fall, hit the cart, grabbed the soap, and snapped off a piece of it for me to find, like Hansel and Gretel.

I don't question it.

I push through the doors and enter an airy sitting room with a small bar along the far wall and tall folding doors that open to the outside. Beyond them is the pool, surrounded by cabanas and a rock wall with an artfully placed waterfall that spills into the water.

I search the tile floor and spy another chunk of soap by the door to the pool deck and sneak outside.

The morning wind blows small ripples across the water, and the red fabric of the cabanas flutters like giant lungs breathing in and out. At the far end is a sunken outdoor bar next to the pool, where patrons can swim up and grab themselves a cocktail.

Beside it is another chunk of soap, and considering its size, most likely the last. If I'm going to find him, I'm on my own from here.

As I cross the pool deck, something splinters the rock of the waterfall behind my head.

It takes me a second too long to realize that I've been shot at—again. I drop hard and roll behind a deck chair, knowing the shooter's aim might be better next time. I drag myself across the pool deck, drop into the bar—and come face to face with Cass.

"Get out!" he hisses.

"No," I respond.

He sticks his gun in my face. "This is *my* spot."

"I don't care. Someone's shooting out there—"

"Why the hell do you think I'm down here!"

"Who is it? Kat?"

He shakes his head. "Same person who took out the helicopter and Robert's guys."

Whoever it is is a dangerous shot, which means we're sitting ducks here. And I don't really trust this guy not to do something stupid. So I poke my head up long enough to scout out the surroundings, and when I think it's clear, I crawl past him and pull myself out the other side, ducking behind the top shelves that house the alcohol.

"Where you going?" he croaks.

"You told me to leave."

"I know, but...."

This guy doesn't know *what* he wants. "Make up your mind!"

He shuffles over, and I scan the area once more before waving him up.

As inconspicuously as I can, I crane my neck around the back of the bar to peer at the clubhouse. The fire has now spread through the back of the building and billows high in the sky. The fire department and police must be on their way.

Bodies lie all over the deck—one is splayed backwards on the stairs and another draped over the railing.

Cass starts whispering. "Sniper took us out from the treeline with a rifle. We tried to flank, but whoever it is kept moving, hiding. Like a ghost."

This worries me, and I glance back to assess the scene, studying the entire area. Sure enough, a lone figure rises from behind a slope along the fairway and looks our way.

"Get down! We've got to hide!"

chapter 134

Cass and I commando-crawl across the pool deck towards the waterfall. The rock formation cuts off our path, but it's the only way out of here that isn't immediately exposed.

"Hit the water but stay quiet," I say over my shoulder, before sliding into the pool like a sea otter. I paddle beneath the surface until I am behind the tumbling spray. I pull myself up close to the pool wall and catch a breath.

Cass pops up beside me.

"No way they won't notice us here," he says.

"Head for the building. Once you're there, you'll find plenty of cover."

"What about you?"

"I'm going after Charlie and Kat."

"What the hell is it with you two? He your boyfriend?"

"No, but—" I begin but fall silent when I see a shadow move across the fabric of one of the cabanas.

The killer?

Doesn't matter. I'm not sticking around to find out.

I gesture at Cass to stay quiet and low before submerging myself, letting out as much air as I dare to sink to the bottom. Cass drops down next to me, already struggling to hold his breath. I point towards the side of the pool with the swim-up bar, and he shoots me a look, shaking his head.

I can't wait around to argue. I push off the bottom of the pool and torpedo across the water until I reach the far wall. I rise slowly enough to break the surface without a splash and silently suck in a big breath of air beneath the bar.

Cass surfaces near me, far less smoothly, gasping.

I shush him and pull him none too gently beneath the overhang too.

I point to where I think the shooter is, and Cass nods.

Finally, he's paying attention.

Moving quickly, I swim to the pool's edge, past the overhang, and poke my head up. It's risky, but if I don't know where the killer is, we're in just as much danger.

I don't see anyone right away, then a dark shape moves on the fairway side of the pool. They carry a large rifle with a long scope, and they're wearing a leather jacket. Their hair is tucked up into a baseball cap, and it takes me a moment to realize it's a woman.

Then she turns my way momentarily, and I see her face. And I understand why Charlie said he knew who the killer was.

"Son of a *bitch*!" Cass grumbles beside me and drags his body out of the water. He's already going for his gun.

"Wait! Don't—" I hiss, but he ignores me, pulling himself out of the pool, dripping, to move swiftly towards her the second she turns away, pistol pointed at the back of her head.

I'm hoping his gun is too wet. A gunshot rings out.

It's not his.

As Cass crumples, the woman turns, rifle at the ready, but she lowers it quickly.

"Charlie?" she asks.

"Careful, Irene," Kat says, hauling Charlie forward in front of her as a shield, gun aimed over his shoulder, the pearl-handled straight razor at his throat. "You wouldn't want to accidentally kill your son."

chapter 135

Irene and Kat square off, Charlie caught between them. I stay low and quiet, hidden in the pool, hoping no one has noticed me yet.

"Let him go," Irene shouts. Her posture and voice hints at the wild animal that's been unleashed over the years since her daughter's death.

"You know I can't do that."

Irene takes aim, and Kat compacts herself tight behind Charlie.

"Lower the gun, or I'm slicing his artery."

The straight razor is pressed against Charlie's throat, and blood stains the neck of his shirt. If he even twitches, she'll probably drop him.

Slowly, Irene complies, dropping the rifle at her feet.

"Good. Now, raise your hands and take a few steps towards us."

Irene follows Kat's order. "It's okay, Charlie. Everything will be okay."

"Yeah, Charlie. Everything's going to be okay," Kat mocks. She pushes him forward, and cuts his hands loose. "Go on. Give Mom a hug—I knew she'd come for you."

Charlie steps towards the shooter, whom he doesn't seem too surprised to see.

Irene reaches out for him, but he pauses halfway.

"No."

Kat clucks her tongue, disappointed. "Why not? Don't you miss her?"

He looks at his mom, then back to Kat, shaking his head. "No, I don't."

"Charlie!" Irene cries out.

"Sorry. But you left when I was a kid. You've been dead to me for a very long time."

His words break her, and she drops to her knees.

But I know him: he's bluffing. He's trying to keep her safe, and if it means hurting her to keep her alive, he'll do it.

Kat shrugs. "Seems like even your son realizes how pathetic you are. And to think I actually admired you once."

"When she killed your father?" Charlie asks, taking a step to one side and turning to face Kat.

Kat follows him with her gun. "When I was younger, he was the most powerful man I knew. But then she"—Kat sneers—"killed him."

"And you realized he was weak? Just like your mother?" He takes another small step away, and Kat turns a little more to keep him square in her sights. What is he up to?

"So why get her to do your dirty work?"

Kat allows herself a low chuckle. "Killing people gets boring—fast. But figuring out how to make someone do it for you? To have that much control? It's one of the most power-ful feelings in the world."

Charlie nods. "You're pretty powerful now, too. You've got us cornered—there's no way we can get out of here without you killing us, so what the heck, why don't you tell me how you got her to do it, to take out all your rivals? Almost no one knew she even existed."

Kat smirks. "It didn't take long for me to figure out who had killed The Falcon."

"You knew? Poor Winston thought he was the only one." Charlie shakes his head, taking another step. He's put a lot of space between the three of them. "Let me guess, you then fished for her through message boards, convinced her to trust you, then fed her the people you wanted out of your way?"

I stare at Cass's body, only a few feet away.

Beside it, his gun.

Charlie knows I'm here! He's making her turn her back, giving me a chance to go for it. Because if I don't, he and his mom are dead.

I pull myself out of the pool, staying low to the deck so the *drip drip drip* doesn't draw her attention.

Charlie sees me but doesn't change his expression. "But why go through all the trouble, Kat? Why even use her? Like you said, she's weak."

Silence.

Kat doesn't answer, and I freeze, hoping she's not onto me.

"Unless…you missed your daddy?" he says.

"I wanted vengeance!" she snarls.

"Because *you* were weak!" he shouts back.

She pounces on him with her knife, and I scramble for the gun.

I'm not fast enough.

Before I can get my hand on the grip, Kat spins, catching me mid-reach.

"No!" Charlie cries out. "Don't."

She waves her gun at me. "Move! Now! Over by his mom."

Various scenarios run through my head: dropping, rolling, trying for the gun again. Maybe I'll make it, maybe I won't.

Charlie glares at me and shakes his head. *Don't do it.*

If I don't do what she says, she's going to start shooting, but she'll start shooting eventually anyway. But if I try something now and she shoots Charlie or Irene first, I couldn't handle the emotional consequences. She's outplayed us.

So I give up.

chapter 136

I stand beside Charlie's mom, and Kat keeps her gun pointed at both of us while she talks to Charlie.

"Now, what was that you were calling me? Weak?" She's all smug smarm. "I'll show you *weakness*. Choose. Choose who dies first."

Charlie doesn't answer.

"Oh, come on, Charlie. Who do you want me to shoot? Your mother or your best friend? Who's it going to be?"

He still doesn't respond.

"Ah, you see the dilemma," she says, drawing it out. "They're both going to suffer a slow, painful death—but whoever you pick first will know you valued them least."

"No . . . ," he mumbles.

"What? You don't think so? Then let me help you."

"Wait! No—!"

She barely acknowledges us when she pulls the trigger.

Irene slumps beside me.

Charlie screams, "Mom!"

I catch her, struggling to hold her up, but her limp body is too awkward, and we collapse to the ground together.

"See? I knew you cared," Kat says with glee. She lifts the gun again, definitely aiming at me this time. "You get any ideas, and your friend is next."

Charlie's a furious storm of rage and pain. I've never seen him like this.

"You feel it, don't you, Charlie? You feel your weakness?"

"You shot my mother—!"

She grins. "Yes. I did."

"I'm going to kill you." His eyes dart back and forth, deciding if he's fast enough to get to her before she shoots me.

"See," she goes on, toying with him, "we've all got weakness inside—"

She turns to gaze at him for only a moment, but it's all I need. I rush her, lifting her up before slamming her to the ground. Her tall, thin frame takes the brunt of the hit, and the gun goes flying. But then the straight razor is in her hand, an extension of her will, and she swings it at my ribs. I block it—barely—but she's nimble, and it's suddenly in her other hand, coming at me from the opposite direction. I'm not as quick this time, and it slices across my skin.

She swings again, and instead of stopping it, I grab her arm and pull her right into a head-butt that nearly cracks my skull. She slashes at my leg and draws more blood, so I shoulder-check her, trying to drop her once and for all, but she hooks an arm around my neck and slices my chest.

I grab her arm as she swipes at my throat, but it's a bad angle, and she's using both hands to thrust it forward. If I don't stop her, she'll sever my artery. I'll bleed out in seconds.

I'm twisted weird—can't get my feet under me to throw her off. One elbow is tucked behind me, and I can't reach her with the other arm. I try to roll, but she's firmly planted.

There's nothing I can do. I'm bleeding out, feeling light-headed, losing strength—

"Get off him, you bitch," Charlie shouts, and suddenly there's a jolt like we've been hit by a stampeding bull. Her grip loosens, and then she's gone, yanked off my back.

I drop and roll and come back up, fists clenched.

Charlie's got her in a headlock. Wild, she lashes out at him with her blade, but he just bats it out of her hand.

His arm is around her neck, and she knows she's in trouble. She claws at him, desperate to pull him away, but it only makes him tighten his grip.

"Charlie...," I mumble.

The fire in his eyes burns brighter than the fire behind him.

"You gotta let her go."

"She shot my mom."

"I know—"

"And what they did to my sister."

"I know. But you can't do this...."

I hear shouts, and police officers race towards us.

Gekas's cavalry.

"Let her go, son!" they shout, guns raised as they run onto the scene.

Charlie looks at me, pleading. "They took my *family*."

"I know," I say sadly. "And they're assholes, and they should pay. But not like this."

"I can't, Tony."

"You can—because I need you. And so does everyone else who cares about you."

Kat's eyes roll at this. It's a good thing he can't see her expression, or that would be it.

"*Please*, Charlie."

His whole body shakes, his brows squeezing tight together as he winces with the physical pain of fighting the battle within.

And then he breaks, letting loose a howl that hurts my soul, and shoves her away. He drops to his knees and raises his hands in surrender, tears streaming down his face.

I kneel down beside him, hugging him hard as the cops swarm us both.

chapter 137

The next few hours are one long slog.

My cuts are bad enough that they take me to the hospital to stitch me up while an officer stands guard. The doctors say they want to keep me for observation, but they're likely also holding me until the cops can get my statement.

Charlie is taken away in a police car, and no one will tell me what's going on. Sure, he almost killed Kat, but he also was the Mob's hostage for more than a week. My guess is they'll probably keep him in a holding cell until they can sort out what actually went down at the country club. I want to think that he's been behind bars enough times that he'll be fine, but his emotional state makes me worry that this time is different.

By the time the paramedics arrived, his mom had lost a lot of blood from the gunshot wound. They tried their best, but she didn't make it. I was glad that the police had been good enough to give him a moment to say goodbye before he was taken into custody.

I watched him standing over her body, unable to imagine what was going through his head. He hadn't seen her for years—hell, maybe even a decade—and now she was dead. Despite their differences and all the bad choices, Irene was still his mother; he must feel an inexplicable loss.

It's nighttime when Mom and Dad knock on the door of my hospital room. Mom fawns over me with hugs and kisses and tears, before wiping them away and checking my chart, then stepping out to talk to the nurse in charge.

Dad stands at the foot of my bed, his face an uneasy mix of sadness and frustration.

"I... I'm sorry about your car," I offer.

He shakes his head. "The car? It's...just...a car."

"It *was* a pretty nice one, Dad."

He grimaces. "Yeah, kind of expensive." He moves closer to sit on the side of my bed, and puts his warm hand on my arm. "But...you... You're...." He struggles to finish.

"I'm sorry, Dad. For everything."

"You saved your friend. No matter what it took."

"But you were right... I can't keep doing things this way."

His smile is gentle and warm and rueful and sad, and he leans across the bed rail to hug me. "I *am* proud of you."

It's only then that I truly feel it's over.

chapter 138

Charlie knocks on my door the next morning, carrying a big brown paper bag. He's showered and shaved, and back in т-shirt and jeans.

"I see you've finally ditched the scuffed suit," I say. "Nice fit."

"Nice robe," he says, pointing at the thin yellow excuse of a hospital gown barely covering me. "I think I see your junk."

I fake swat him, and he ducks away, laughing. He reaches into his bag and pulls out two coffees and a container of pancake bites. "Wally, Nick, and Jerome send their regards."

He rolls the side table over and opens the bag, plunking himself down in the chair beside me. He kicks his shoes up on my bed. Classic Chucks. No more Crocs, I notice.

"Careful of the arm," I caution.

"Oh, enough, you big baby. You're not getting any sympathy from me."

"Hey, man—I took these cuts to save you."

"Yeah, and I once got stabbed a bunch to save *you*."

"Are we comparing wounds now?"

"Maybe," he says with his trademark grin. "Does your new girlfriend like your scars?"

"Hey, she's not my girlfriend."

"Well, not yet anyway. Your scars, plus the Shepherd charm? She won't know what hit her."

"Enough!"

The grin widens.

"So, the fact you're here must mean you're not under arrest," I say.

"Are these the crack detective skills you used to find me?"

"All right, enough." I put up my hands. "What did happen?"

He runs a hand through his shaggy hair. "They took me in, asked a lot of questions. Pretty sure they were trying to make something stick, but...."

"What?"

"Gekas's statement pretty much cleared me."

I wince. "Damn, that must have been tough to swallow."

"Yeah, well, maybe she's okay." He grins again.

I want to say something about his mom. "Charlie—"

"Nope, we're not doing this again, Shepherd."

"But—"

"No. I know what you're going to say, and I appreciate it. But I've kept a lot a shit from you."

"I get it," I tell him. "I haven't had your life—can't even imagine what you were dealing with."

"Well, I should have trusted you more. I just—"

"Charlie, don't worry about it."

"Fine, but can I at least say thank you?"

"I don't know. *Can* you?" I ask, smirking.

He glares at me, then we both break into laughter.

"What's so funny?" Mom asks as she and Dad bustle into the room.

Before we can answer, Dad zeroes in on the pancake bites. "Excuse me, what are those?"

"Hatley's finest—and only decent—breakfast food," Charlie replies. He digs into the bag and pulls out a second, smaller, bag of them, and hands them to Dad. "I figured you and Mrs. S. deserved some of your own."

Dad opens it up and takes a big whiff before Mom grabs the bag and steals the first one.

"Very tasty, Charlie," she says, leaning in to give him a hug. "We're very relieved you're safe."

I've seen Mom give Charlie the occasional embrace, but never has he ever received it without a stiff spine. Not this time. This time he relishes it, giving her a quick tight squeeze in return.

Dad pats him on the back. "What say we work on getting you two boys home?"

"Sounds great, Mr. S."

chapter 139

By late afternoon, the doctors have released me, along with a stack of pain meds and antibiotics, which I'm grateful for. The stitches make getting dressed torture, and walking to the car is no better.

"You move like an old man now," Charlie says.

"Hey, if you want to carry me—"

"Nah, the exercise will do you wonders. Right, Mrs. S.?"

"Don't you bring me into this."

"Oof," Dad mutters under his breath. "It's going to be a long trip, I can tell already."

We drive to the hotel to check me out. Mom and Dad had offered to do it earlier, but I personally wanted to thank Gabe for his kindness.

Charlie accompanies me, and Juno greets us before we can even get to the front desk. Actually, I should say she greets Charlie and nearly ignores me. Charlie drops to the floor, face level with the pup, who gives him plenty of licks.

"I've never seen her like that with strangers before."

"Well," I say, "my friend is special. Probably has food in his pockets too."

Gabe studies my bandages. "When I heard the news about the country club, I wondered if you were involved."

I force a smile, not sure how to answer. Strangers coming into your town and burning down buildings is never a good look.

He goes on. "A lot of people around here were suspicious of the new developments. Turns out they had good reason to be," he says. "Although I don't know the details, I feel like we owe you."

"I thought you weren't too fond of Hatley?"

He chuckles a bit. "Well, a town full of rednecks is a heck of a lot better than one filled with a bunch of gangsters, at any rate."

"Time for me to check out," I say. "Thank you so much for all your kindness."

"Don't worry about your bill. It's already been paid."

That's a surprise. "By who?"

"Didn't say. Just got a stack of cash delivered by courier. They left a very large tip, too, so whoever your friends are, thank them for me."

Charlie and I glance at each other and shrug. He's got no clue either, but we're not going to argue.

We go up to my room—walking up the stairs sucks balls, and I'm sweating by the time we reach the top—but it's all worth it for Charlie's reaction when he sees my room.

"What the hell, Shepherd? I was sleeping on cement floors in basements and being knocked around, and *this* is where you were staying?! Did you order room service, too?"

"Absolutely. If we had more time, I could even take you down to the spa."

Charlie helps me pack my bag, shouting out, "Oh, have I missed *you*!" when he yanks up his backpack from the far side of the bed.

He unzips it for a quick but thorough once-over. "What the hell? I had a system of organization, and you messed it up!" But he shrugs off this slight annoyance with good grace and swings the backpack over his shoulder before grabbing the rest of my stuff.

As we descend the stairs, one thought runs through my head: Didn't I leave his bag in the car? How the hell did it get here?

chapter 140

Turns out, Dad was right. The trip home *was* long, but not for the reasons I expected.

Charlie and I are asleep in the back seat when my phone rings.

Dad is driving and answers the call. "Hello?"

Silence.

"Hello?" he repeats.

"Hello . . . is Tony there?"

Shit! It's Lakshmi. My phone is attached to the usb!

"Wait, is that the girl?" Charlie shouts as he scrambles to keep the phone away from me.

"Which girl?" Mom asks.

"Son?" says Dad.

"Hello?! Lakshmi?!" I shout.

"Tony?" she answers.

"Charlie, give it to me!" I demand.

But he doesn't and instead calls out, "Hi, Lakshmi! I'm Charlie, Tony's best friend—"

"Stop it!"

"And Mr. and Mrs. S.—his mom and dad—are here too—"

"Charlie!"

"Hello, Lakshmi," Mom and Dad say in unison.

"Do *not* make me tear my stitches," I growl, jamming out my hand, palm first.

Charlie grins and hands over the phone.

I quickly unplug it and tuck myself into a ball behind Dad's seat. "Hey there. Sorry about that," I say in a hushed voice.

She can barely contain her laughter. "No worries. Did I catch you at a bad time?"

"Nope...sorta...whatever. It's good to hear from you."

"You too. So, Charlie...?"

"Yeah, he's the friend I mentioned." He peeks over at me like a curious dog, and I mouth, "You're dead."

"So, the fact that he's with you must mean things are better."

"Yeah."

"And his storm? Has it passed?"

"I think so. I hope so."

"That's good." We're both silent for a moment. "So, you're heading home?"

"Yeah." The idea that I'm putting a province between us sucks. "But..." I look at Charlie and my folks, who are all watching, "if you ever happen to be in the neighbourhood, please give me a call."

"Oh, I will, Tony Shepherd. You can count on it."

We say goodbye and hang up, and I finally acknowledge all the curious eyes.

"I thought you were out here looking for Charlie," Mom says.

"Yeah, Shepherd." Charlie's enjoying every second of this.

"Okay, enough. We're not doing this," I grumble.

"Oh, we're doing this for many weeks to come." He leans over the seat to Mom. "Uh, Mrs. S., no particular reason at all, but could I get Heather and Jodi's numbers—?"

"You're *not* calling my sisters!" I shout, and the car erupts in laughter.

Oh, yeah. It's going to be a very, *very* long trip home.

chapter 141

A week after we return, we bury Charlie's mom.

Mom and Dad had offered to pay for her body to be shipped home, but Charlie insisted that she be cremated. They still covered the cost, on the condition that he allowed them to buy a plot in the local cemetery. When he tried to object, Mom had simply said, "I just think it'd be nice if there was somewhere you could always visit her."

He didn't argue.

The graveyard service is simple and low-key. Mom, Dad, Charlie, and me. Elaina offered to be there too, but Charlie said he'd catch up with her later.

After it's done, Charlie speaks with Dad, and then he and Mom leave Charlie and me on our own.

"I hope you don't mind, but I told them we'd walk home."

"Charlie, it's almost forty degrees out, and we're in dress clothes!"

"Yeah, we're going to be ripe by the end of it."

His smile fades, and he stares at the small marker beside his mom's grave.

"It's weird. I never had answers. I never had closure. I barely knew her. And despite all the shit I did to Melanie, she's more of a mom than Irene ever was."

I keep silent, letting him talk.

"But Dad told me stuff about her, about the times before…," he pauses, and I can see him struggling. "Before everything happened with Sophie, and she sounded pretty awesome."

I smile, but there are tears in my eyes.

"Losing my sister destroyed us. As a family and in our own separate ways."

His voice breaks, and I put my arm around him. He doesn't fight it. "I just didn't want it to happen to anyone else."

I want to say how grateful I am, how he's made this world a better place, but I don't. Not because I'm embarrassed to, but because I don't need to.

"So, you ready to go?" he asks. "It's going to be a good two-hour walk."

"Charlie…," I groan.

"By the way, did you see in the news about the guy who went missing—"

"Can we at least wait until my cuts and bruises heal?"

"Fine. But let me at least tell you about the murder scene…."

epilogue

I stand in front of the mirror of my bedroom, examining my scars. They've healed up well, the map of my journey sketched across my torso and obliques. A couple of years ago, I'd been preoccupied with my looks and strength; now I'm just grateful for a body that has mended this well and kept me very much alive.

Charlie bursts in. He too is relaxed, rested, and healthy after his ordeal. A comfortable bed and solid meals have done him good.

"Could you knock?" I say, giving him the gears.

He slowly raps the door with his knuckle, staring at me and smiling the whole time.

"Dick," I say.

He shrugs. "Maybe." He nods at my shirtless reflection in the mirror. "Would you and your war wounds like a minute alone?"

Although his sass should be annoying, I'm grateful for it. "I had a minute, and you interrupted it," I retort, throwing on a button-up shirt that falls loose over my cargo shorts.

"I suppose it's better for me to find you playing with yourself than for your mom. Speaking of which, she sent me to get you."

I look up from doing up the shirt. "What's the rush? There's still time."

He holds his hands up in truce. "Hey, chill. I'm just the messenger. And this *is* your graduation barbecue, Shepherd. Should've been weeks ago, but noooo, you had to be a hero."

I throw a towel at him, and he dodges it.

Mom yells up the stairs. "Anthony!"

"Shit!" Charlie mumbles.

"Charles? Where's Anthony?"

I point at him, grinning. "You're in trouble!"

"No, you're *both* in trouble if you don't get down here."

"How does she do that?" Charlie remarks offhandedly as we go downstairs together. "It's like she's psychic."

Mom's chopping lettuce while Dad preps burgers. Heather's home for the weekend, and as she zips past, she points at two coolers. "Mind grabbing those, little brother?"

I stare down at her.

"Okay, okay—you're not so little anymore," she laughs.

I grin and grab one of the coolers, and Charlie follows with the other.

Outside, a big banner of gold balloons hangs in the back-yard, along with a photo booth, picture frames, hats, the whole nine. We set the coolers next to a large table stuffed with salads, side dishes, buns, and dessert.

"This all looks delicious, Mr. and Mrs. S.," Charlie shouts back through the open sliding door.

"Make sure Ollie doesn't get into it," Mom cautions, but our pup doesn't seem too interested. He's napping in a shady spot under the tree, living his best life.

Dad shouts, "Can I get an extra set of hands?"

"On it," Charlie replies.

The front doorbell rings.

"Anthony, could you—?" Mom calls from inside.

I pass through the house and answer the door. A delivery person is standing there with a large basket.

"Anthony Shepherd?"

"Yes. That's me."

After a quick signature, he hands it over.

"Whatcha got there, Shepherd?" Charlie says over my shoulder. He's already peeling off the cellophane.

I grab the card before he loses it: "Ms. Lamay extends her congratulations. K."

"Who's Lamay?" he asks.

"*Ms.* Lamay," I correct him. "Let's just say I have friends in high places."

"I'll say." He pulls out a bottle of Dom Perignon, expensive chocolates, and a pink plastic card. Charlie studies it, "Wait, I've seen these in the cars at . . . ." He stares at me, speechless. "Damn, Shepherd, you really *have* made some connections."

The doorbell chimes again.

I open it. It's Gekas.

"Anthony, congratulations." She smiles, shaking my hand. I think she'd maybe give me a hug if it didn't seem so awkward.

"Charles, how are you?" She puts her hand out to him too.

"Pretty good," he says, shaking it. His defences are down and he seems genuinely himself, calm and content.

Maybe things are changing.

She hands me one of the two gift bags she's holding. "This is for you." Inside is *Meditations* by Marcus Aurelius. "I thought you might like it."

Charlie nods. "Some good stuff in there."

She pauses, a bit uncomfortable. "I also wanted to say... I should've listened to you, Tony.... Acted sooner."

"It's okay," I tell her. "I would probably have done something stupid anyway."

We all stand there, uneasy, unsure what to do next, until she lifts the other gift bag. "This is for Ben and Keya...."

"They're in the kitchen."

"Thank you." She leaves us, and Charlie and I stare at each other, wordless.

The doorbell chimes again, but before we can open it, Elaina and Melanie let themselves in, still in the midst of conversation.

"Trust me, the Shepherds *want* us to make ourselves at home," Elaina is saying.

"Are you sure?" Melanie asks.

"Thank you for picking Melanie up," Charlie puts in, taking Elaina's hand in his.

"No problem. She shared a little story about you, something about ice cream and sticky fingers."

Charlie glances at Melanie. "She did, did she?"

"Oh, yeah. I think she and I are going to get along *great*."

Charlie rolls his eyes, then the three of them wander into the kitchen, where they're immediately put to work.

I stand back and watch it all with happy gratitude.

As the party unfolds, the sun moves across the sky, and the backyard ebbs and flows with food and stories, people, hugs, gifts, and well-wishes. It's more than a graduation party.

It's the coming together of a family.

The landline rings, and I'm close to the door, so I go inside to answer it. Jodi had said that she and her husband, Bryan, would probably call later on—although I thought it'd be by video.

It's not them.

"Hello, Tony Shepherd."

"Cousin Rachel?" I glance at Charlie as a chill runs down my spine. "You're *alive*?"

"Let's skip the Cousin Rachel bit," she says. "That part of my life is behind me. Call me.... Actually, you know what? Don't call me anything."

Charlie sees me looking his way and senses something is up. He casually stands and makes his way over.

"How did you survive?"

There's a bark of laughter. "Turns out I'm tougher than I thought. Doctors patched me right up. Just won't be winning any beauty contests in the near future."

"Why are you calling?"

"First of all, to congratulate you on your graduation."

Yeah, right. "And?"

"Well, to thank you. You helped me finish the job."

"You're welcome...?" I say cautiously.

"Who is it?" Charlie mouths.

"Oh, is that Charlie? Excellent."

How the hell does she know he's here? He hasn't said a thing. I glance up. One of Dad's security cameras is pointed right at us.

"Hey there," she says.

"What do you want from me?"

"Actually, I'm calling for your friend. Put him on."

I hold out the phone so that it's between us.

"Perfect. You'll both want to hear this." She pauses and groans in pain. "Ugh. Crime does *not* pay."

"What do you want?" I repeat.

"All right, all right. Relax. I'm getting to it. But once I've told you, it's the last you'll hear from me."

"You promise?"

"Absolutely. I have another life, a *real* life—with a husband and a kid that I want to spend the rest of my days with, and I'm not going to waste it worrying about two dumb punks who don't know to leave well enough alone." Another groan.

I sigh. "Okay, so what is it?"

"Just that when I visited William, we had a good long chat, and he told me quite a few interesting things."

Charlie grabs the phone. "If you hurt him—!"

"Relax," Rachel repeats. "I'm here to help. Now, it took me a while to make sense of everything he said, and even longer to piece it all together with other information—"

Charlie swallows hard, and his voice shakes as he asks, "What did you find out?"

"That your sister is alive, Charlie Wolfe."

acknowledgments

Writing a book creates many questions, and along with them come the people who can help answer. In no particular order we would like to thank Sheri McEachern, Mercury Kapp, Kristin Koroluk, Marianna Kyriakoulias, Joshua True Goff, and Cst. Dana Adams and Cpl. Keith Malcolm, for their expertise in a variety of areas.

Thank you also to Tom Liagridonis, Shaun Broom, and Tricia Martin for their kindness and answers to professional queries. And a big thank you to Kevin Johnson for being a pillar for Counios & Gane.

We adore our publishing team, Lori Burton, Donna Grant, and Heather Nickel, and are so thankful for all their edits, guidance, and endurance. Don't get too busy—we've still got one more of these to go!

Angie is indebted to Maria Plastaras and Katerina Voyatzis for their support in this book's early writing stages, as well to Patra Barlas for her incredibly positive attitude, hospitality, and generous spirit. Heartfelt thanks go to Kevin Leflar for his quiet, steady support and love—and to the Creator for the strength and focus to carry on this story-writing journey.

David would like to thank his wife and kids for always being supportive of his creative journey. He's also immensely grateful for Angie's patience while he struggled on his part of the work. This was a long and humbling process. Lastly, he's immensely thankful to the readers for continuing to support us after all this time.